the Catalain book of Secrets

the Catalain book of Secrets

JESSICA LOUREY

The Catalain Book of Secrets
ISBN-13: 978-0-9908342-0-5

Cover designed by Scarlett Rugers Design, www.scarlettrugers.com.

The Catalain family tree as well as the pages from the actual Catalain *Book of Secrets* were designed by Tony Van Den Einde.

TOADHOUSE
BOOKS

DEDICATION

To those with the courage to choose joy.

"Time makes more converts than reason."
-Thomas Paine

"Trust your instincts."
-Your mother

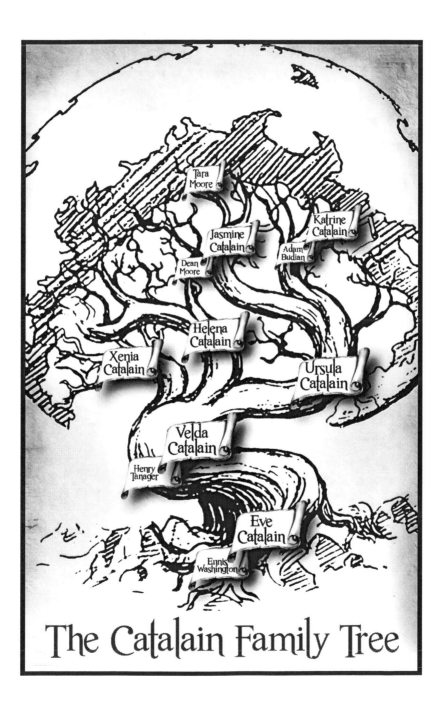

The Catalain Family Tree

PROLOGUE

March 1965

Ursula was twelve years old when her mother asked her to murder a man.

Child, I need you to make me something.

Ursula's eyes lit up behind her thick glasses, the desperation in them palpable. Her brown hair was braided on each side, her purple cotton dress simple. Outside their rambling Queen Anne mansion, a Minnesota spring wind taunted the oak trees, slapping their leaves against the grand house. The air smelled of metal and storm. The earth had been rumbling for days, and everyone in Faith Falls knew what that meant, either from experience or from story: the snakes were coming.

Every few decades, on a timeline known only to the snakes, an early spring blew into Faith Falls, hot and jittery. Shortly after, the U.S. Geological Survey in Mounds View would measure unusual Richter readings in the area. Then, like clockwork, tens of thousands of red-lined garters would unravel from a great, underground writhing ball and slither topside, devouring every small creature that crossed their paths. Locals saw it as a quarter-century inconvenience that didn't outweigh the bucolic charm of their river town. Scientists called it an anomaly. The superstitious worried that the town had been built on sacred Ojibwe burial grounds.

Ursula had felt the recent temblors and heard the whispers about the snakes' return. But what was happening outside of the Queen Anne didn't matter. Her world had narrowed to this single chance to earn her mother's love.

What do you need me to make?

Poison.

For a rat?

Yes. A big one. But the poison can't have any taste, or the animal won't drink it. Can you do it?

Ursula worshipped her mother back then. Velda didn't reciprocate. Instead, she would joke over Sanka and cigarettes that the fairies must have switched her real daughter for plain, thick-waisted Ursula, with her glasses and hair as straight as a bone, a plain lump next to her mother's grace and style. Ursula was always within hearing distance. She would look down at herself and know her mother was right.

But here, finally, was the moment Ursula had been preparing for her whole life: Velda *needed* her. Her heart smiled. She would make the most glorious poison for the rat, and Velda would realize that she wasn't a mistake. She flew to the kitchen and set a pot of water on the gas stove to simmer. Racing to her room after that, she rifled through the pouches of herbs she'd been collecting since she'd cut her knee on a river rock six years earlier.

Her parents had kicked her out of the house that day, first her dad, and then when she went to ask Velda if she could help with anything, her mom. Velda was hugely pregnant with the twins, uncomfortable as a grounded moon.

You're always underfoot. Go find something to do. I don't want to see you again until it's dark.

Ursula had started to cry, her fingers kneading the hem of her paisley dress, before she remembered that both habits made Velda angry. She wiped her face and straightened her clothes. The day was hot. She decided to go swimming.

She played her favorite game, the one where she pretended to be a fish with a whole school of friends. Some of the imaginary fish were six years old, like her. Others were older but still played close. Her pretend friends enjoyed the rainbow feel of cool water on hot skin, just like her.

She was smiling when the rock sliced her foot.

She paddled to shore, stepping tenderly on her bleeding heel as she reached the bank. That's when she spotted it: the horsetail lining the river's edge had morphed from its normal green to a bright, pulsing blue.

Her mouth dry, she plucked some, smelled it, rubbed it in her hands and then—moving quickly before she changed her mind—shredded a bit and dropped it into her wound. The bleeding slowed and then stopped. On her walk home, every plant that could help her shone the same bright blue—willow bark for the pain, juniper berries for an antiseptic wash. She giggled as she skipped along the dirt road, gathering all the blue-washed herbs in the pockets of her summer dress.

Over the next six years, she discovered that with practice, she didn't need to be experiencing the pain to identify which herbs would heal it. She began haunting the library, devouring the botany books. The more she learned, the more she collected plants and seeds against future possibilities.

Velda may have noticed, but she'd never spoken of it.

Until today.

Ursula's breath was shallow as she pawed through her repository for a special plant, one that was a sedative in small doses. She spotted the labeled packet: *conium maculutam.* She'd discovered the weed in a ditch last July and harvested, dried, boiled, and condensed it until it was a deadly brown paste, never imagining she'd have a use for it so soon. She also snatched an envelope of lavender to disguise the bitter, carroty taste of the hemlock.

Back in the kitchen, she dipped an eyedropper into the now-boiling water, withdrew three globules, and squirted them into a spoon. Then she dropped the pea-sized pasteball of hemlock into the hot liquid, followed by a sprinkle of powdered lavender and a touch of honey. The blood galloped through her veins as she mixed the concoction with a toothpick, stirring until it was a quarter teaspoon of murky liquid the consistency of maple syrup. When it was complete, she poured it into a blue glass bottle.

Here. She handed the mixture to her mother, her expression a muddle of triumph and shyness. *Pour it over cheese, or in a dish of milk, and put it near the rat's nest.*

Velda accepted the spoon, her eyes glittering with tears. She'd sent the now six-year-old twins to spend the day and night at a friend's house. The left side of her face was a swollen tapestry of yellows and blues. Her left arm was in a sling. Her right arm shook as it held the spoon.

Mom?

He watches you sleep, you know.

Ursula tipped her head, one braid falling over her shoulder. She pushed her glasses up her nose out of habit. Her expression turned to slapshock when Velda tipped the contents of the spoon into Ursula's father's favorite beer glass, the one embossed with a 12-point buck on its side.

Mom? No response. *Mom!*

Go to your room.

It had never in her life occurred to Ursula to stand up to Velda. Why would a bug argue with the sun? So she stumbled out of the kitchen and cowered behind her bedroom door, every nerve so tender that she was sure she'd been skinned. She tried to lean into the door, to become part of it, to absorb the comfort she'd always felt inside the Queen Anne erected by her grandparents. Outside, the fierce wind screamed. She'd be cleaning up branches tomorrow. She wished the storm would break already.

He wasn't a great father, Ursula recognized that. Some days he was a savage, other days loving, but overall, he'd been as distant as Velda, until lately, when he'd begun paying attention to Ursula, telling her she was pretty, asking her about her day and pulling her onto his lap, even though she was more woman than girl. The new attention tasted like stolen candy. She loved to hear him say nice things in his slow drawl, sweet and lazy like Mississippi honey. What did Velda mean that he watched her sleep?

When the front door slammed, Ursula jumped, pressing her ear against the rough wood of her door. The sounds that assaulted her were not new: crashing, yelling. A popping sound. Velda's cry. Then the worst sound of all: quiet.

The silence shook her bones. When she couldn't stand it any longer, she snuck downstairs. Her father was at the kitchen table drinking beer from his favorite glass, the one that held the poison. He scowled at her, his face handsome and angry, his chin three days past a shave. Her mother was seated across from him, bleeding from her nose. Ursula dropped next to her. She reached toward Velda, yanked her hand back, and then rested it on her mother's knee. Velda leaned into her.

Side by side, they watched him grimace and swallow his beer, muttering about *goddamned women, should have known better* before opening another. The hiss of that second cap popping would be a sound Ursula could forever after call up at will.

The end was not pretty. Before the second glass emptied, he knew. His eyes bulged, and they landed on Velda.

Why? The single word was raw, the straight letters a plate for his fury.

Ursula didn't think her mom was going to answer. She didn't know if she'd hear her even if she did, so loud was the bloodthumping in her ears.

You're a snake, Velda finally said.

To Ursula's eternal surprise, her father laughed. The sound was horrible, torn from his throat and bile-soaked. And then he lunged, but not at Velda. He came for Ursula.

The hemlock had robbed him of grace, but he managed to reach her, a hand to her throat. He pressed his nose to hers, his breath a bitter cloud, his eyes growing milky with the poison. She screamed, and he tightened his grip.

You did this to me you goddamned little witch, didn't you?

She was too scared to breathe. Her heart skipped, and the urine trickled out of her. He squeezed harder.

You'll pay for this, he said, his eyes now the yellow of pus. A fit of wet coughing overtook him, but he didn't loosen his grip or break his stare. His spittle flew, each drop landing on Ursula's face, sizzling her flesh. *I'll come back. I will never stop walking this earth, and every time the snakes rise, I'll be here to take the power away from every one of you goddamned witches. You will never have a better man than me, not one of you Catalain women down the line.*

Not one good man.

Thick coughing rattled him again, this time with such power that he fell to his knees, releasing Ursula. She sucked in a great gasping breath. Her heart restarted. She began to cry. The terror of what was happening exploded her, and then the loss of hope emptied her. This could not be fixed.

Velda stood to the side. She lit a cigarette, her hands shaking. *Take it back, Henry Tanager,* she said through the acrid smoke. She could not seem to locate her mouth with the cigarette.

His laugh was dark and empty. *Take the poison back,* he said, collapsing onto his stomach. He clawed toward the phone, but it was clear he wouldn't make it. The skin of his hands was shriveling, revealing the rigid angles of his finger bones. His voice was wet and loose. *I will take your power when the snakes rise. Your children will pay for this, and their children.*

Take it back! Velda screamed. Her smoking cigarette dropped to the ground.

I will return to make you pay. Not one of you can stop me. The poison was eating him, devouring his flesh, leaving skeleton and hair.

He tried to stand, lunging at the phone, but his body was overcome by spasms, and he fell back to the floor. By the time he vomited, he was paralyzed from the waist down. He yelled, but his words were gone and it was the incoherent roar of a terrified animal. Velda led catatonic Ursula into the living room and closed the door behind them. Out of sight of her dying father, Ursula became aware of the cold urine soaking her underpants.

When his screams took on a pleading tone, his garbled voice escaping in rasping gurgles, Velda led Ursula outdoors to the banks of the Rum River immediately behind the Queen Anne. The air was preternaturally warm, but the wind had died down, leaving behind a path of stripped leaves and twigs. The storm had never broken. Ursula and Velda walked side by side, not touching, the dying branches crunching underfoot.

Velda finally spoke. *He was the only man who ever saw through my charms. I loved him for it, married him six weeks after we met and was pregnant with you two weeks after that.*

Ursula was empty—of feelings, words, light—so she remained quiet.

You know what this means, right? With him gone, we can finally move out of that damned house. It was your grandparents'. Your father insisted we live there. I never wanted to. The place has always carried a curse, if you ask me. It's a mausoleum. She laughed without humor and lit another cigarette.

Ursula knew the gorgeous Queen Anne held secrets and prayers. It was the only consistent comfort she'd ever had, the only home she'd ever known. She loved it. Overhead, a blue moon appeared. Bats swished through the evening ink. The air smelled of wild roses. The world hadn't stopped along with her father's heart. How could that be?

Then the ground began to rumble underfoot with such force that Ursula was thrown against her mother. It wasn't until the earth began to swell as if giving birth that Ursula realized what was happening. Her mouth fell open. The soil was pulsing, rising, leaves and branches rolling down the sides of earth split with the force of labor.

And then, it burst forth.

It was a ball of snakes, at first disoriented, then unraveling and lunging away from their birthing. Ursula screamed until her throat was raw. Velda simply watched, letting the snakes run over her feet like water. Eventually, she told Ursula it was time to return to the house.

If Ursula had ever fought for anything in her life, it would have been in that moment. As much as she wanted to escape the snakes, she didn't want to witness her father's corpse, to smell his vomit, to feel the stone of his body, but she could have recovered from even that. What was causing white hot terror in her was the thought that he wouldn't be dead. *I will take your power when the snakes rise.* He would be waiting for them, a rotting zombie with a bottle of poisoned beer in one hand and an accusing finger leading the other.

No. Ursula's voice was quiet, almost erased by the sussorous snakesong.

What?

I don't want to go back. Please. What if he's not really dead?

Don't be stupid. And don't ever tell a soul about today. Family doesn't tell on family. Sharing a secret makes it worse. Do you understand?

The words branded themselves across the back of Ursula's eyes. *It's our secret. Don't ever tell a soul.* She accepted it as fact.

When they returned, Henry Tanager was sprawled on his back on the cracked linoleum of the kitchen floor, his lifeless eyes open and staring at Ursula, his body nothing more than skin-coated bones. A distant part of her, the murky animal motor that kept her heart beating and her breath going when everything else was shutting down, took note: she was a girl who had crafted the poison used to murder her own father.

Fate and time worked desperately to craft a bubble where this didn't have to be the end of Ursula's self-love. If, in that moment, Velda had acted, had in any way stepped out of her own misery to comfort her daughter, to take responsibility, to explain, Ursula could have worked her way back to herself.

Instead, Velda turned away from her husband's death stare to call the police from the wall phone, wailing into the mouthpiece, throwing herself into the role of unexpected widow as completely as she had any other character in her life, as only Velda could do. She left Ursula to soak in the iciness of her father's lifeless gaze, and just like that, any intimacy mother and daughter had developed that day was severed. That golden thread that joined Ursula to her mother was the same strand that connected Ursula's heart to her body.

Snip.

I'll be back.

Summer

Chapter 1

Katrine
August 2014

The dome of the Volkswagen Beetle glided alongside the prairie grass like a giant scoop of French vanilla ice cream. The car was a rental, the smallest in the Budget stable. Katrine had started out the evening by parking the vehicle in the far corner of the lot near the airport and huddling inside, worried that jet lag, the witching hour, and a habit of driving on the opposite side of the road would pull her under. The car contained everything she owned in this world: a laptop, two suitcases of clothes, jewelry, and toiletries, a box of records and notes, and a framed newspaper article.

An hour had passed like water dripping as she'd stared at the ceiling of the vehicle, focusing on an oily black stain the size of a quarter three inches forward of the interior light. Her chin trembled, and she couldn't seem to swallow past the thickness in her throat. When she couldn't stand being motionless for another second, she'd propped up her seat, twisted the key in the ignition, and pointed west.

Once the car was in motion, zooming away from Minneapolis on I-94, she'd allowed the familiar scent of a Minnesota summer night to stir her memory. The peppery spice of corn silk. The clean warmth of wheat waving in the evening breeze. The elemental freshness of lake water. The smells reminded her of sailing on a tire swing over the river, the sweet and glittery crunch of watermelon rock candy, and her first kiss, stolen by Gregg Hansen during the middle school version of homecoming. She'd been 13, wearing tight corduroy pants and a flowing white blouse that felt pretty. He was two years older and just starting to fill out his faded jeans and REO Speedwagon t-shirt. His lips had tasted like sweet apple wine before his braces scraped her lip, forcing her to yank her head back. They'd stood outside the school gym. She remembered hearing the bass thump of Prince in the background and a thrill shooting through her like silver.

Unexpected tears bubbled up at the memory. She wiped them away and rolled up her windows to fade the smell of the past, also shutting out the bewitching night air. She jabbed at the radio until she located NPR. The soothing monotony of the newscaster's voice steadied her heartbeat. Even so, her hands appeared odd on the steering wheel as she drove, and she had the distinct feeling of staying in one spot as the road rushed past her, a set car on a child's movable track. When the radio produced more crackling than words, she switched it off, afraid to search for other stations, to stumble across a song that would trigger the seditious tears.

An hour out of the Cities, her head began to baby-wobble. She had to stretch her legs or she'd be asleep at the wheel. She exited the interstate, taking the St. Augusta exit ramp so fast that she almost squashed the frog hopping across the high-beam-lit road. She slammed her brake pedal to the floor. The pick-up truck behind her was forced to swerve to miss the cream-colored bug, honking his horn and flipping her the bird as he squealed past. She ignored him, stepping out to transport the leopard frog to the far ditch.

Frogs. She'd always felt a connection with them, been compelled to save them. Maybe she was hoping one would turn into a prince. She laughed at the thought, or at least made the dry sound that passed for her laughter these days.

She returned to her car, stopping at an all-night station before driving due north. All four pumps were open. She topped her small tank and strode inside to pay. The convenience store was empty except for the attendant behind the candy-laden counter. She tried to catch his glance, to feel real, to be seen. He never looked up from his handheld. On impulse, she walked to the rear and grabbed a frosty bottle of root beer from one of the coolers before approaching him, feeling disassociated from the cold bottle in her hand.

He still didn't look up. She felt the tears returning, but then the shiver of a million fingers tickled her skull. *If Kallie doesn't make it through surgery, I'm alone.*

Her defensiveness melted. The attendant wasn't ignoring her. He was in crisis. "It's going to be fine," she responded. She wanted to set him at ease, to comfort the worry in his belly. "Your sister's operation is going to go really well."

"What?" His head shot up from his phone, his expression a paint-bucket blend of surprise and fear. He did the same double-take most men did when they first laid eyes on her, and then his face slipped back into confusion.

She focused fully on him for the first time, her eyes blurry from 42 corrugated hours without sleep. He hadn't spoken until she'd addressed him, hadn't even held eye contact with her until this moment. She wanted to make a joke to break the tension (*For my next trick, watch me pull a foot out of my mouth.*). "Nothing. Keep the change."

She slid him a twenty, her last, and hustled out the door. She had only jingle left in her purse, no paper, and a credit card that had sidled past its limit two weeks ago. She'd called in a favor to buy the London-to-Minneapolis plane ticket, a kindness she hoped she'd be able to repay. In front of her glowing computer, searching for a flight, she'd told herself that it didn't matter where she went, as long as it was *away*. That had been a lie. Since the moment she'd discovered Adam's betrayal, her world had become a pulsing black, accented by the red of fear.

She'd been too tired to shop for groceries. She hadn't worked in two weeks. Her friends were worried about her, begging her to leave her flat, grab a cup of coffee, meet them for lunch, smile, shower. (*Hey, think how much money I'm saving on water,* she'd said, but no one had laughed.)

Muscle memory urged her to move forward, but she couldn't remember how. The sorrow of love lost, of duplicity, of feeling like a fool on her most basic level, lay in her gut like a bitter stone. She'd swallowed it whole when she'd first found out, and it had gathered spit and blood, growing as it pushed down her throat. By the time it reached her stomach, it was a black fist, cooking in her stomach acid until it was hard and heavy, continuing to grow. She didn't belong anywhere.

And there it was.

It was finally time to go home, to return to a town that she'd abruptly left fourteen years ago and was returning to just as suddenly, a town where she'd never known her father— not even his name—and where she'd grown up in a haunted Queen Anne perched on the edge of everything, complete with a witch's workshop in the rear. Once the idea planted itself in her brain, it grew in urgency. She was being called back, finally. The relief was balm to the muscles around her heart, surging through her bloodstream, lubricating the stone in her belly, not strong enough to erode it but at least shifting it.

The final leg of her journey home was anticlimactic. Faith Falls, Minnesota, was a nowhere town, constricting, outside the flow of life. She'd considered returning over the past fourteen years, had promised herself and her mom and Jasmine that she'd visit for Christmas, or a birthday, but then something always came up.

Has it really been fourteen years? She shook her head. Thinking about all that time made her feel like a shit. As she tried to get a bead on the exact reason she hadn't come back, not even for a single visit, the thought would become slippery, and she'd be left wondering what she'd been trying to remember. But, as she neared Faith Falls, she had the sensation of crossing the bubble of a force field, and whatever had called her home began to burble in her veins.

With relief, she saw Faith Falls hadn't changed much.

Settled in a river valley, the first visible landmark was the Our Lady of the Lakes' soaring steeple. The spire had been a point of pride with the Catholics who'd built it with tithe money in 1973 to show the Lutherans who was closer to heaven; unfortunately, the church itself was embarrassingly modest and so the whole structure had the appearance of an upended turtle struggling to maintain a giant erection (which the Lutherans were quick to point out, privately and in more colorful terms; you can't beat a Lutheran for body part euphemisms). She'd had friends from both affiliations growing up and never understood the earnestness of either.

The sky was turning a murky lavender when she wound down County Road 77 and into town. On a whim, she twisted open her bottle of root beer, the sharp kiss of released carbonation loud inside the VW. She hadn't drunk a root beer since high school, hadn't even known she'd missed it. It tasted like caramel and a good joke. Bubbling in her stomach, it gave her a tiny vein of hope, the first she'd felt in months.

She continued to drive, noting the new trailer park that pocked the north side, the anonymous housing development sprung up next to the river, the fast food restaurants and box stores now ringing the edges of the town like tinfoil jewelry on a queen. She had to pass through the haunted Avignon neighborhood, the rumored site of an Indian burial ground. She held her breath until she was through the neighborhood, something she and Jasmine had done since they were children to keep the bad luck at bay.

When she motored into the heart of the old downtown, she was surprised to feel respite, an alien emotion this past year, akin to discovering she had wings. If she could hold the thought long enough, she imagined she'd left Faith Falls because it had smothered her. It was a flat dead-end, lacking the allure of the great wide world. It was fear of the town's suffocating smallness that had kept her away, that must be it. So why did that limitation suddenly feel like an embrace?

River Street was almost as she'd left it, three blocks of old-fashioned, sleeping storefronts, wide sidewalks, and brass sculptures of otters no taller than her knees. Bradley Willmar, owner of Willmar's Apothecary, had convinced the Chamber of Commerce to buy the statues to liven up the downtown. Rum River was thick with otters, and reminding folks of these playful creatures would bring more people to the area and add to the village's charm, he'd argued.

It was no coincidence that his drugstore, in the family for seven generations, was planted in the middle of River Street, with Hobbes Theater on one side and Belinda's Boutique on the other. Across the boulevard was a divided office shared by an accountant and a chiropractor, Juni's Salon, Ragged Cover Used Bookstore and

Coffee Shoppe, and Farmers & Merchants County Bank. Turned out brass otter statues didn't affect the business prospects of a single one of them, for good or ill.

Katrine had worked at Hobbes the last two summers of high school, ripping tickets and scooping popcorn. She'd loved it. She'd watched every movie that came through for free, sometimes twice, and would sneak Jasmine in on slow nights. She tried to remember what had been important to her then, what had made her heart race and lit her eyes, but she'd been a firefly in her youth, soaring from one perch to another and leaving a trail of light in her wake. Introspection and magic had not been her game. She'd left that for her sister.

She steered past downtown, scanning the streets for a familiar face, but no one was out at this hour. She hadn't expected anything different. She drove toward the river, turning without thinking, until she spotted it, the house built by her great-grandparents, the beautiful, restored, dignified old Queen Anne.

Looking at it, Katrine felt as empty as a fresh-dug grave. But she'd get to see her sister. After all these years, she'd finally get to put her arms around Jasmine again. That was her beacon.

CHAPTER 2

Jasmine

The white curtains fluttered in and out with the breath of the wind, carrying the honeydew-scented, pre-dawn August air. Jasmine watched the curtains inhale and exhale, inhale and exhale. She was working during the wee hours. She didn't have to—her accounting business was not demanding in late summer—but it was that or look at the empty spot in her bed. Up until three months ago, he'd be sleeping next to her every night that he wasn't on the road, snoring like a sailor.

That was before he'd left her, and their perfect life in their perfect house. She'd upped her dosage of antidepressants without consulting her doctor. They fogged her ability to reach out to the solid, humming center in each human, a talent she'd never had as strong as Katrine anyway, though her sister had always underestimated her own powers. The drugs silenced the whisper in Jasmine's fingers and ears that had always helped her to choose the perfect ingredients for her roasts and cakes and sense just what temperature and how much time her magic required. She wanted this deadening.

The green and white pills allowed her to live in the world like a normal person, walking on it instead of with it. The mental scaffolding she'd built over her past was shaky, but she balanced on it as best she could, fighting not to look down. Once Katrine had moved away from Faith Falls fourteen years earlier, taking hope and risk with her, Jasmine had required the anti-depressants to keep her equilibrium.

She'd been surprised at how quick and exquisitely painful the separation from her past self and her magic had been. It took three weeks of the drug, bitter smooth capsules sliding down her throat, through her stomach and into her blood where they cloaked every bit of bright blue alchemy, leaving a brownish-gray sludge that washed out in her urine, stinking of forest decay and ink. If any power had remained, any of the cellular keys to the great mystery she'd been born into, the cotton of the drug stuffed her brain and absorbed her juices, making it impossible to concentrate on magic.

Or to care.

It was hard, this stigma she'd chosen, but it had its rewards above and beyond not having to look back. Her husband, for one. No way would stable, normal, average Dean Moore have married a Catalain in her full power. Not many men were that brave, and even if they were, the Catalain women seemed to attract the bad and repel the good when it came to the men in their lives. And their daughter, Tara, would have been denied opportunities if her mother was still a Catalain witch in name or deed.

Jasmine vividly remembered her first day of ninth grade, when she and her class went from the shelter of elementary school to the jungle of Faith Falls High. Heather Lewis, two years younger than her and Faith Falls royalty, had convinced a junior boy to throw a bucket of water at Jasmine outside of the school. Jasmine, who had gotten up early that day to curl her hair and apply her make-up.

She'd been excited to start a new chapter in her life. As her mascara ran with her tears, a ring of boys circled her, pretending to be flying monkeys.

Katrine had barreled through all of them and led Jasmine away, but it was too late. Jasmine was labeled a witch. She didn't possess the sense of humor or popularity needed to shake such a tag, and so she did the best she could to make herself invisible. It helped, but the teasing continued throughout her school years.

She was a Catalain, after all.

She would fight to protect Tara from ever having to bear the curse of the name, just as she'd fought to protect her sister by casting her final spell before she'd forsaken her magic, the spell that had banished Katrine to the other side of the world.

She sighed, missing her sister with the same powerful ache that visited every day, but content in the knowledge that Katrine was safe as long as she stayed in London, away from Faith Falls.

She would protect her sister where their mother, Ursula, had not.

CHAPTER 3

Ursula

The nighttime smells in Ursula's garden were heaven, sweet as basswood honey. The warmth of yesterday's sun still radiated from the silky black earth even though it was nearing dawn. She whispered a quiet blessing, equal parts hope and gratitude.

Sweat trickled down her neck, curling the short gray-black hair around her ears into question marks. The gardening was not strenuous, but the level of concentration required to hold the blessing while handling the enormous white flowers was considerable. And she didn't want to lose any of the pollen. The soft yellow crystals clinging to the stamen were precious and rare. She required a great deal, at least an ounce, to brew remedies to see the town through the winter, and even that would not be enough for everyone.

Ursula finished with one moonflower and moved to the next, the last of them, cupping the sparkling white bloom firmly, its petals great butterfly wings reflecting the starlight. She tapped it over the blue decanter. The pollen tinkled like a thousand fairy bells when it landed. The golden dust could be gathered any night the moonflower bloomed, July through September in this part of the Midwest. For Ursula's purpose, however, only the flower dust gathered under a full moon would do. Tonight was doubly auspicious: it was a blue moon, a second full moon in a single month. Once every three years thirteen full moons fell in a calendar year.

Ursula rested on her heels and rubbed the back of her hand across her forehead, leaving a streak of dirt-stained dew above her glasses, which had begun to slide down her nose. She was done for the night. All the flowers had been groomed, and it would be four more weeks until she could return to collect more pollen, unless an early frost snapped the blossoms before then. She held up the decanter to the moon. The pollen mottled the sides of the cobalt glass and settled on the bottom in a soft coating of pure sweetness, shuddering in the moonlight like a newborn.

Ursula's knees creaked as she adjusted her weight. She'd been tending this garden, tucked on the property between the main house and her moss-covered workshop, for more than half of her 62 years. When she'd moved back to Faith Falls in 1979, pregnant, a steel-forged woman already bearing her life's scars, she never stopped by to tell Velda she was back in town, though she knew her mother was living in the same bungalow she'd moved them all to after her husband's death. The single thought that brought her peace was the idea of living in the gorgeous old Queen Anne her ancestors had built.

By then, the house was abandoned, the cost of upkeep and heat proving too much. To most townspeople, the lines of the house now appeared ragged, like a photo unfocused at the edges. Occasionally, a person out walking their dog or jogging past would pause on the cracked sidewalk in front of the house, puzzling whether it was a trick of the eyes or something about the paint that gave the grand old home a blurry look. Soon, though, they'd forget why they were standing there and move on, sure they had lost something, checking their pockets for keys, wondering if they'd turned off the oven, running down a list of their ballerina dreams.

Ursula bought the house before Jasmine was born. She'd learned young that money was the way to remain independent of her mother and to keep those she loved safe, and so she'd worked long hours marketing her elixirs during the day and crafting them in her one-room apartment at night, saving every penny she didn't absolutely need. It was enough for a down payment and renovation materials.

She began the painstaking process of remodeling the interior of the Queen Anne, which was more neglected and abused than she could have imagined. She started by stripping dirty white paint off original crown molding, digging out the hand-carved banisters from the attic and restoring them, knocking out walls, and peeling away flowered wallpaper, first while heavily pregnant and then with her newborn cozied to her chest. The house began to purr and preen.

It was while she was refinishing the wooden floor where her father had breathed his last that she discovered the *Book of Secrets*. She'd been laying heavy on the sander, sweat running down her back, melding her shapeless dress to her like a second skin, going at a particularly rough spot when her damp hands lost control of the machine.

It careened into the nearest wall of the foyer between the kitchen and the dining room, tripping a switch. A thick maple panel slid open with a whoosh and an exhalation of air that smelled of salt and roses, revealing a secret alcove as large as a bread box. Ursula recognized the same blue glow emanating from the cove as surrounded the plants she harvested for her potions. Heart fluttering, she reached in.

The secret space held only one thing: a book so thick that she couldn't hold it with one hand. The outside cover was worn brown leather that always felt warm to the touch, like the skin of an elephant. She opened it with shaking hands. The paper inside was linen, and the secrets handwritten in fine, scrolled black calligraphy. No author was credited, though it looked to Ursula like at least two different types of handwriting were in the book, along with a third who had drawn vibrant designs of flowers, vines, and plump vegetables at the edges and in the corners.

She tried to start at the beginning. A different page fell open, and the silky promise of answers pulled her in. She lost a whole day to the book, reading of spells and potions, and barely put a dent in it. Magic was familiar to her—every Catalain woman was born with some—and so she accepted the book as she had accepted the house. It was a sentient thing, powerful and independent. She told no one of the book, vowing to open it only when she had a question or needed help, and went back to refinishing the house.

She hired a local handyman to scrape paint the color of a smoker's teeth from the exterior. He tinted the turret and first and second floors a rich maroon and the third story malachite green. The recesses and trim were painted cream except for the many window frames, which he shaded the green of the turret on the first pass and deep purple on the strip closest to the window.

It took two years, but when she was done, she had reclaimed the storybook house of her imagination. It was in focus for the first time in a half century, a crisp form against the plum-and-cream of a dusky sky, and people commented on what a beauty it was, so well-kept. Of course, they whispered, it must be terrible to heat in the winter, those old houses always were, and thank goodness that wasn't their problem.

Ursula chuckled. She could do that now that she had the Queen Anne.

With the house restored, she tackled the garden, an overgrown tangle of animal waste, crabgrass, and cigarette butts. She burnt off the top layer, letting fire cauterize and the ash seep deep into the dirt like balm. Then, she raked until she was sure all the glass and garbage were removed. Finally, she turned the soil with hand and spade, not willing to let the unnatural drip of a gasoline-powered tiller pollute what she was creating. When her work was complete, the plot was half an acre, abutting Rum River and half a mile north from the 20-foot waterfall that had given the town its name. The freshly-turned soil was as deep and soft as velvet, crawling with plump earthworms, swollen with minerals.

The cottage was her final project, the building little more than an oversized garden shed and draped with thick, spongy moss from which emanated the intoxicating scent of petrichor no matter the weather. Rather than disturb the drowsy moss, she instructed the carpenters to build up from the inside using wood and stone. They also added a small greenhouse onto the back, and leading to the front, laid river rock stepping stones to connect the tiny bungalow with the clematis-tangled back gate and the rear door of the Queen Anne. The result was a crooked garden cottage straight out of a fairy tale.

The inside of the cottage became a rustic but sturdy laboratory, the walls lined with bottles and herbs, books on alchemy, glittering charms, tables strewn with drying herbs, and containers of sweet oil that undulated even when the bottle was still. The smell was of humid earth and exotic plants, sewn together with a chemist's tang.

She divided her days between the garden and the cottage, her sweet, serious Jasmine playing with hand-sewn dolls at her feet or chewing sticks and tasting herbs. The baby would reach up with chubby hands when she was hungry, and Ursula's face would break into a surprised smile, as if she had forgotten she had a child.

On either side of her property, bland colonial ramblers sprang up, so Ursula built a six-foot tall cedar fence to shield her garden. And it was perfect. She grew no vegetables, only herbs and flowers, spicy bright things that winked and flirted with the sun and worshipped the moon.

When everything on the property was ready, Ursula invited her beloved twin sisters to live with her. The year was 1982, and she was eight months pregnant with her second child, father unknown, even to her.

Ursula's sisters arrived together, Xenia driving a yellow moving truck and sunny Helena steering their cornflower blue minivan. "The Catalains are back in town," people whispered. It was funny because Velda had been around for years. She had just done an exemplary job of massaging the town's memory. And of course Ursula had been back for over two years, quietly building her nest and raising Jasmine. Something about the four women in town together for the first time in over a decade caused a critical mass.

Their combined presence dipped the townspeople a little more deeply into the muddy gray puddles of their lives than they liked. This is the way of all small towns, forever. Too much brightness reminds people what they don't have, and so they fight to extinguish it. The whispers of witchcraft, so prevalent immediately after Eve and Ennis had built the Queen Anne and then disappeared, began to recirculate.

The twins ignored the rumors and talked Ursula into letting Velda visit when she wanted, and all four of them lived their lives. Faith Falls, for its part, spent the next twenty years in an uneasy truce with the Catalains. Men and women came and went from their bedrooms. Ursula's daughters, Jasmine and Katrine, grew.

When the snakes returned to Faith Falls in 1990, as they did every 25 years since time remembered, Ursula held her breath, but of course her father's corpse didn't reanimate and enact revenge upon her and her children. The thought was ludicrous. Ursula believed in the science of magic, not the superstition of curses, and the recollection of her father's murder faded to a daguerreotype gray.

Comforted by the embracing sweetness of moonflowers and the familiar rhythm of her oasis, Ursula pushed one hand into the rich soil. The pulse of the earth caressed her fingertips as she searched downward. Her stretching fingers passed earthworms and beetles and plunged through the crust into the first level of the water table. She let them dance there for several seconds before yanking her hand back, startled by the sound of a car.

It was 3:00 in the morning, and in a town of 10,000 people, traffic this late was as rare as a police siren. A lonely man must be lost, or a pair of hormone-drenched teenagers was searching out a quiet spot for late-night necking, though she doubted that's what kids called it nowadays.

She shook the dirt from her hand, grabbed the blue decanter by its neck and stood. The glass hummed. "Oh, you old knees," she whispered down at her legs. "What am I going to do with you?"

But her voice was playful. She was in her favorite place, and everything was now as balanced as she could make it. She even smelled a hint of rain in the air, the pregnant promise of a storm to feed her rootlings. But then she sensed something more. She sniffed to be sure, but there it was, a scent that made her shoulder blades draw up: a hint of sandalwood and cucumber. She cocked her head, searching the air with the antenna of her intuition.

That smell could only mean one thing: Katrine was here.

The Catalain Book of Secrets:
Digging

Humans have an inclination to confuse pain, coal, and paper for something of value. Don't despair if you can't tell the difference between real treasure and fool's gold, or worse, if you start treating the ill luck that's befallen you like a diamond to be hoarded. The answer is the same, no matter what you hold in your hands: don't bury it.

If you find yourself drawn to the same patch of dirt—either in the earth or in your memories— locate a sturdy hand shovel and dig until you either find what you're looking for or you feel foolish for putting it underground in the first place.

In either case, let it go.

CHAPTER 4

Ursula

"You sure you don't need anything?"

"Mom."

It sounded like a four-letter word the way Katrine said it, piercing Ursula. She had vowed to herself before she even knew she was pregnant with Jasmine that she would never criticize her daughters the way that Velda had put her down, never control them the way her mother had done to her. So Ursula nodded, and did more than bite her tongue; she swallowed it, turning away from the daughter she hadn't seen in over a decade and closing the bedroom door behind her.

She walked downstairs, unable to shake the image of how tired Katrine had looked when she'd arrived twelve hours ago and how she still looked, her lovely cheekbones sunken into themselves, the gray dust coating her skin, the dimness of her eyes. It hurt Ursula's heart, and so she soothed herself the only way she knew how. She'd been thirteen when she lost her virginity, fourteen when she started sleeping with men twice, sometimes three times her age. Velda hadn't noticed.

Ursula's latest lover was a plumber who lived on the south side of town. After running to the store to purchase all of Katrine's favorite foods, Ursula drove to his house and watched him and his wife through their bay window, the light of the TV flickering across their faces. He was a potato-faced man, she a kind-hearted woman who'd grown tired with life. When the wife went to bed, Ursula left her car and tapped on the glass.

Startled, his head jerked toward the window. His eyes widened when he saw Ursula, traveled in alarm to the door his wife had gone through, then landed back on Ursula. She didn't move. He met her at the front door.

"What are you doing here?" His voice was a heated stage whisper.

She took his hand and yanked him toward her car. This was their fourth meeting; the first had been when he'd stopped by three weeks ago to fix the water heater and the second and third were when he'd stopped by to do "follow-up work." She had chosen him by the same criteria that she chose all her men: they were already taken and so there was no risk of a relationship, and the women they were married to had already strayed. He tried to pull back from her now, outside his home, but she placed her hand on his crotch, squeezing hard. His shoulders softened.

"Fine, but hold up. I need to tell Myrna I've got an emergency call."

He slipped into the house, exiting a few minutes later with his plumbing tools in hand. Ursula was leaning against her car.

"Can you at least hide, for Christ's sake?"

She stared at him coolly. "If you don't want this, you didn't have to come out."

He glanced over his shoulder, then back at Ursula. His expression blazed with a particular heat she'd become accustomed to in the eyes of other women's husbands. "I'll meet you at the north edge of City Park."

She beat him there, yanked open his pick-up door when he arrived, and climbed on top. She changed his radio to an oldies rock station before she unzipped his pants and guided him out. She wasn't wearing underwear. Her movements were confident and aggressive. She rode him with her eyes closed, imagining he was someone else, until the wave of pleasure began to build in her stomach, searching higher, higher, until it overtook her. Her peace was complete, but temporary.

She climbed off without so much as a goodbye, leaving the plumber with his mouth and pants open. There was nothing more to be had from this man. She would end their trysting the way she always did, by giving him a potion that would reignite his love for his wife, turning it into a consuming passion where the only way he could earn respite was to treat his wife like a queen.

When she returned to the Queen Anne, she still couldn't sleep. Her daughter had been gone for too long. The woman sleeping upstairs felt like a stranger. Ursula didn't know what she should do for her, and so she lay in bed, eyes open, ears tuned to the slightest sound from Katrine's room.

The sun rose, and still no sound filtered from her daughter's bedroom. She tiptoed downstairs and was relieved to find Helena and Xenia were up and busy fluttering around the kitchen. The sight of her sisters bustling loosened her chest, and she pulled her first deep breath of the day.

"Katrine walked like a ghost who didn't know she was dead, didn't she?" Helena asked Ursula by way of a good morning.

"You don't have to be so dramatic," Xenia, Helena's twin, cut in, reaching behind her sister to grab the coffee beans from the cupboard. Where Helena was round and comfy, Xenia was lean as a jaguar. Helena's hair was thick blond and curly, and Xenia's was black and straight as a sword, with encroaching gray above each ear. Ursula had allowed her twin sisters a tiny vegetable plot on the side of the house. Helena couldn't bear to pull any of the tiny carrot shoots when they first sprouted, even if they were suffocating each other, but Xenia gutted them.

The twins had lived together since the moment of conception, and other than their devotion to one another and their malachite-green eyes, could not be more dissimilar. Despite the vast differences in their appearance and personality, they could be picked out as Catalains from across a crowded room. It was in their eyes as well as their quiet confidence, not the slightest hint of apology in the swing of their hips.

"She was just tired," Xenia continued. "Jet-lagged."

"Dead tired." Standing at the island in the center of the Queen Anne's grand old kitchen, Helena was using a metal spatula to coax the divinity off the parchment paper. She waved the spatula in the air when Ursula glanced at the candy. "Don't even tell me it's too humid to make divinity. We need this specific candy for the clarity it provides. Soothing, too. See the soft blues and greens I used?"

Ursula nodded and glanced at the clock. Katrine had been in her childhood room for nearly twenty-four hours with barely a squeak to anyone. She sighed and returned her attention to her sisters, her love for them a constant. She'd raised them, after all. An old thought, one she hadn't considered in decades, flitted across her brain pan: would her sisters still love her if they knew she'd murdered their father? She stuffed the black idea back into whatever hole it had crawled out of.

"What do I do about Katrine?" Ursula asked simply.

"Let her sleep," Xenia began.

"Then throw her a welcome home party," Helena finished.

"But—" Ursula started, but before she could complete her sentence, Helena tossed a puff of divinity into her mouth, and the sweetness melted into her tongue like an answer. Such was Helena's magic.

"Who wants to tell Jasmine?" Xenia asked.

"You don't think she already knows?" Ursula leaned into a cupboard to grab a coffee cup when a muscle spasm tightened her right arm. She must be doing too much mixing in her shop. Or maybe it was the thought of her oldest daughter, who had grown from a serious and gifted child to a disconnected one, despite living only across town. Jasmine didn't have her grandmother's gift for mirroring or her shallowness, but in so many other ways reminded Ursula of Velda.

"There's a lot that girl doesn't know since she started medicating." Xenia reached over and chose a kiss-shaped candy, a wisp of seafoam green, and popped it into her mouth. "I'll call her."

"Maybe we should invite her over for dinner? And Tara?" Helena had a habit of ending her sentences in questions, especially when she was talking to her twin, the yin to her yang, the shadow to her light.

"And Velda," Xenia said.

Ursula clenched.

"And Velda." Helena reached into the cupboard for pecans and brown sugar. "I'll get started on the patience candy."

CHAPTER 5

Katrine

Katrine wasn't asleep.

She guessed that her aunts were downstairs right now worrying, and that her mother was wishing she could brew a potion for her to ease the weight at her chest and throat, but she couldn't find it in herself to leave her childhood bed just yet. Her room was a chantry of memories, her body a jittery cord of electricity under the Mariner's Compass quilt. It took all her will to keep her eyes shut as her thoughts raced around her skull like caged fox.

The sharp, clean scent of sage threaded the cool cotton sheets and pulled her spirit outside along the whispering banks of the Rum River behind the house, where she and Jasmine had spent summers back when the earth was a softer place for children. They'd play at rock skipping, toad hunting, flower picking, and daring each other to swim out to the center where the current shot swift and silver like mercury sluicing down a hill. Playing chicken drop, they'd call it.

Katrine always ventured out the farthest in chicken drop, would let the force of the river carry her to the rocky whorls where the water washed over her head, bouncing her from side to side. She wouldn't dare it when the water was so high that it rushed the banks, but if the summer had been dry, she'd let the river propel her to the edge of Faith Falls. They were Minnesota falls, neither high nor theatrical, twenty feet of foamy, roiling water that plunged down in steps rather than in a single dramatic drop.

One summer when Jasmine and Katrine were still pig-tailed and freckle-faced, someone had tossed a garbage bag of newborn puppies in at the public access, 600 yards north of the falls. Three of the retrievers had managed to paddle their way to the opposite shore, but the fourth had plummeted over the falls, where his body was found battered and bloodied.

When Jasmine and Katrine heard the story, they'd cried, and then spent hours planning tortures for the perpetrator. He or she was never caught, which was their good fortune as the girls had settled on a mixture of battery acid, razors, and a turkey baster.

"You're going to go over!" Jasmine would squeal every time Katrine took on the river in chicken drop, her voice drowned by the rumble of the falls. Once Jasmine realized her sister was going to do it, was really going to let the current take her, she'd shadow her along the bank, her colt legs poking out of her dripping shorts as she darted downstream.

Katrine heard her sister every time but dared not open her mouth or the river would rush in and through her, embracing her inside and out. Instead, she would flash the thumbs up, feet poised forward to allow her to bounce off of rather than crash into rocks. Her target, a low branch ten yards on the safe side of the falls, rushed to meet her. Each pass she had one chance to catch it. Every time she did.

"Goll, you're crazy!" Jasmine complained one day the same summer the puppies had been dumped in the river. She watched as her sister hauled herself hand over hand along the length of the branch, white foam swirling around her soaked shirt. The rapids gnashed their teeth in thunders of frustration, but Katrine ignored them, towing herself along the branch until it was shallow and calm enough for her to stand.

Katrine laughed when she reached the shore. She stood, her breath short from the work of it, and shook herself like a dog, her heart thumping pleasantly. The sun warmed her summer-tanned skin. "It's fun. You should try it."

Jasmine never did. She was the older of the two, a rule-follower since she was born. At nine, that meant grown-ups listened to her more than regular kids, talking to her instead of around her. Her constancy shaded Katrine like an umbrella, protecting her from adult eyes and giving her the confidence to skin her knees and pop up to try again, to ring doorbells and run on a dare, to make up ghost stories featuring fairy princesses and hook-handed pirates, and to wear too-short dresses because she liked how free they made her feel.

Even at a young age, Katrine recognized this gift her sister gave her, generous Jasmine who possessed more magic than anyone in their family, Ursula included. Katrine barely had a spark in comparison, but she had Jasmine.

"At least swim with me," Katrine begged. "You were already in the water, anyhow. We can walk back up where it's shallower."

Jasmine shook her head, shoving her toe in the mud. "I don't want to."

"We could make a Popsicle raft and float a frog down on it?"

Jasmine's eyes widened before she erased the expression. "You wouldn't."

"I might."

"You'd *never* hurt a frog. Everyone knows that. Anyway, I'd tell Ursula."

"Would not. Anyhow, I wasn't going to do it. I just wanted to keep you away from that bitchy hole you were falling into."

Jasmine stuck her tongue out. Nine wasn't too old for that, as long as no one else was watching. "It's time to get back. Ursula's taking us to get our hair done for the dance. Remember?" They'd always called their female relatives by their first name, even their mother. Especially their mother.

"I probably remember better than her."

But Jasmine was off, grabbing her picnic basket before striding upstream toward the house. She'd been a constant presence in the kitchen since she was old enough to walk, asking Ursula what she was stirring or Helena why she boiled toffee longer than caramel. She baked her first pie at age seven, an apple tart with homemade crust that tasted like autumn and cured Xenia's allergies.

It was Jasmine's gift, her magic, to create food so delectable that it made you forget your pains, which was all Jasmine wanted it to do. Katrine sometimes wished she possessed a powerful magic like that, but all she had was a fritzing, unreliable ability to read some people's emotions, and sometimes their thoughts. Jasmine, on the other hand, had the whole world of food, and the power to make the eater do anything she desired. For today's picnic, she'd packed creamy egg salad sandwiches accented with bright dill and celery, spread it on homemade wheatberry bread, and complemented it with a side of crunchy salt pickles that she'd canned herself.

The meal was the perfect mix of textures and flavors, and eating it made Katrine feel precious, as well as gave her a vision of where she'd left the amber ring she'd been seeking for over a week. Not for the first time, Katrine was grateful that Jasmine loved her, because she could really mess a person up with her witchy cooking if she wanted to.

Katrine walked behind her sister, following the bank, listening to the song of the river, watching water bugs slide and skate across the surface. Her nose itched, and she wondered what it would feel like to be able to fly. "See, I knew you thought the same. She won't be there."

"What?" Jasmine had stopped for her sister to catch up and was scowling.

"I was agreeing with you. I don't think Ursula will be there either. She has that client coming over tonight, and you know how she gets with new clients. Always in her workshop."

"You stop that, Katrine Catalain."

"Stop what?"

"Get right outta my head." Tears gleamed in Jasmine's eyes, crystal drops escaping the sheltered pool around her heart. "If Ursula isn't there, Helena will take us. We'll still get our hair done."

Katrine shrugged. She wasn't a mind reader, not really. She only caught scraps of other people's thoughts, the punch line to a joke here, a secret shame there, each thought fleeting but written across her frontal lobe as plainly as a newspaper headline. She knew she had the weakest gift of the family, but it didn't take a mind reader to understand that her sister was worried their mother would let them down. Again. Ursula tended to her daughters like the sun tends to the planets—distantly, almost as an afterthought, by nature of proximity rather than intent. Katrine knew Jasmine felt it like a new hurt every time their mother chose a customer over them.

"I don't care about any fucking haircut," Katrine said, trying out this particular swear word for the first time. It tasted delicious and a little bitter, like dark chocolate. Her goal had been to shock her sister out of one of her sad tempers, but once uttered, she thought she might like to drop the f-bomb more frequently.

But Jasmine was gone, running toward the house. Katrine didn't follow, instead searching and stooping to collect the translucent red river agates that always cheered up her sister. Her fingers grew muddy digging for the stones, and she bent more than one fingernail back trying to pry them loose from the earth. When she had a handful, she rinsed them in the river. The water burbled its approval.

At some point, the cushiony claws of sleep coaxed adult Katrine from these river memories, pulling her down, through the mattress, outside the room of musty wallpaper and crown molding, high school yearbooks, a treasure box brimming with smooth stones, bits of river glass, a dusty bird's nest. She found herself in a smoky bar, a place she'd never been before yet was as familiar as the tops of her knees. She smelled cigarettes and sour whiskey fermenting in the floorboards.

A man was beckoning to her, a tall figure wearing a cowboy hat, a guitar slung over his shoulder. She elbowed her way through the laughing crowd, weaving around people who were clinking their beer bottles and twirling the ice in their sweating glasses of bourbon, but the man never seemed to draw closer.

When a door slammed open in front of her, she knew that's where the cowboy had gone. She strode through, instead discovering her husband Adam on his knees, his head between the thighs of a familiar woman. She screamed herself awake, ripping open her eyes and embracing the merciful gray of twilight.

She'd gone from a girl who'd play chicken with waterfalls to a woman afraid to leave her bedroom.

She needed Jasmine. It was Jasmine who had called her home. But why now?

CHAPTER 6

Jasmine

On a sunny day, Jasmine's lawn held the shadow of Our Lady of the Lake's mighty spike, the tip of it pointing toward her house like an accusation. The planned neighborhood she lived in with her husband and daughter had defined the edge of town after World War II, row upon row of tiny identical bungalows ordered from the Sears and Roebuck catalog and erected by the newly-hired employees of the Samaras Motor Company. Tivadar Samaras had arrived in America from Greece in 1942, oblivious to the war, following a black-eyed girl with hips like a lyre. The affair didn't last long, but he stayed where he'd landed—New York.

The woman with dark eyes turned out to be one of many beauties he fell hard for, but he had the good fortune to impregnate only one: the daughter of a wealthy hotel magnate, whom he met while cleaning the elevator of the New York Hilton. She encouraged his dreams, including his passion for developing a car with seats that folded into a double bed. They drove west to Minnesota, the land of cheap real estate, mosquitoes, and abundant water, and the Sam Car was born.

Tivadar filled his Faith Falls factory floor with World War II veterans and his office and bed with their wives. His business went great guns for the first five years, until his investors caught up with him and realized that only 947 of 10,000 cars had been sold. Apparently, Midwesterners wanted to keep their beds in their bedrooms, where the Good Lord intended. Tivadar fled back to New York with his wife, leaving behind 145 unemployed and an empty factory with an underground tunnel system leading from it to each two-bedroom bungalow on Sam Street. The tunnels had been another of his dreams. He'd envisioned a workforce that was never late because they could walk under the weather, avoiding the slicing winter cold. Like all of his ideas, it was still searching for its time.

Over the years, many of the original Samaras Motor Company employees had sold their houses. Some of the new homeowners boarded up their basement entrance to the tunnels. Rumor had it others left theirs open, and that each generation of Faith Falls' teenagers had completed the rite of passage of sneaking through the creepy passageways to the abandoned factory with its shattered windows and cavernous rooms to drink sweet, syrupy liquor and smoke menthol cigarettes.

Before Jasmine and her husband moved into their single-story, pale-green bungalow on Sam Street, she'd ordered him to brick over the already-boarded-up entrance in their basement, worried a criminal might sneak in while they were sleeping. She'd had bouts of curiosity about what lay beyond the portal, but the antidepressants shushed those thoughts.

August was a slow month, and today, rather than working, she was staring out the kitchen window at the shadow of the church spike, preparing supper and planning Tara's next geology unit, when the phone rang. The unexpected trill turned her breasts cold, which is what passed for nervous with the pills driving her brain stem. She was surprised by the emotion. She'd been jittery all day. Jasmine pulled her white cardigan tighter and rested the knife she'd been using to mince garlic. She was preparing chicken alfredo, Dean's favorite. He preferred the store bought version, but she'd discovered that if she added a sprinkle of sautéed garlic to the generic sauce, he didn't know the difference.

It wouldn't matter as he wouldn't be joining them, hadn't eaten a meal at his own table in three months. It was her unhappiness, he'd said. He couldn't take it anymore. She'd protested, explaining that she had everything she wanted. He'd shaken his head, his eyes so deep and sad. And he'd left. To Tara, she explained that her dad would be traveling more and so she wouldn't see him as often. To everyone else, she said everything was fine.

She rinsed her hands under warm water and tensed, waiting for the phone to stop.

Besides chicken alfredo, she was preparing his favorite sides: crisp head lettuce with ketchupy Western dressing and uniformly square garlic croutons and fresh-baked Pillsbury breadsticks. The house smelled like store-bought bread. It was a canned smell, no match for the rich aroma of the hand-kneaded bread she used to make, but it would do. She'd even picked up a frozen cheesecake for dessert.

Heather Lewis should be dropping off Tara soon as well. It had taken five years of hard work and personal sacrifices for Jasmine to win Heather's confidence, but it had been worth it. Heather hailed from the most powerful family in town, and befriending her ensured Tara's popularity. Jasmine drove their daughters to religion class, and Heather drove them home. With both girls starting viola lessons, the routine had transferred to their Sunday night music classes.

Even so, Jasmine was afraid that the mooring that was Tara would cleave from her if she didn't watch over her child, as if without active attention, her daughter would float off into the ether. Jasmine reminded herself that there was more to her than being a mother, and when the day came for Tara to move out and on, she would remember what that was. Until then, she home-schooled her daughter, ferried her to Immanuel Lutheran Church on Sundays and Wednesdays and music lessons on Tuesdays, and provided Dean updates when he called from the road and asked to schedule time with his daughter.

The machine clicked over. "Jasmine? It's Xenia. You're probably busy, but, well…Katrine is back in town. Can you believe it? We'd all love to have you and Tara stop by tomorrow for supper. Dean too, if he's home. No need to call, or to bring anything. Just show up if you can make it."

Jasmine returned to her cutting board and took up the chef's knife, mincing the already tiny garlic flecks until they were juice and the board was etched with grooves. Her sister was back in the path of danger. Even worse was the unexpected electric surge of betrayal: Katrine broke the spell on her own, which meant she could have come back at any time and had simply never wanted to enough.

CHAPTER 7

Tara

As Tara watched her mom brutalize the garlic, her stomach knotted. Here's what she knew: her mom had had one best friend in the world and it was her sister, Katrine. Then something terrible had happened to Jasmine. That awful thing had somehow sent Katrine across the globe and driven Jasmine to antidepressants. It was also the same reason Jasmine wouldn't talk to Tara about her Catalain magic, wouldn't even acknowledge that Tara might have some.

Might have *a lot*, in fact, enough for her to know things about people that they didn't even know about themselves. Enough to know that her dad had left three months ago. Enough to know that if her mom didn't open the door on her heart and release the secrets that were poisoning her that nothing would be all right again.

Tara had been watching her mom all day, noticing her jerky movements, the way she snapped and then apologized, how she forgot what she'd gone into a room for. Even now, as Tara watched her mom cook, she understood that Jasmine was strung as tense as a piano wire, so taut that she didn't even notice Tara on the other side of the breakfast nook.

When the phone rang, they'd both jumped. Tara had itched to answer it, but she sensed she'd learn more by watching her mom. Jasmine stood rock-still.

The ringing ended, and Jasmine had exhaled a shaky breath.

Then Xenia's message had played out. Jasmine had begun to obliterate the garlic.

And Tara had stopped breathing. *I get to meet Katrine.*

Chapter 8

Katrine

She held a snowglobe in her hand, turning it upside down, letting the flakes whirl around a diorama of Faith Falls, then turning it rightside up so the snow could settle. She'd received the gift from her aunt Xenia for her eighth Christmas.

There had been so much food and so many people—clients of Ursula's, Helena and Xenia and Velda's lovers—that they'd had to move into the Queen Anne's massive drawing room to hold it all. The table was creaking under lavender-infused Duck L'orange covered in crispy, sweet-salty skin, tiny quails stuffed with sage dressing, wild perch drizzled with onion jam, garlic soup with poached eggs, freshly-dug garden potatoes in browned parsley butter, their skin so tender that it melted when you bit into it, haricot verts in a lemon-almond sauce, roasted butternut squash, delicate mushroom caps filled with salty bacon, wild rice, and poached raisins, fresh spinach dressed with poppyseed vinaigrette, a wild lettuce salad speckled with sunflower nuts and bits of bright, fresh orange, platters of grapes, apples, nuts, and cheeses, and two loaves of oatmeal bread and another two of crusty French, all four loaves steaming. Ten-year-old Jasmine had cooked it all, and everyone who tasted it felt safe and loved.

Conversation had been lively, flowing as sweetly as the wine.

Katrine remembered being so happy that she'd felt like the color pink. She'd missed her family desperately. She couldn't wait to see Jasmine again, Jasmine who had called her back, who was in crisis but who would also make everything right, like she always had.

CHAPTER 9

Ursula

The woman reached toward the cool doorknob of the cottage tucked behind the Queen Anne, and then let her hand dangle in the air. She wore slouchy suede boots, a matching skirt, and a navy blue blouse that made her eyes appear almost black. At her wrists and neck, chunky, blue plastic jewelry deflected the sunlight. Ursula watched the woman from the kitchen window. She arrived at the back gate as they all did—tentatively—and had made her way to the cottage before standing in front of it, uncertain.

This visitor owned the Chinese restaurant in town. Probably, she'd overheard customers talking about Ursula. Most of her marketing was whispered word of mouth. Ursula speculated briefly on what had brought the woman here, and whether she would have the courage to approach the back door of the Queen Anne once she realized there was no one in the cottage.

She did.

Ursula waited several beats before she opened the back door of the house. The woman stood there, a scared animal ready to bolt, her eyes on her feet.

"Hello," she whispered.

"Can I help you?"

The woman still didn't look up. Ursula let the silence grow heavier than the woman's fear. It took less time than she'd guessed it would before the woman dragged her stare up to meet Ursula's gaze. Her eyes widened, and the words poured out.

Her name was Diane. She and her husband had fled Vietnam after the war. She'd concealed all her jewelry in her youngest daughter's diaper and managed to keep it hidden on the long journey to America. Her husband had brought them to Minnesota, where he sold her precious gold to buy a restaurant in a river town where everyone looked the same.

She was proud of her cooking and her ability to honor the principle of five elements in every dish—five spices and five colors corresponding to five organs, senses, and elements. Her specialty was *lau canh chua*, a bright, sour soup simmering with slivers of shrimp and crab, cheerful pineapple floating against deep red tomatoes, bamboo shoots, and a hint of tamarind paste.

Her English was good enough to converse with her regulars, the people she cooked special dishes for and those who came for her sweet-n-sour pork. She didn't tell them the latter was not a Vietnamese dish; they liked knowing only what they knew. She smiled when she talked, a big toothy grin, and to all her customers, she was cheerful, forever happy, the perfect hostess. On the surface, this was true. Her daughters were ungrateful, her husband sullen, her son living across country, but she recognized that she was lucky to be alive and a day didn't pass when she didn't thank Jesus Christ for her family's safety and their new country. But she wasn't happy, and her dissatisfaction had nothing to do with her family.

She was sad in her secret soul because she'd never sung in public.

She'd saved for years, stealing pennies here and there, to purchase her own home karaoke machine. Her husband mocked her, asked why'd she buy something she wasn't going to use. Her daughters played around with it for a few weeks but grew bored. None of them knew that she stole downstairs when they were asleep, mouthing the words to "Dancing Queen" with headphones cupping her ears. It made her heart soar, but it was just practice for the day when she was brave enough to pick up the microphone at the VFW on Karaoke and Taco Tuesday.

Her speech over, she drew a shuddering breath, her gaze still locked on Ursula's. "Please. You help me?"

In helping people, Ursula could scrub at the spiritual stain of her father's death. It felt even better to help when they were good people, like Diane. If she was quick, and she always was, she could give this woman what she needed and still have plenty of time to prepare for Katrine's party tonight.

Ursula smiled. "I think I have just what you need."

The Catalain Book of Secrets:
Stage Fright

Every great dream carries with it an
equally powerful fear. This is the natural
balance of things, as every front requires
a back. The danger comes when a person
confuses the fear for the dream and spends
more time imagining, dreading, and planning
for the bad than the good. A balanced tincture
of yellow jessamine, peppermint oil, and lunar
caustic, with 190 proof Everclear as the solvent,
will dissolve this fear and anxiety. If you find
yourself short on materials, you can eliminate the
jessamine, peppermint oil, and lunar caustic.

CHAPTER 10

The Queen Anne

Velda was the first to arrive. She came empty-handed, always, her once jet black hair now a glorious grey, her petite form barely brushing the surface of the Queen Anne's wraparound porch. The boards of the steps creaked a greeting. At her side walked Artemis Hartshorn Buckley, a tiny man, lean as beef jerky, whose name was bigger than he was.

Artemis was known across five counties as the man who'd tied 523 helium balloons to his favorite lawn chair and floated up and across the highway to Pelican Lake, where he'd come down in twenty feet of water.

When asked why he'd done it, he'd said, "It's life. You can't wait for it."

That was last summer. Velda had tracked him down after she'd read about him in the *Faith Falls Gazette*, and they'd stuck to each other like tree sap since then. She'd tried to seduce him at first, but he'd talked her out of it, and they'd settled into a steady friendship.

"Squirrel meatballs," Artemis said, handing Helena a steaming crockpot at the door. He lived downriver in a cabin he'd built with his own hands. He made a living as a carpenter but didn't require much as he lived off the land where possible.

"Oh. Do they taste like chicken?" Helena offered a helpful smile.

"Nope. Taste like squirrel. You look mighty sharp tonight."

Velda nodded in agreement as Helena covered her surprised expression and smoothed the flowered, lemon-yellow dress over her ample hips. "Thank you. Make yourself at home."

"Don't mind if we do." Artemis led Velda to the drawing room to the right of the foyer, the central gathering place in the house after the kitchen. The drawing room was an enormous space with dark, hardwood floors and high ceilings. Two walls were decorated with bookshelves, and the other two were hung with rich oil paintings in mahogany frames mixed with watercolors Helena had created in a community ed class and even some framed finger paintings from when Jasmine and Katrine were younger. Mismatched but comfortable chairs and two couches were arrayed throughout the room, and a fire flickered in the marble fireplace. The flame was small and unnecessary during warm summer evenings, but it created a sense of coziness in the gigantic room.

The smell of woodsmoke twined with the roasting chickens and corn on the cob in the backyard barbeque pit, which could be accessed by walking through the open French doors on the far side of the drawing room. Sweating bottles of white wine, beer, and water poked out of a tub of ice near one of the French doors. Artemis grabbed a Leinenkugel and poured Velda a glass of Riesling. Velda accepted the cool wine and added three limes. Helena mixed herself a white wine spritzer, and followed her mother, still nervous after all these years. When Ursula and Velda got together, even the air held its breath.

Xenia, sensing her sister's distress, came out from the kitchen, her hair pulled back into a tight black bun, a bag of sourdough rolls in her hand. "Good to see you, Mother."

Velda stood on her tiptoes to hug her and then stepped back. "Is Ursula grilling?"

The twins nodded, their eyes bright. They would have been surprised to know that they were standing in identical stances, arms crossed, heads cocked.

"I'll go say hi." Velda strolled out to the barbeque pit, the twins following close behind. Ursula was bent over the smoking grill, spatula in hand.

"Smells good enough," Velda said.

Ursula ignored the comment. "She's been in her room since she arrived," she said, nodding up at the second story of the house.

Velda glanced at the second floor window. It was open, white curtains fluttering out into the soft breeze. "Ever think about going to talk to her?"

"Xenia and Helena have both been up there, trying to comfort her. She told them she wants to be alone to rest, and I respected that. I peeked on her between clients, and she was asleep."

"It's true," Helena interrupted. "She's been sleeping straight through."

Velda clucked, ignoring Helena's interjection. "Being a mother never did come easy to you."

Ursula's posture crumpled, but she kept turning the corn. Artemis, who had followed Velda outdoors, watched both women, his face keen.

When she didn't get a rise, Velda sighed and began walking toward the house. "I wish, just once, you'd show some fight, Ursula. I'll go get Katrine. Sometimes you need someone to pull you back into the game."

Helena scrambled straight to Ursula, tut-tutting with worry and holding out a tray that she had grabbed from the picnic table. "More candy?"

"You've been pushing that patience candy on me all day," Ursula said, her voice kind but strained. "You know I don't like pecans."

"Divinity, then?"

Ursula smiled at her sister. "No. Thank you. I'm fine."

"We'll have to be sure to not ask Katrine too many questions, isn't that right?" Helena asked no one in particular, voicing the exact opposite of what she was dying to do. She offered her tray of sweets to Artemis, who took two brown patience candies and a dollop of divinity, made a sandwich with them, and popped it into his mouth. "She's had a long trip and doesn't need us all landing on her like flies."

Xenia stepped over and patted her twin on the shoulder. "We're all as worried as you are, but I think it's the best plan. We don't want to scare her off again. She'll talk to us when she's ready, though it'd be nice to know how long she's planning to stay. I hope it's for a good long time. Family's where you need to be when things turn sour."

Velda glided outside within minutes, toting her withdrawn granddaughter. Katrine wore a beautifully-cut taupe pantsuit, but walked like a grounded bird. The Queen Anne remembered her as the prettiest girl in town growing up. She'd attracted boys and envious stares equally, and while there was a shadow of that insouciant glamour still there, her hunched spine and travel-worn hair pulled into a messy pony tail spoke of exhaustion rather than beauty. Even her Catalain green eyes, the color of the secret parts of the ocean, were faded.

Before Katrine's aunts could form a protective barrier around her, Artemis appeared in her path and offered his hand. "Name is

Artemis. You must be Katrine. How're you doing?" He had a fleck of divinity stuck between his front teeth, which were otherwise white and evenly-spaced.

The women, all but Velda, stared, their hair swollen and standing up at their necks. Helena moved forward with her tray of candy, but before she reached her niece, Katrine turned to Xenia in lieu of answering Artemis. "I wouldn't mind a glass of summer wine. Can you point me in the right direction?"

"I'll get it for you," Xenia said, disappearing through the French doors.

Katrine returned her tired attention to Artemis, who despite his forthright manner, occupied his space comfortably, like a rocking chair or a favorite sweater. "I'm fine."

He nodded. "You've been living in Europe?"

"London, actually. I moved there after I graduated from college. A long time ago."

"They've got good beer there, yuh?"

"I suppose."

"Welcome home." Artemis rubbed his elbow and glanced around at the group. "Anyone need a fresh drink?"

The women exhaled. Ursula spoke first. "I'll take some red wine. The chicken must be about done. Katrine, I've prepared grilled mushrooms and corn for you."

"I'm not hungry. Just the wine for now."

Xenia returned with a glass of Riesling for Katrine and claret for Ursula. She exchanged a quick look with Helena. "Jasmine might be coming, too. But we won't wait for her if the food is just about ready. Why don't we go inside and set the table?"

Velda kept her eyes on Katrine. "We should eat dinner outside. One night off of a full moon, and the frogs are singing."

"I wouldn't mind eating outdoors," Artemis said. "It's best to soak up August before winter sucks all the heat out of your bones."

"Great idea," Helena agreed. She returned seconds later with paper plates and flowered napkins, and Artemis helped her set the picnic table. When he winked at her, she flushed and looked away. "And I've got a new candy recipe I want you to try. Later. After we eat."

Katrine smiled. It wasn't up to the standard of her old grin, which stopped men and women in their tracks, but it was a start. "I can't wait."

The house creaked, almost as if it wished for arms to hold them.

Chapter 11

Katrine

The small bonfire, set off from Ursula's garden, crackled in the starry night. Beyond it rested Ursula's work cottage. Behind that, the river gossiped and crooned, trying like a child to gain Katrine's attention, but she was too deep inside herself to hear. The guests were warm from wine and food, and circled the fire in a companionable silence, broken when Artemis wondered how long Katrine would be staying.

Her response, when it came, prickled. "I don't know."

"Honey, you don't have to know," Helena said. "You can stay as long as you want, right? This is your home."

"It is quite the home," Katrine said absently, looking at the grand old Queen Anne through the flicker of the fire. She realized she didn't know the story of it before her mom remodeled it. "Your parents built it, right?"

"Eve and Ennis Catalain," Velda said.

"Tell me everything," Katrine said. Her question was prompted by a desire to not have to talk more than curiosity. Across the fire, Ursula's eyes glittered.

Velda's reluctance was written on her face. She kept it short. Her parents, Ursula's grandparents, moved to town in the early 1900s, when it was an established hub. They were rich, and they were loved, at least at first. They wanted a large house to entertain in. Like many of the homes constructed by wealthy Midwesterners at the end of the nineteenth century, the structure was a solid, drafty, rambling Queen Anne-style Victorian. Eve had wanted a turret, cantilevered gables, and a wraparound front porch. Ennis had added second-story oriels and on the third story, deep-set porthole windows surrounded by ornate trim. The result was the enormous, nooked and crannied, magical gingerbread house mansion.

"I spent the first twenty years of my life in that mausoleum," Velda said, indicating the house whose shadow they rested in.

Ursula only nodded. Velda was now in her element. She wanted an audience, not a conversation.

"Nobody knew where Eve and Ennis came from. Some said New Orleans, others claimed Boston, but whatever the city, everyone knew they came from money." Velda's expression grew distant. "Your grandmother was a beauty. Stunning. She threw elaborate parties and organized town dances and the annual mummer's parade. Her homemade liquor was legendary. In fact, a charming rumor began to circulate that her mulled hard cider was so delicious that it could turn back time, though surely only those who drank too much believed it." Velda allowed a small smile.

"Ennis was handsome, too. He and Eve travelled, bringing back new styles, felted and feathered Homburg hats, silks from the Orient. One year, after a particularly long absence, they brought back a daughter. Me." Velda's voice was bitter. "I was as pretty as a doll and just as biddable. People begged to hold me, would brag for days if they could coax a laugh from me. That's what Eve told me later."

Despite herself, Katrine was leaning forward, hanging on Velda's every word. Such was her grandmother's magic. "Where did they go?"

Velda cut her eyes to the side. "Died. Car accident."

Xenia had heard the story before and had little patience for repetition. "You can help us out at the store," she offered, putting the focus back on Katrine. "We need extra hands this time of year. The tourists are crazy about Helena's chocolates."

Helena smiled with pride. "They come for your dresses, Xenia, and you know it. They just buy the candy so I don't feel bad."

"I'd love to see the place," Katrine said. "Seven Daughters, right?"

"You've never been to it?" Artemis asked.

Katrine shook her head. She'd been in a different world. She had the good grace to feel ashamed of how disconnected she'd become from her family, even if it hadn't been intentional but rather death by neglect. She knew she wouldn't like herself much if she were meeting herself for the first time, and the image almost made her smile. *Well hello, Katrine. So nice to meet you. How long have you been this uptight and controlling? A couple years? How wonderful. And self-involved, too? Great. Your dance card must be super-full.*

"Well, then Seven Daughters is as good a place to start as any in reacquainting yourself," Artemis said. "It's the only store that seems to be riding high, no matter the economy."

"I'm sure the store is great. I don't know how long I'll be around, though." Thinking about her next move felt like too much of a commitment, or like admitting to failure. Both the past and the future were overwhelming. She wanted to be still.

"Still too cool for Faith Falls," came a voice from the side of the house.

Katrine turned, her pulse lifting. "Jasmine?"

Her sister stepped into the light. A teenager was at her side, looking so much like a Catalain that she could only be Tara. Both had Helena's curly blonde hair, but the firelight hollowed their cheeks and flickered on their lean frames, bringing to mind Xenia. They both had the jewel-green Catalain eyes.

The sky snapped. It was the first time all seven had been together: Velda with her glamour, Ursula who concocted potions, Xenia the maker of dresses, Helena the candy crafter, Katrine with her sporadic mind reading, Jasmine and her forsaken cooking magic, and Tara the wild card.

"We can't stay long," Jasmine lied. "Dean's waiting for us."

Katrine stood and moved forward, her step tentative but lighter than it had been since she'd arrived. She didn't know who she wanted to hug first, her sister or her niece, and the palpable strength of her love for both scared her. To protect herself, she stopped, indicating the covered dish in Jasmine's hands. "Please tell me that's your apple cake."

She hadn't known how much she'd been craving it—moist, packed with morsels of still-warm apple, the cream cheese frosting laced with cinnamon and nutmeg. It could cure a sore throat on contact and, if you took seconds, it gave you the church giggles. Katrine hadn't tasted it since she was fourteen years old.

"Pie. This is my daughter Tara, by the way."

The girl studied Katrine with steady eyes. She was fourteen, all elbows, knees, and front teeth, but she stood with her back straight, a student of life already. Katrine nodded at her, a tiny smile flickering at the corner of her mouth. This was the first time she'd laid eyes on her niece. The girl was a beauty. "Pleased to meet you. The photos your mom sent don't do you justice."

The girl nodded back.

"Dean is a trucker. You probably forgot that. Anyhow, he's only home until tomorrow morning, and we can't stay very long."

Jasmine's words rushed out, little chunks of emotions getting trampled by her false syllables. "We stopped in to say hi. I'll leave the pie on the counter."

"You can stay and eat some with us," Ursula called from beside the fire. Her words were neutral, threading the thrumming tension.

Unable to stand the distance a moment longer, Katrine stepped forward, her arms outstretched. Her need to be held by her sister left her breathless. *This* is what she had come home for.

Jasmine rejected the embrace, shoving the cold and heavy pie plate into Katrine's open hands. Confused, Katrine reached out mentally to make that connection to her sister. Jasmine was closed off.

"You can at least have a piece of pie, Jazzy," Katrine said. She was surprised to hear she was pleading. *Come on, let's do the chicken drop together. Please. I feel safe when you're with me. Let me in.* The words bounced back at her unheard, tinkling to the ground like broken glass.

"Please, Mom." Tara tugged at Jasmine's hand, but couldn't drag her eyes from Katrine.

Jasmine pursed her lips and turned her back to the family, striding to the house. "Fine. But we can't stay long," she said over her shoulder.

They all followed except Ursula, who murmured about needing to tend the fire. Helena's jittery energy was palpable, and Xenia put out a hand to calm her sister.

"What kind of pie is it?" Xenia asked, striding ahead of the group to grab clean plates and silverware.

"Cherry," Tara offered. "Right, Mom?"

Katrine accepted a plate, the first food she'd eaten since arriving. She found herself salivating, remembering the amazing food her sister had cooked throughout her school years. Jasmine's roasted garlic soup brought neighbors over to see what smelled like heaven, her fresh bread was so soft it invited naps, and her casseroles were gone before most potlucks began. Her food didn't just taste good; it healed.

Katrine dug into the sweet wedge, perfect round balls of cherry oozing out the sides. As she lifted the fork to her mouth, one blood-red circle broke loose and rolled across her plate, leaving a viscous pink trail. She chewed, her eyes widening in surprise. The words passed her lips before she could weigh them. "This tastes like shit."

Katrine noticed Helena step toward Jasmine and then stop, halted by the grim light of satisfaction in Jasmine's eyes.

"I know someone at the newspaper," Jasmine said, not responding to Katrine's comment. "I could help you get a job. Call me if you need me." And she took Tara's hand and pulled her daughter out of the Queen Anne.

CHAPTER 12

Katrine

Ursula had always provided house and food for her sisters. In return, Xenia sewed all the clothes for the five females and Helena cooked all the food until Jasmine was old enough to take over. For spending money to go the movies or buy books, Helena sold homemade candy out of the Queen Anne kitchen and Xenia tailored clothes in a small room off the kitchen that she had converted into a sewing space. Until she was five and started kindergarten, Katrine was convinced that all kids were allowed to eat their fill of decadent candies and play dress-up in the most glorious dresses.

After Jasmine and Tara had left the party, Katrine was reeling. Seeing her distress, Xenia and Helena distracted her with the history of their store. They had rented the space for Seven Daughters' Candy and Clothes two weeks after Katrine moved away to Chicago to pursue her English degree. They built a burgeoning clientele on word of mouth, and it hadn't taken much convincing for them to make it official once the girls moved out. Seven Daughters was launched. The store was small, a renovated restaurant two blocks off downtown River Street. Helena revamped the kitchen, outfitting it for candy-making and retained the old-fashioned dessert coolers that had housed cinnamon rolls and pies for many years, instead filling them with tantalizing truffles, her specialty.

Helena bragged about Xenia, describing her chocolates as delicate affairs, each no larger than a wild plum, shaped like sea shells, flowers, and intricate animals, or arcane symbols like trishula, the horns of Odin, and Celtic crosses. Some had fillings, from smooth buttercream to crunchy roasted almonds, fluffy ganache to exotic sugared mango, and they came in white, sweet, or dark chocolate. Regardless of shape, color, or flavor, every chocolate made the eater's mouth dance, massaged her heart, tuned her senses. Helena's Lilac Love chocolates were the most popular, crafted of a chocolate so dark it melted down your throat like an elixir. Helena shaped the chocolate to resemble the delicate flutes of lilac petals, and injected them with a crystalline sweet center she crafted from distilled spring flowers. Those who'd eaten a Lilac Love swore that one bite revealed your soul mate.

Peppermint Secrets were the second-best seller. They were crafted of white chocolate molded into a delicate leaf shape with veins of exquisite green mint laced through. Helena recommended those for people whose stomachs were upset by guilt. She demurred when asked for her recipes, made no claims about the properties of the chocolates other than that they would taste delicious. And they did, always, as beautiful to the tongue and belly as they were to the eye.

Over the years, she'd gleaned a lot of information from her customers, more than a bartender or even a hairdresser would hear in the course of their day, and she often stayed late to concoct special orders for the woman whose husband was cheating or the teenage boy who wanted a gift for the girl he was too shy to ask out.

When customers weren't sharing their most secret desires, according to what Helena swore to Katrine was the truth, they were worshipping the racks of gorgeous dresses in Xenia's section of the store. Though they shared the same till, Helena limited the face of her business to the dessert coolers. Xenia spread her wares over the rest of the main room, setting up dress racks where diners used to swap farm stories over coffee and homemade cake donuts.

She displayed ten racks. They contained sundresses and wrap dresses and formal gowns and slinky dresses, and each one was unequivocally flattering to the woman who bought it. The mayor, a short and top-heavy Finn, had purchased a black, empire-waisted dress for her husband's Christmas party and discovered that she had beautiful strong arms the moment she donned it. Juni, owner of the salon one block over, was sure that the local kids had invented the word "cankles" purely to terrorize her and her alone, until she found that Xenia's green pleated minidress displayed her magnificent thighs, which made her ankles purposeful atop a pair of strappy sandals.

Women and the occasional rococo male traveled from as far away as St. Louis to browse Xenia's racks. The demand for her designs expanded to the point where she had to register customers and impose a limit—one dress per person per year. Some maneuvered around it, but on the whole, the ladies in the know were willing to support each other.

The store sounded glorious, but it wasn't enough to puncture the deep sting of Jasmine's rejection (*she called me home she needs me what's happened to us?*). Nonetheless, Katrine found herself outside the store the next morning. She didn't actually know what had brought her downtown in the first place. She had a hangover and wasn't sure if it was from the wine or the cherry pie. She had no plan, no desire or aversion when she thought of working for her aunts. It'd be the route of least resistance, putting in seat time at Seven Daughters, protected, outside of life's current. She craved easy. But it would mean more hiding, and she was starting to grow sick of herself. She needed to resuscitate her heart, even if the stimulant she used was a resurrected love of writing, or she'd be halfway to cat lady before she knew it.

So, she knocked on the locked door of Seven Daughters. To her surprise, it was opened by a tall, awkward boy of 16 or so with eyes like a baby wolf.

"Hello?"

"Hi," she said. "I'm Katrine Catalain. Helena and Xenia are my aunts?"

"They're running errands, I'm afraid." He stepped aside to let her in. "Is there anything I can help you with?"

After the initial stare, it had taken him only a single blink to look and talk to her like a regular person. He had something about him, something that pulled Katrine out of herself and made her want to engage, despite the pain her sister's reception had set up inside her.

She ran her hands over the silk of a honey-colored sundress nearest the door, so soft it felt like a living thing. Even on the rack, she could tell it would hang beautifully. "Gawd, I missed these gorgeous dresses. If only Xenia would go international."

Leo shook his head. "Xenia said she's an artist, not a salesperson."

"What errands are they running?"

"Helena went to Cashwise to buy sugar. Xenia is making copies of a flier for some classes they'll be offering here in the basement." He paused, blushing. "I've been working here all summer, and it's the first idea of mine that they took. I told them they should pass on their gifts to the people of Faith Falls. You know, teach them to cook and sew. Xenia said she'd do it, but only if she could call them End of Times classes. She said that the only way the people of this town would be interested in sewing and canning was if it were post-apocalypse and they had no choice."

Katrine chuckled, amazed that she still had laughter in her. This boy must have some magic of his own.

He ran his hands through his hair, still blushing. "Did you want to look around the store?"

She sighed. Some part of her did, but she was worried by the thought of being in one spot for too long. "No, thank you. Will you just tell Xenia and Helena that I stopped by?"

He nodded happily. Good-byes had never been her strong suit, so she turned and left the store without another word.

"Whoa!"

Katrine found herself immersed in soft cloth over hard flesh, the clean scent of soap, clumsiness. She had charged into a man coming out of the store next door. Catching her balance, she stepped back.

"No, it was my fault," she said. "I should have been watching where I was walking." She felt herself flush. There had been a time when she'd not only known who around her was coming and going but also, sometimes, what they were thinking and feeling.

"Hey, it's okay." His voice was concerned. "I just barreled out of there. Are you hurt?"

She wiped her eyes and glanced at him. His thick hair was curly brown laced with gray, though he wasn't old, maybe 36, with eyes so open and blue she expected to see waves in them. She noticed his big hands, long-fingered and strong, with a contrasting delicacy that reminded her of cascading piano music. He was handsome, in a goofy way.

"You work here?" She indicated the store he had come out of, Ren's Watches, Unique Timepieces Sold and Repaired.

"More often than not," he said, a smile crinkling the corners of his eyes. He held out his hand. "Ren Cunningham."

She nodded at his hand but did not take it. "I'm sorry for bumping into you." She stepped around him and continued walking up the street, unsettled by the encounter and the buzzing in her stomach.

"You're sure you're all right?" he called after her.

She raised a hand but didn't turn. If she had, she would have seen him stare after her, puzzled, before stepping next door to buy one of Helena's Lilac Love chocolates, a sudden craving for which had propelled him out of his store moments before, leaving an antique pocket watch half-assembled.

Katrine continued down the street, ignoring a momentary pang in her chest, a charged sensation somewhere between leaning over a cliff and jumping across it. *Must be something I ate.* She walked into the yellowed offices of the *Faith Falls Gazette*, unsure whether her sister had told them she was coming or not. It wouldn't matter. The newspaper either needed another reporter or they didn't. Besides, she didn't know if she even wanted to work here. She just didn't have anywhere else to *be*. The place stank of ink and instant coffee. Behind the front desk, a Fleet Farm calendar was one month out of date.

"Hello, may I speak to the editor?"

The curvy receptionist, her body perfectly suited for life in a chair, turned from the computer screen and flashed Katrine a wide smile. "You're in luck. She came back early from a meeting. Whom shall I tell her is here?"

Who, thought Katrine, years of training rearing up like a rash, *who shall I tell her is here.* "Katrine Catalain. I'm interested in applying for a job."

The receptionist's eyebrows shot up at the name, and she gave Katrine a full once-over. "We're a pretty small paper."

"I understand." She didn't offer any more.

The receptionist shrugged and waved Katrine back, past the particle-board desks and wood-paneled walls, until she reached an open door decorated with a brass plaque that read, simply, "Editor."

The woman who locked eyes with Katrine when she entered was familiar. Her hair was done up Texas-cult style, serving as a tall, poofed stage to full lips and a nose like the tip of a paper airplane. Other than make-up-creased wrinkles shading her eyes, she appeared the same as she had in high school. Katrine was surprised at the strong reaction she had, her stomach muscles clenching as if she were a Faith Falls High freshman all over again, enduring the taunts: *Don't eat me! Where are you hiding your warts, Catalain?* Or her personal favorite and clearly the result of protracted group brainstorming, *which witch bitch?* She forced herself to stand straight.

"Katrine Catalain, as I live and breathe. How are you?"

Heather Lewis kept her voice level and her hands out of sight. Her mother was a Gottfridsen, and Gottfridsens were Faith Falls royalty, the spine and fingers of the town, had been since Albrikt'd opened the saw mill 120 years earlier. Their rivalry with the Catalains went nearly as far back, starting as a deep friendship that went sour after Eva and Ennis disappeared, leaving the town too much time for self-reflection, too much room to wonder at the magic that the Catalains seemed to possess.

The Gottfridsens had passed the bitterness down to their children in their genes along with red hair, a missing pinkie knuckle, and an inclination for heart disease. Heather hadn't inherited the little finger deformity, but her red hair blazed like a corona. She had also demonstrated a knack for making Katrine's and often Jasmine's life miserable in high school.

Their rivalry had been legendary, both of them pretty but Katrine with the edge, winning homecoming queen to Heather's princess, voted "most likely to succeed" to Heather's "best smile." Heather had her small revenges, and being the chief namecaller was only one. She'd also taped "Lick me, I'm a Catalain" signs to Katrine's back, told boys that Katrine was easy and girls that she was stealing their boyfriends, and had even convinced her that their sophomore year picture day was actually 1950s Dress-up Day. It had all transpired a lifetime ago, and Katrine wondered why it had ever mattered.

"I'm well, Heather." Katrine turned to go. She was too numb to grovel.

"Wait. Your sister called me."

Katrine stopped but didn't respond. She wondered what deals with the devil Jasmine had made to befriend this woman who had made their school years a hell on earth. *Jasmine, who are you now?*

"She said you need a job." Heather's voice climbed a note higher. The pencil she was gripping made a tiny cracking sound. "Do you?"

Katrine turned and scanned the office. The venetian blinds shading the window behind Heather were dusty, and they sliced a view of the brick wall of Fenlason Portrait Studios. Somehow, the light made the sliver of an office seem smaller, barely large enough to house the desk, three file cabinets, and office chair. The desktop was cluttered with paper and a chipped mug full of pencils, a stapler, office implements. Photos of family clung to the walls like barnacles, and two more balanced on the corners of the desk. They were all of the same two girls, maybe 9 and 11 in the most recent one. There was no photo of a man. Heather's ring finger, which she'd worked so hard to conceal, was bare.

"For the past three years, I've been an editor in the London offices of *Vogue*. Fashion writing wasn't my plan, but it's where I landed. Don't bother calling them for a reference because I walked out three weeks ago without notice. I can write feature articles and take my own pictures. I don't know how long I'll be in town."

Heather licked her lips. "I can't hire you full time, but if you want to be an on-call reporter, I'll pay you per piece. It's not glamorous work, and it pays for shit. You'll cover football games, open houses, church events."

"Thank you."

Heather leveled her eyes at Katrine. They gleamed. "You can start on Friday. There's a bead shop just opened up on the edge of the Avignon neighborhood. You remember the Stearns Banks that used to be there? The bead shop's there now. They offer crafts classes Friday afternoons."

Katrine automatically held her breath at the mention of the haunted neighborhood before realizing how ridiculous she was being. She wanted to ask Jasmine if she still held her breath against bad luck, and the thought made her ache. Would Jasmine even talk to her?

"You listening? The store just opened, and they're offering their inaugural class on Friday. I'd cover it myself but I already have plans. That's how big news like this is in town. The only bigger story will be when the snakes come back next spring."

A picture fell from the wall, and Katrine had the oddest feeling of falling with it. When it hit the floor with a crash, she didn't jump—she'd seen it coming—but Heather almost leapt out of her skin.

"Should I take that as a sign?" Heather laughed uncomfortably as she leaned over to pick up the duck painting. "Maybe I'm supposed to be the one covering the bead shop? It has been a while since I've gone out."

"Did it break?" Katrine remembered the snakes. She'd only seen them once, when she was ten, in 1985. She shivered at the memory of their rasping, reeking takeover of the town. Most people stayed inside, if they could. How could Katrine have forgotten about that unique Faith Falls weirdness? She vaguely remembered being told the snakes came every twenty-five years, or maybe she'd dreamed that.

"What?"

"The painting." Katrine pointed at it. "Is the glass okay?"

"It's fine." Heather hung it back on the wall, adjusting the edges. "So, you want the job or not?"

Katrine hesitated. For four weeks, almost to the day, she'd been fighting the gray sloth that wanted to keep her in one spot and force her to remember. She'd stayed in motion out of habit, but she had no illusions about what activity would get her. She'd still be here. Adam would still be gone.

"Kat? You want the job or not?"

Katrine leaned closer to the weak pilot light still flickering inside her. A strong gust, and it'd be gone. She cupped her hands to shelter it. "I'll get you the article."

The Catalain Book of Secrets:
Alteration

Change for good and change for bad feel the same, at first. They both hurt, and the harder you hang on, the longer the pain draws out. A basic trinity spell is the best remedy for the discomfort of flux.

1. First, select three stones. They should fit in your palm, and when held, they should ignite a sensation in the part of you that hurts— throat (indicates you aren't being understood or aren't understanding), heart (indicates you've been misused), or belly (means someone tried to steal your strength). Don't worry if the rocks aren't pleasing to your eye. Feel them.

2. After you've chosen your stones, gather a small pouch, a candle, and some sage, if available. (Plain dried grass and cinnamon powder will suffice if not.)

3. Find a quiet spot outdoors. Burn sage or your cinnamon-dusted grass. Inhale deeply as it burns.

4. Then, turn three circles, like a dog ready to nap, until you figure out which direction you want to face.

5. After you've decided, sit down, cross-legged. Put one stone on each side of you and one behind you, all within arm's reach.

6. Place the candle in front. Light it.

7. Close your eyes and think about how holding those stones made you feel, and tell yourself you're grateful for the change in your life, whatever it is (Even if you don't mean it. Especially if you don't mean it.)

8. Reach past your throat, your heart, and your gut, right to your glorious spirit, and ask for some balance and clarity. Sit with that for as long as you're comfortable, then place all three rocks in your pouch, tie it and seal it with the wax from the candle before wrapping the pouch in a bit of cloth that makes you smile.

9. Sleep on that package for three nights.

10. When you awake on the fourth morning, you'll feel the itch of healing begin. Unwrap then unseal the bag.

11. Display the rocks where you can see them, and when you look at them, remember that itch of healing. It'll grow stronger every day.*

*Because here's the splendid truth: it doesn't matter if you make a wrong choice or a right choice, as long as you take action, because all change is good. (Of course, knowing that is one thing. Believing is a whole other matter.)

CHAPTER 13

Jasmine

Two days after she'd fed store-bought cherry pie to her sister, Jasmine found herself on the other side of the bricked-over tunnel entrance in the basement of her home. Growing up, the root cellar shelves of the Queen Anne had been stacked with vegetables, salsas, and jellies canned by Jasmine's own hand. The single bare bulb would glitter off the jeweled purple of the grape jam, or the quart jars of tomatoes so red you'd smell spicy summer just looking at them. She remembered all the food stores making her feel safe, and proud.

Here, in her box house, the basement was a family room with faux wood-paneled walls and a rough carpet that smelled faintly of wet. She'd wanted the wood paneling to cover the brick of the tunnel, too, but Dean had broken three drill bits trying. She settled for having him install a book case in front of it and filling the shelves with porcelain knick knacks.

She normally came to this wall to dust, but today, a sound had brought her here. It was faint, but loud enough for her to hear it from the living room where she'd been ironing. She'd padded downstairs, first thinking it was the hum of the air conditioner she was hearing. She'd reached the bottom step before she'd remembered that Dean had disconnected the wheezing air conditioner last fall and never gotten around to hooking it back up before he'd left her.

She cocked her head, trying to figure out where else the noise could be coming from. She was drawn to the brick wall. The sound was low, almost below the level of hearing, but the closer she stepped toward the wall, the louder it became. She pushed aside two porcelain piglets so she could stick her ear against the cool brick. *Yes.* A hissing, she was sure of it, like air leaving a tire.

I will take your power when the snakes rise.

The words the man had whispered in her ear rose, unbidden, icing her blood, and just as quickly, with the help of decades of habit and medication, she squelched them, and the sick thud of her heartbeat. She wouldn't let that secret eat her, and she wouldn't infect anyone else by sharing it with them. She would bury it again and a million times more if she had to.

Kids, playing in the tunnels. It must be, though she'd never heard any sound from there before. She made a sideways fist and pounded the brick. The noise was swallowed by the dusty stone, and, as if to mock her, the hissing grew louder.

"Hey!" she yelled.

Tara came to the top of the stairs. She was holding a book in one hand, her finger marking her page. She was wearing gray sweats and a Guess t-shirt that Jasmine had bought at Goodwill. "Yeah?"

Jasmine stepped back from the wall. Why was her heart beating so fast? "Nothing. I…I was just cleaning."

Tara shrugged and disappeared. Jasmine returned the two pink pigs to the shelf, one balancing on its two front legs, the other a swollen, milking sow, its eyes comically wide as if to say *how'd this happen?* Jasmine hadn't intended to collect ceramic pigs, but ever since she'd picked up a salt-and-pepper piglet set at a garage sale the year after Tara was born, Dean had decided that pigs are what he would buy for her whenever an occasion called for a gift. And she'd decided she loved them.

Jasmine kept her hands on the shelf. The murmuring sibilance had stopped, but she still felt shaky, threatened. She forcibly relaxed her shoulders and told herself it was okay that she'd agreed to let Helena and Xenia take Tara to dinner and then the movies tonight. She shouldn't have let Helena talk her into it, shouldn't have allowed her to plead that a family night would be great fun for Tara and that it'd be good for Katrine, too. In reality, it was neither love for her daughter nor hope for her sister that had broken Jasmine's resolve. It was Helena saying that she'd heard Dean was coming back to town, and that he and Jasmine could have a date night if Tara went to the movies with her aunts.

Date night. Michelle Jakowski had used the term just yesterday, when she was telling Jasmine about her husband tramping around, looking for love elsewhere.

"Think he'll be attracted to me again if we have a date night?" Michelle had asked.

"It's worth a try," Jasmine had replied. Michelle didn't believe in divorce, and Jasmine thought that was a fine way to be. Date night sounded so normal. She'd had to cajole Dean, to convince him that they were meeting to talk about Tara, that she wasn't expecting anything else from it. And that's why tonight, she would have a date night with her husband to see if she could win her good man back, and Tara would go to a movie with her aunt and great aunts.

The doorbell's shriek set her heart to pounding again. She forced herself to walk, not run, up the basement stairs. The front windows of the house were open to let in the sultry, late August breeze. The air smelled like nectar and river. Jasmine scratched her nose and opened the door.

"Jasmine! Thanks so much for letting us steal your beautiful girl." Helena beamed at her, wringing her hands in front of her banana-colored pleated dress, sewn by Xenia. Jasmine couldn't help but return a shrunken version of that same smile. Helena had been a loving constant her whole life, a warm pillow of affection. Of course Helena still relied on the magic that Jasmine had denounced, but she was her favorite aunt nevertheless. Xenia stood behind Helena, glancing toward the church steeple, and next to her was Katrine.

"We're going to have a wonderful time," Helena continued, "and so are you."

Jasmine nodded, noting that some color had returned to her sister's cheeks, though they were far from the plump roses she remembered. She thought again of the buzz in the tunnels. It had sounded hollow and mean. "I'm sure Tara will enjoy it. PG-rated movie, no pop, okay?"

Tara appeared next to Jasmine. She was now wearing a worn purple terrycloth jumper, also from Goodwill and five years out of style. Jasmine could feel her daughter trembling, a horse ready to bolt its pen. "I'll be fine, mom."

Xenia raised her eyebrows. "That outfit ought to preserve her virginity."

Jasmine grimaced. "Have her back by 10, all right?"

Tara rolled her eyes, but Jasmine could see her heart wasn't in it. She was too busy beaming at Katrine. Jasmine shot another look at her sister. "You go to the newspaper?"

Katrine focused her gaze, and Jasmine steeled herself for the liquid tingle of her sister's attention, but it never came.

"I'll probably do some freelance there," Katrine said.

"Great. Heather said she'd help you if she could." Jasmine watched for her sister to flinch at the mention of their old rival, but it never came. It made her sad, in a distant way, that her sting hadn't left a mark. Realizing where her thoughts had taken her, she grew even sadder. She hadn't realized how much anger she'd stored up against Katrine for leaving all those years ago and for never before returning, even to meet Tara. She knew it was unfair. After all, she'd cast the spell that had pushed her sister. "Well, I better finish getting ready. No telling when Dean'll get home, so I have to be prepared. I'll take a hug, Tara."

Tara obliged. "Thanks, Mom," she whispered, and pecked her mother on the cheek before leading the way down the sidewalk.

Jasmine turned without another word. In the kitchen, she slid a cup of onions into a microwave-safe bowl, cooked them for three minutes to the second, and sprayed the air with honeysuckle air freshener to cover the scent. Her plan was to sneak the onions into the lasagna she was premaking for supper tomorrow. If she cooked them down now, Dean wouldn't have a guess that they could be in his food the next day, if she could talk him into eating at home. He liked his food simple.

Kitchen clean, she returned to her ironing, the hissing in the basement forgotten.

CHAPTER 14

Katrine

They'd enjoyed a spicy but delicious dinner at the Great Hunan and were now in the lobby of the Hobbes, which was buzzing with patrons scrambling to buy chocolate-covered raisins and oversized sodas, smiling in anticipation of the evening's escape. The smell of popcorn and butter oil was overwhelming and as welcome to Katrine as laughter. She followed her aunts to the candy counter but demurred when asked if she wanted anything.

"You don't like popcorn," Tara said, but it was a statement rather than a question.

Katrine glanced over. In the short time she'd known her niece, she'd already observed that the girl possessed her grandma's habit of disappearing by mirroring those around her. Now she wondered if Tara was a people-reader, too. "Not the taste, but I love the smell. Reminds me of working here when I was a teenager."

"Did you like it? Working here, I mean."

Katrine felt a tickle at the rim of her heart. Her niece was beautiful, with her big liquid eyes and pointy chin. Katrine wanted to simultaneously protect her from the world and take her shopping for clothes that didn't look like they had been handed down from an orphanage. "Yes, I really think I did. You work?"

"I wish. I'm only 14."

"Don't wish your life away." On impulse, she grabbed her niece's hand. The smile she received in response was radiant. With her free hand, she pointed toward theater three. "It's filling up fast."

A form emerged from her peripheral vision to join her aunts at the counter. It was Artemis. He was wearing a worn newsboy cap and an ironed button-up shirt in deep blue. His hands were shoved into his pockets. He nodded as if he'd planned to meet them all along. "Thought it would be a nice night to catch a movie. Care if I sit with you ladies?"

"Not at all," Xenia said, leading the way. Artemis hung back to help Helena with her two brimming buckets of popcorn, one glistening golden and the other naked except for salt. Katrine and Tara trailed behind. They managed to find the last five seats together three rows back from the screen and strained their necks watching a modern romance where they were supposed to laugh at the woman tripping in her high heels and the man being emotionally distant but sensible.

Halfway through, Katrine found herself growing sad, and then, even worse, disconnected. She'd felt that way last night, lying in her childhood bed, disassociated and rootless, the feeling she'd hoped to escape by returning to Faith Falls. The sensation left her so anxious that she'd gone to the paint room in the basement, selected a half-used can of pine green that Ursula'd bought earlier in the summer to touch up the porch trim, and returned to her childhood bedroom in the dead of night. She pulled all the paintings off the wall, moved the furniture toward the center, lined the floor with newspaper, and started painting over the creamy walls.

Each stroke made her feel safer. The dark color kept her in the house, at least while she worked, and the acrid smell reminded her she was grounded in her body. But then the walls were painted, and she found she was still disconnected. It was terrifying, a mixture of claustrophobia in her skin and agoraphobia in the world.

And so, after painting, she'd done what she promised herself she'd never do, but the only move that promised her relief: she texted Adam. It was the first contact she'd attempted since she'd left London. She told herself it was to let him know she forgave him so she wouldn't have to carry the burden of him anymore. Her hands shook, making it difficult to type.

Hey. It's me. I moved home. Thinking of you. Wishing you peace.

She hit "send." Her heart raced into her mouth and throbbed there. All the images of him that she'd been keeping at bay flooded her. Adam. No facial hair, a smile that made her thighs buzz, skin that smelled like cinnamon. They'd talk for hours, holding hands, whispering, giggling. She waited three months to sleep with him, sure this one would be different. Oh yes, it would be different. She knew this looking up at him the first night they had made love, at his glorious naked chest, his eyes closed in concentration, caressing her, whispering her name, telling her she was tight, she felt so good, she was the most beautiful woman in the world.

They'd met at a photo shoot, she covering it as a staff writer for *Vogue* and he in charge of lighting. He'd come to her wounded, his heart sliced by a critical mother, two ex-wives, and a tour of duty serving the British Army in Iraq. She would fix it, mend it, decorate it with her toothbrush and an overnight t-shirt. She helped him enroll in the university, encouraged him to begin talking with his mom, tracked down a volunteer job for him working with veterans at the Royal Hospital Chelsea. They'd be everything for each other, no matter what. He would owe her that much, after all the help she'd given him.

Sometimes she worried she didn't know what true love looked like or that maybe he didn't support her dreams as much as she would like, but when his head was between her legs, it sure felt like the real thing. *Make love to me*, she'd cry, when she couldn't stand it any longer.

He'd laugh, and his hot breath would send her over the edge, shivering, quaking. He'd crawl up beside her. *I was*, he'd whisper in her ear, his voice husky.

Three years into the relationship, she was offered a full-time editorial position at *Vogue* and took it as a perfect sign that it was time to get married. She'd wanted to be a writer since her first journalism class in college. She'd assumed she'd be covering politics, or human interest stories, as those were her passions. Still, the money at *Vogue* was good until something better came along. She proposed. They married, small ceremony, only close friends invited, before renting a flat in West Hampstead together. The first two years of marriage had felt blissful, with the extreme highs and crashing lows she'd come to associate with love.

And four weeks ago, he'd started fucking her intern, a pretty Asian girl named Lucy whom Katrine had taken under her wing. At least, Katrine had discovered the affair four weeks ago. It could have been going on for months. She'd discovered her husband in Lucy's flat when she stopped by with soup and tea. Lucy had called in sick for work, had only lived in London for eight months and didn't know anyone, was flat-bound. Or so Katrine had thought.

The true horror of it was that Adam wasn't a bad person. Or maybe the horror of it was that she could still make herself believe that, and that most days, she wanted him back. He wasn't the first. Her past was littered with the retreating backs of the emotionally stunted men who told her how beautiful and smart she was, who sucked her in, who cheated on her and then left. There was Quint, the 18-year-old stunning, sleek farmer's son who'd taken her virginity when she was in tenth grade, and that of her best friend, Samantha, a week later. She took him back afterward, felt like a queen in his arms, loved the way he loved her body, wept for days when he skipped town with the substitute English teacher with big boobs.

Then came Jerry, ten years older and driving a Harley, all snaggled teeth and a too-quick laugh. He hunted her like a deer, charmed her with his crazy jokes and obsessive attention, and had her pretty much living with him her senior year. Jasmine had missed her around, she knew that, but Ursula didn't seem to mind she was gone. As soon as she was all but moved into his house, though, he was out prowling for someone else.

Craig had been different, a college professor, reserved at first, which was surely a sign of maturity and ability to commit. They made it as far as engaged before she found the hundreds of porn sites on his computer, the secret emails from women looking for an anonymous screw while their husbands were away. She waited five years to commit to a serious relationship again. That relationship was Adam, who'd waited until they were married to cheat.

In her childhood bedroom, though, now painted deep green and smelling of bitter, creamy paint, she couldn't lie to herself. She had messed up again. She had believed that she needed to sacrifice to be loved, and then she'd chosen an unfaithful man. It was a fool's dance, one step removed from Laura Ackerdan, nicknamed "Get-lucky Laura" in high school, a girl who would give a blowjob to any guy who asked—even the ones who must have giggled with nerves and scratched at the scabs on their arms while she went down—in the desperate hope that one of them would *see* her. Probably each one of those boys could better describe the part in Laura's hair then her face, and why would any girl let that happen to her?

Shit. She hadn't thought of Get-lucky Laura in at least a decade. That's what coming home will do to you. Roil up your brain like a river, unearthing liquid muck that you thought you'd built over, turning everything into a wet flooded mess.

Adam.

Something about him had made her feel like the only person in the world, capable, beautiful, necessary. They fought every other day, but that had seemed temporary. Their love was the real thing.

The deal was, it was one thing to recognize a pattern, a whole other to own it, and as likely as learning to fly to change it. It hurt, what she'd let Adam do to *her*, a people reader. Sure, her gift was unreliable, but she thought she'd have an inkling. On good days, she'd been able to sense the desires, fears, and everyday thoughts of those closest to her. She didn't want dishonesty or infidelity, right? No one did. So why hadn't she been able to read *those* qualities in Adam? What had compelled her to pluck an unfaithful nowhere man out of obscurity and weave him into the fabric of her life, blind to the harm he'd do her?

Her phone buzzed in the middle of that thought, an arriving text bringing her back to the pungent scent of fresh paint. She'd removed Adam's contact information in a fit of rage the day she'd discovered the affair, and then written it in ink in her journal, overcome by fear that she'd forget it. As if she could. She recognized his number. Her heart hammered. He had written a single word: *thanks.*

She shrank inside herself, and she heard something like the raw, wet pop of gristle releasing from bone.

thanks.

It was his first communication since she'd discovered his duplicity and kicked him out of the flat. After she'd first found out about his cheating, she'd alternated between walking past his workplace, hoping to run into him, and sobbing on her floor, praying she'd never see him again. She'd sustained that for a month before breaking her lease, giving away the few possessions she owned other than her favorite clothes, her laptop, toiletries, and a framed copy of a newspaper article she'd written in college. The frame was bulky, but she loved that story, an investigative piece she'd written on unfair housing practices. It had resulted in two families in the local homeless shelter being approved for rent-stabilized apartments and a Journalist-of-the-Year award.

Her meager possessions in hand and her life a smoking mess in her rearview mirror, she'd returned home.

She glanced back at his text, and the truth of it dawned on her. She hadn't texted Adam to forgive him. She'd reached out to make him feel better, hoping that he would do the same for her, that he'd save her from herself, from this green room, from this haunted house, from her suffocating hometown. He hadn't. He wouldn't. He was a selfish, emotional child.

And so the tears came, tears of anger at herself. She missed him. She wanted him back.

The crying was starting again, only now she was in a theater watching a ridiculous romance with her family, three women who felt like strangers, wearing a Chanel dress that cost more than the car they'd driven here in. She felt Tara's eyes on her. Her niece was watching her like *she* was the movie.

"Stop it," she hissed, suddenly angry. Her niece jerked her head back as if slapped, and Katrine stood, turned toward the audience, and repeated, "Just stop it!" in a louder voice. The whites of a stranger's eyes flashed at her in the dark theater, but she ignored them and stomped out, unable to tolerate being still for a moment longer.

The constriction in her chest eased only slightly when she got into the humid August air. She was doubled over, one hand on the brick of the Hobbes, the other trying to loosen an invisible scarf from her neck.

"Are you okay?"

Katrine knew her eyes were rolling like a panicked cow's. She looked up and down streets both familiar and strange, feeling like the world was swallowing her whole. She forced herself to focus on the man who was talking to her. He was tall and worried-looking. She drew a breath. "You're the same guy I bumped into outside of Seven Daughters the other day."

He nodded. He'd followed her out of the movie theater, but now that they were standing on the sidewalk, he appeared uncertain what to do.

"Robin?"

"Ren," he said, the shadow of a smile on his lips. "But close."

"Sorry." She indicated the theater behind her. "Did you witness that star performance? The one where I made an ass of myself in front of a theater full of strangers?"

His eyes held hers. He repeated his question. "Are you okay?"

She stood upright, running her fingers through her hair, her breath still shallow. What was she doing back in Faith Falls again? "As good as can be expected. You don't have to miss the movie for me."

"It wasn't that good."

Her brain was roiling. She couldn't shake the trapped sensation. She didn't know anything about this man with his curly hair and kind smile, but he felt safe. "Can you give me a ride home?"

He looked at his watch. "My daughters are inside. Let me go tell them where I am, and then I can. The Catalain house, right?"

She nodded. *Where else?*

Chapter 15

Tara

Helena reached across the empty movie theater seat to pull her grand-niece closer, and whispered to Xenia, "Should we follow her?"

"Let her go," Xenia whispered back. "We'll PINC her later."

Artemis kept eating popcorn, his eyes trained on the movie screen.

"What's pinking?" Tara asked, forgetting to whisper. She was shushed from behind.

"Tell you after," Helena mouthed.

Tara nodded and returned her attention to the screen, but her mind was racing elsewhere. She'd witnessed it in Katrine, the fist-sized barbed thorn curved like a fishhook and resting just below her aunt's heart, near her stomach. It was bone-white, sharp, and deeply embedded. The flesh around it was brackish and bruised, stretched tight from infection. Tara had always been able to see people's wounds, but never one so vivid, and never one that the owner actually *moved*. Tara had seen her aunt tugging on it, but she'd been pulling on the smooth rather than the barbed end, causing the whole works to swell even more.

Tara shook her head. She'd wanted to tell her aunt that she could pull it loose if she yanked the barbed end and suffered through a bit of pain, but she was intimidated by Katrine's beauty. She was so pretty, and exotic, and smart. Her aunt had power pulsing through her and emanating from her like blue electricity, but Tara knew she was only focused on the barb.

Forty-five minutes and a happy ending later, they were out on the street, enjoying the pleasant bustle of being in a group of people all heading home.

"So what's pinking?" Tara asked again.

"PINCing, not pinking," Xenia said, unbuttoning the sweater she'd closed to ward off the chill in the theater. "It's a code of conduct, not a color."

Helena smiled. "It stands for 'Pretend It's Not Crazy.' Like, when we had to dig a new well and didn't have running water outside the house for two days? It was the hottest summer ever and no place to hook up the hose. We could have run it from the kitchen sink to the garden and watered everything in a flash, but Ursula decided she didn't want an old hose attached to her beautiful new kitchen faucet and running through her clean house for an hour.

"So instead, she had us truck in and out with buckets, lugging them by hand, banging everything around and tracking in about a hundred pounds more dirt than we would have if we had just attached the hose to the faucet. It was crazy, but Xenia and I pretended like it wasn't." She shrugged, palms in the air. "We PINCed her and let her do what she'd made up her mind to do. Women PINC each other all time. It's part of the unspoken code."

Tara rolled the concept around in her head, examining it from all angles. "Why wouldn't you just tell Grandma she was being unreasonable and show her there's a better way?"

Artemis had been standing to the side, seeming not to listen until he spoke. "It's not often you can convince someone who's made up their mind that your way is the better way. You can just love them and hope to lead by example."

Xenia smiled one of her rare smiles, slow and cool like a cat's stretch. "Exactly And here's the thing about being a strong woman: you get so used to pushing up against everything just to be heard that sometimes, you push when you don't need to, or see a fight where there isn't one. PINCing is our way of helping each other conserve energy for the fights that matter."

Tara didn't understand what Artemis or Xenia meant, but she liked Xenia's smile and so she stored their comment away. "What happened to Aunt Katrine to make her so sad? Mom won't tell."

Xenia sighed and glanced at her sister, who appeared to be leaning toward Artemis for strength. "She left her husband. After she found out he was cheating on her with a friend."

Tara nodded. That's what she'd thought.

The Catalain Book of Secrets:
Blue Glass

Store spells in blue glass because of
its powerful magnification and healing
properties. It used to be only women
were allowed to handle the blue glass. The
world might be a better place if that were still the
case, but people forget about its nature and pour
anything into it, liquor, bile, cheap perfume. Its
purpose is holier than that, and do not forget it.
And remember that the heart is like blue glass,
a vessel for magic, hope, and dreams. It's at its
weakest when it's empty. Deny it its due and it'll
break on a turn; fill it with chance and magic and
it's indestructible.

CHAPTER 16

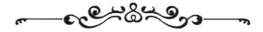

Katrine

They sat in his compact car outside of the Queen Anne. Not for the first time, Katrine was struck by how the windows of the house were arranged to look like a smiling face. She'd always felt like the house watched her. Sometimes she liked it, other times she didn't. "You ever been inside?"

Ren kept the car running, his hands on the wheel. He shook his head. "I didn't grow up in Faith Falls. I moved here with my wife and daughters seven years ago."

"Oh." Katrine put her hand on the door handle. She started to pull it open. "Thanks for the ride."

"You're welcome."

She stopped halfway out of her seat. "I'm not always...I'm actually a pretty stable person." She laughed, but it sounded too high, artificial. "Anyhow, I don't usually throw fits in a movie theater. It's been a...challenging year."

He glanced over at her for the first time since they'd been in his car. She felt the tug of his blue eyes again, the invitation of the great wide ocean to come swim in its waves. She couldn't look away.

"My wife committed suicide two years ago."

Her cheeks grew hot. "I'm so sorry. Jesus, I'm behaving like a child." Tears pushed at her eyelids. The man had lost a wife, probably an amazing one. All she'd lost was a shit of a husband who she should have known better than to love in the first place.

He shook his head, tossing a curl into one of his eyes. The slow, kind smile made its way back to his face. "I didn't say that to make you feel bad. I understand challenging years, is all. Go easy on yourself."

She didn't know what to say to this stranger, and the suffocation was back, its fingers circling her neck. She slammed the car door and ran to Ursula's cottage.

Chapter 17

Ursula

The sharp yellow scent of a match being lit dominated the space around Ursula. She'd been smelling it on and off since Katrine had returned, and none of her potions could eliminate the sulfurous odor. She knew what it meant, what fire always meant: change.

She wasn't afraid of change. She knew better than to get attached to anything or anyone. So why did her heart feel lined with ice? She envisioned her sisters, daughter, and granddaughter safely at the movies tonight and Jasmine dining out with her husband. She didn't sense any particular alarm when concentrating on each of the five women.

The Catalain Book of Secrets was out on the rough wooden bench in her workshop. Today, the book had opened up to a page titled "Mind, Body, Spirit":

The connection between the holy trinity
has been forgotten as humans camp
in their own minds like a baby afraid
to be born. Until the brain is forced
to again share with the heart and the
two are reminded that they are children
of the spirit, fear will dominate. It will
be expressed in many ways: anger, anxiety,
melancholy, a need to control or fix, exhaustion.

To balance the holy trinity, you must bypass
the mind and speak to the spirit. (Dancing and
laughing are the best ways to achieve this.) The
more people involved in this communion, the
better it will work.

You'll know when you've succeeded because you
will sleep deeper, forgive quickly, and roll
in abundance.

Ursula slammed the book shut. Entries like that annoyed her. It was a mixture of basic knowledge and vague instructions. She already understood that most people with mental disorders that responded to treatment, like depression or anxiety, were simply without guides. They felt and heard too much without understanding it was their own magic, and so became lost in their heads. Once they were trapped in their minds, medication became the route of least resistance. A form of this had happened to her beautiful Jasmine, and because her daughter was an adult, all Ursula could do was watch, and be present if Jasmine sought her help.

But this idea that one could overcome the mind's prison by dancing or sitting around and laughing, *that* she didn't have time for. Ursula had a chemist's sensibility, and she liked clear measures. She slammed the book shut and reshelved it.

She tightened the apron over the worn but still beautiful dusty plum, empire-waisted dress Xenia had sewn her ten years earlier. People told her it made her black, silver-shot hair shine and brought out golden flecks in her eyes. She liked that it was comfortable.

She was returning to a tincture of hempseed oil and peppermint, checking the blend with a whiff and a light touch against the glass tube, when she heard the footsteps coming down her stepping stones. She recognized them; her only question was whether or not Katrine would knock.

She didn't. The door swung open, and Katrine stepped inside, closing it behind her. She didn't wrinkle her nose, as she had done when she was younger to convey her distaste at the strong, spicy smell of the workspace, the odor of alcohol, sage, and mystery. Keeping her eyes on the hundreds of tiny blue glass bottles lining the shelves, she spoke.

"You've been busy."

Ursula's heart tugged, and wondered what this moment would be like if she was a mother who embraced her children, asked them how the movie had been, how their marriage had gone wrong. Ursula was not that woman, and Katrine's emotional barricades were as visible as the bundles of thyme hanging from the rafters.

"How are you?" she asked by way of response.

Katrine picked up an empty bottle and held it in front of the window. The moon shot through it, reflecting the blue in a pale cerulean square over her right eye. "Don't suppose you have anything for a broken heart?"

Ursula studied her daughter. She was gorgeous, more beautiful even than Velda had been in her heyday. She could use some more meat on her, but her sharp cheekbones would only grow prettier as she aged, and her full lips and sea-glass eyes had bewitched many boys and then men throughout her life. The gray dust over her skin made her seem more precious, like a forgotten jewel waiting to be discovered. Ursula felt pride for her baby girl swell her throat.

Yet, she knew Katrine didn't want a spell. Her daughters had always refused their mother's elixirs, initially out of childish spite, and then out of habit. She'd never forced her potions on them, vowing to always let them have their own choice in that regard and all others.

"He wasn't the man you thought?" The family had been informed of the wedding ceremony after the fact, the infidelity shared almost as an afterthought when Katrine came home.

Katrine snorted. "I didn't see it coming, if that's what you're asking. The Catalain magic doesn't work consistently. Especially mine. You know it's weak."

"Maybe it isn't, and you simply didn't want to see this coming."

Katrine dropped her hand so the glass was no longer reflecting the moon through the window. She gripped it so tightly that her hands shook. "You ever make a mistake with your potions?"

For the second time in a week, Ursula thought of the father she'd murdered. Her shoulders tensed. "Not in making them, though I don't always give them to the right person. I'm sorry about Adam."

Katrine turned her gaze on her mother for the first time. The green in her eyes was storming. "You never met him."

"That was your choice, not mine, and I can still be sorry you're hurt."

Katrine opened her mouth, then closed it. She set the thin blue bottle on the table. It was warped by the indentations of her fingers, and the air was tinged with a faint char of melting glass.

A knock at the door broke the mood. Katrine's face cleared. "Guess your real purpose has arrived."

She slipped out the door, not even tossing a glance to the woman waiting on the other side. Ursula considered running after Katrine but then remembered the weight of Velda's "advice" on her own shoulders. She squared her shoulders. She would be here, always here, when Katrine was ready.

Ursula turned her attention to the woman standing on her cottage steps, backlit by the moon. She was an exotic creature, her head heavy with black, gold, and copper dreadlocks laced with jewels and metal rings. Her eyes were amber-green tiger eyes, but one stared off another direction than the other. Her body arced like a cello, and she held herself with a dancer's poise. If her eyes had treated each other like sisters, she would be so stunning that she'd be difficult to look at. As it was, the visual defect was too pronounced, and such a contrast to her beauty, that your average person was inclined to feel superior when looking at her, as if it was preferable to be average than to fly so close to the sun and fail.

Ursula felt her hand go to the *Book of Secrets* high on the shelf. She rested it nearby, though she was itching to open the book. "You want me to fix your eye?"

The woman stepped into the workshop and closed the door behind her. Her left eye, the one that Ursula had taken to be the weak one, swirled in its socket twice before landing on her. The woman's gaze felt like butterfly fingers, and the sensation almost made Ursula smile.

The woman shook her head, and her jewels and metal rings jangled like fairy bells. "No."

"Then what?"

"I just realized that if I found out I had a year to live, I wouldn't change a thing. It's made me so sad that I don't want to go on living."

Near Ursula's hand, the *Book of Secrets* laughed.

Chapter 18

Jasmine

Jasmine watched her precious daughter play the viola, unaware that the soft smile on her face was identical to Tara's. When Tara missed a note, Jasmine stuck her fingers in her ears. "Is it supposed to sound like that?"

"Mom," Tara said, rolling her eyes. "I'm *learning*, remember?"

Jasmine kept the teasing expression on her face. "You make it hard to forget." She longed to stroke her daughter's hair, but it had been a couple years since Tara'd let her get away with that. She kept the smile on her face. She'd felt lighter since dinner with Dean last night. It had been an uncomfortable meal at first, as if they were playing themselves on stage.

"Pass the salt?"

"Of course." Their hands touched. He looked into her eyes, and she thought he was going to ask to move back home. Instead, "Will you see a counselor?"

She was surprised at how distant the words felt. They were meant for someone else, someone who couldn't stop turning on and off light switches or who wanted to fall asleep in their garage with the car running. She was neither. She was content, as long as she kept Jasmine close and there were no surprises.

"What for?"

The pained expression on his face was more eloquent than he, but he tried. "You keep yourself small, Jasmine, and you're doing the same to Tara. That's no way to live."

A thousand needles of surprise pushed through her skin, and her eyes grew wet. She didn't know he had that depth, though she'd suspected. He wasn't the most handsome man, or the smartest, but he was a wonderful dad, and he was honest. She'd never doubted him for a second. Most importantly, he didn't keep secrets. Everything he was to her was displayed in his open heart.

"Okay," she said. There was nothing a counselor could do for her, and she'd expended too much already in her daily fight to keep her past out of reach. But if seeing a counselor would bring Dean home, she'd go through the motions.

He squeezed her hand. They finished their meal. Before he left his own home for the evening, he'd kissed her forehead. "I love you." It was enough.

"Hey, can Brittany come over later? To watch TV with me?"

Jasmine blinked. She'd been feeling the warmth of her husband's lips on her. "Did you finish your homework?"

"Yeah, you already looked at it, remember? The hydroponic tomato science project."

"I remember." She did. She just liked to hear Tara talk. It seemed like her daughter was growing up so quickly.

"And maybe you could teach me to make spaghetti sauce with the tomatoes I grow? Helena told me you used to make spaghetti sauce so delicious that it could heal a broken heart."

Jasmine felt a twinge. She wasn't sure if it was guilt or fear. Tara knew about the Catalain witchcraft rumors. She couldn't live in Faith Falls and avoid that, but Jasmine had been careful to dispel them at home, and to redirect any of her daughter's skills that seemed to verge on the supernatural. She was going to protect Tara from the pain she'd experienced, at any cost. "That'd be some pretty good sauce. I can't promise anything like that, but I can show you how to mince onions, and steam-peel fresh tomatoes. Add a little of both to store-bought sauce, and it'll taste better than homemade."

"Thanks, mom."

The trust in Tara's eyes was almost too much to bear. Jasmine leaned forward to turn the page on Tara's sheet music. Someone knocked at the front door. Jasmine directed Tara to keep practicing.

It was a delivery person in a brown uniform. "Jasmine Moore?"

She nodded.

"Sign here."

She took the package with her to the living room.

"What is it, mom?"

"I don't know." She reached for a scissors and split the shoebox-sized cardboard package. Inside was another box, and inside that, pink tissue paper. Inside was a ceramic dancing pig with ruby lips wearing nothing but a white mesh tutu. Her front hooves joined together under her chin in a saucy gesture.

"Mom, it's so cute!"

Jasmine held it up to the light. "I love it," she said. She was referring to this life she'd built for herself, one where she could look forward rather than back, and where there was no magic.

CHAPTER 19

Katrine

Katrine wasn't sure what to bring to the interview. It was her first gig for the *Faith Falls Gazette*. She was scheduled to meet with the owner of the new bead store a half an hour before the class, ask her some questions about her new business, and then take photos of the beading class. Heather had told her the owner's name. It was something Midwestern, and she'd forgotten it. She settled on bringing a laptop, the *Gazette's* staff camera, a steno pad, and a thin black pen. She hadn't written a newspaper article since college, but how hard could it be?

Helena had agreed to let Katrine borrow her car until she could cash in her retirement account, something she'd forgotten about until she'd opened a stack of mail forwarded from a friend in London. Her heart had thudded when she'd recognized the *Vogue* London offices in the return address spot.

She needn't have been worried by the letter. It was from HR, informing her how to access her retirement fund and some legal documents pertaining to the files she'd left behind. They could have all of them, every silly bit of research on Paris fashion and Ivory Coast silk and Peter Pan collars making a comeback. She couldn't believe she'd fallen so deeply into that world that she'd neglected her family. Still, she promised herself she'd go to the post office today to change her mail forwarding address to the Queen Anne so her friend would no longer need to deal with her mail.

It was temporary, living here. Just for now.

When she pulled up front, the old Stearns bank building was all scuffed edges and stately columns, a mini-Fort Knox well past its prime, the rainbow-lettered "Stacy's Beads" sign incongruous against the dusty brick. The movie theater owners had done all their banking here, and she'd been inside often to make deposits. She stepped from the hot sun into the cool of the bank building, curious as to how different it would be inside.

Her eyes took a moment to adjust to the dim light, and so her first sensation was the smell: dust and money. It made her feel safe. The building had been gutted, all the teller counters removed and replaced by tables of beads glittering like pirate's treasure in the high-ceilinged space. A woman behind the counter flashed a smile before returning to her work organizing a bead tray.

To Katrine's right was the only familiar object from the days of the bank, and she was delighted to spot it. It was a grandfather clock made of polished maple; instead of ringing on the hour, a little rabbit wearing spectacles would pop out and chime. He used to ring a gong, legend had it, but the gong hadn't been seen for decades. The clock had been an anomaly in a bank but fit right into a bead shop, though it must be under the weather because a tall man with his back to her had his head shoved in the famous timepiece.

Katrine walked up to him. "Ren?"

He stood too quickly, cracking his head on the inside of the grandfather's clock. He was rubbing the spot when he turned around. His face broke into a lopsided grin when he saw her. "Hey!" He pointed his screwdriver toward the ceiling. "What's a nice girl like you doing in a place like this?"

The blush crept up his cheeks at his own dorky joke, and she couldn't resist matching his smile. "You don't get out a lot, do you?"

He shrugged, still smiling. "Work keeps me busy. It's nice to see you."

In one of her rare flashes of complete clarity, she knew he meant it. The knowledge warmed her. "I wanted to thank you for the ride home the other night. You didn't have to do that."

"My pleasure. Really." He kept his smile in his eyes.

She felt her face grow hot. *What is wrong with me?* "Well, yeah. So thank you. And hey, work is why I'm here, too. I got a job at the paper. I'm supposed to interview the owner. You know her?"

Ren glanced over her shoulder, toward the back of the store, and lowered his voice. "She's at the counter, doing her best to pretend she isn't eavesdropping. You being back in town is definitely bigger news than a bead shop opening, if half the gossip I heard at church is true."

The words spilled out before she could stop them. "You go to church?"

He leaned back a millimeter, and her hand flew to her mouth. "I'm sorry. That sounded judgey. My other friends in London weren't church-goers. I forget what it's like here."

He tipped his head, his smile softening. "I do go to church. I bring my daughters. I wanted continuity in their lives after Laura died."

"I'm a donkey," Katrine said, her stomach tightening. "An absolute, horrible goober. I don't know why I keep saying the wrong thing around you."

"I don't mind. Does this mean we're friends?"

She tried to follow his train of thought. "What?"

"You said most of your friends in London weren't church-goers. I am, and the implication was that I'm different than your other friends."

She stuttered for an answer before realizing he was teasing her. She put out her hand, fighting the smile that was tugging at her cheek. "How about we start all the way over? Hi, my name is Katrine Catalain, and I'm a recovering goober."

He took her hand, grinning broadly. "Pleased to meet you. I'm Ren Cunningham, chief greeter for the Goober Rehabilitation program here in Faith Falls, Minnesota."

Katrine was chuckling deeply for the first time in weeks, but when his warm flesh moved against hers, she was struck with a vision so powerful that it knocked the laughter right out of her. He moved forward to catch her, concern in his eyes.

"Are you okay?"

She pulled her hand over her eyes to clear the vision, her stomach fluttering. She'd seen secrets shaped like frogs raining down from the sky, each one of them a vivid emerald green, women laughing as the frogs turned into butterflies just before they hit the ground, and air so clean that it smelled like water.

She had absolutely no idea what it meant, but the vision left a thrill like kisses on her skin. She hadn't had one since she'd met Adam, and before that, they'd been sporadic at best. "Fine. Must have been a static shock. The air has been so dry lately. Um, I better let you get back to work. Talk to you later?"

He started to respond, but she turned to hide her discomfiture and made her way to the counter to complete her interview. Goodbyes had never been her strong suit, but even so, the guy deserved better.

If I was Ren, I'd go out of my way to avoid someone as messed up as me.

Chapter 20

Tara

Tara watched the commotion outside the bay window of Seven Daughters. She knew from overhearing her aunts speak that picketers were not uncommon, though she couldn't figure out why they bothered the store.

She had lied to her mom to come here, the first lie she'd ever told. But she knew her great-aunts needed help setting up for their End Times class, and anyhow, the air seemed looser since Katrine had returned, like anything was possible, like rule-bending was not only acceptable but created a space inside which miracles could happen.

And so once she'd found out Helena and Xenia's regular assistant was busy, Tara had agreed to help them clean the tomatoes and sanitize the jars for tonight's inaugural End Time class, which would focus on canning, as long as she could be home by supper-time. She was excited to learn all she could. She'd told her mom she'd be at Ursula's helping around the house, which was only a small lie.

Today's class would be held in Helena's kitchen so they could use the stove. Tara reviewed the necessary ingredients list for the first class: three five-gallon buckets of plum tomatoes smelling like spice and earth, four dozen quart jars and lids, two five-gallon pots, a pressure cooker, and tongs and ladles. Because of the acidity of the tomatoes, they wouldn't need vinegar, Xenia had told her. They would, however, need onions, salt, and celery for the stewed tomatoes, and Xenia had asked if she'd like to come along to purchase both.

Tara tried to convince her great-aunt to sneak out the back door so they could avoid the three women who had been perched outside the storefront window for the past hour. Tara knew that the Queen Anne Catalains were different, and saw how certain people around town were almost scared of them, but to her, they were family. She couldn't make sense of why anyone wouldn't also love them, or would want to boycott Seven Daughters.

"I'm too old to sneak," Xenia said. "Besides, I didn't do anything wrong. Come on."

It was a beautiful late-summer afternoon, and the sun was still high in the sky. Tara recognized two of the women from her church. They didn't hold eye contact. Meredith Baum, mom to Jasmine's good friend Heather Lewis, did not look away. She stormed right up to Xenia.

"You're going against God's plan."

Tara recoiled. Her parents never argued. In fact, Tara had never heard her mother so much as raise her voice, let alone confront somebody. She tensed, waiting to see what Xenia would do.

Xenia smiled pleasantly. "Nice to see you, Meredith. How's your husband doing?"

Meredith looked like she wanted to spit. Instead, she pointed a shaking finger at Xenia. "Witch," she said, loud enough for the other two women to hear.

"No shit," Xenia said, and strolled forward as the two shocked witnesses parted to let her through.

Tara followed, a bitty smile settling into the corners of her mouth.

The Catalain Book of Secrets: Putting Up Food

1. Sterilize your jars by washing them in hot, soapy water and then placing them along with your lids in a boiling water bath for ten minutes. Remove the jars with jar tongs but leave the lids in the water bath so they don't come in contact with other surfaces.

2. Clean your freshest vegetables. Scrub cucumbers, peel tomatoes, clean and trim beans, get the dirt off. If you're going to pickle, have pickling mix on hand (2 qt. water 1 qt. white or cider vinegar, 1 cup canning salt, and 3 tablespoons of the following mixture: 2 tablespoons black peppercorns, 2 tablespoons mustard seeds, 2 tablespoons coriander seeds, 2 tablespoons dill seed, 2 teaspoons allspice berries. Also, put a few cloves of garlic, a grape leaf, and a dill head in the bottom of each jar). If you're going to make jellies,

plan on having 1 part juice, 2 parts
sugar, and one package of fruit pectin.

3. Fill your jars with produce, packing
them in tightly and leaving an inch at
the top.

4. Unless it's a jelly, pour boiling water
or pickling solution to cover all the produce.
Wipe the rim, making sure it's clean and dry.
Put the lids on.

5. Place the jars into water preheated to 180
degrees, making sure the glass doesn't touch
and there is one-two inches of water above the
lids. If you're using a pressure cooker, follow
the time and temperature instructions for
your chosen produce. If you're using a pot
of boiling water, see the following page for
required boiling times.

6. Once you've boiled for the
appropriate length of time, remove
your glorious jars. Line them
up on a counter. As each pops,
indicating it is sealed, give thanks.

CHAPTER 21

Katrine

The interview had been straightforward, the only odd point when Stacy Reller, the new owner, invited Katrine to a séance later that same evening. Apparently, the Stearns Bank combined with the Avignon neighborhood had been enough to generate an interest in the occult for the women of Faith Falls. "It's like a book group, only with Ouija boards and scrying stones," she'd said. Katrine had politely declined.

Ren had fixed the grandfather clock ahead of Katrine but had made a point of saying goodbye before he left, his gorgeous smile as open as a door. Thinking about a person like him in the world made her happy. If she was honest with herself, she also felt disoriented, as if she'd developed the bends from descending into her past life too quickly. Still, discombobulation was more fun than self-pity, and she rode the sensation all the way to Jasmine's house.

She felt awful about how she'd treated Tara at the movie theater the other night. Looking back, she couldn't remember what had made her so upset. But even more than apologizing to Tara, she had to connect with her sister, despite whatever was making Jasmine push her away. She craved the bond like oxygen.

As children, no one had been closer than the two of them. When they hit the double digits—Katrine couldn't pinpoint the exact age—they'd grown apart a bit, but still been each other's closest friends. She understood she'd taken that for granted when she moved away, and she'd gotten self-involved and lazy in maintaining their relationship. She wanted to fix that, starting now.

She'd waited after Ursula's party for Jasmine to come to her, for her to smooth everything over the way she'd done when they were children, but Jasmine hadn't. And so, Katrine was going to her.

Her stomach clutched and tumbled as she pulled into her sister's driveway, same as it had when they'd driven in the day before. There was something horrible about the normalcy of the little box house, with its brown grass, dingy paint, and plastic flowers in the window boxes. Everything about it said "I've given up," and it made her sad for the person her sister used to be. What had happened to them?

Katrine punched down those thoughts and turned off the car. She should have called first, but Tara was homeschooled and Jasmine didn't have a life, so where else would they be? She rang the doorbell. It echoed inside, and then the house became as quiet as a grave. The waiting silence was followed by a puppy rumble of footsteps tumbling down stairs.

The front door was yanked open. Tara stood in the entryway, a cheap oak closet door on one side of her, a key rack on the other, and a carpeted living room decorated with matchy, scratchy Midwestern furniture in graying pastels behind her. Her face lit up at the sight of her aunt, and that made Katrine feel even worse.

"Hey," Katrine said, trying on a tentative smile, "I wanted to stop by and say I'm sorry for how crazy I acted at the theater the other night."

Tara grinned like she'd just been handed a present wrapped in blue paper. "It's okay. Helena and Xenia taught me how to PINC."

Katrine wrinkled her nose. The term sounded familiar. Then she remembered where she'd first heard it. Back when Katrine was in high school, Helena had caught the tail end of a documentary on orphaned red pandas. She'd decided on the spot to sponsor all seven that the San Diego zoo had adopted, sending the zoo regular checks and even flying out to visit the pandas two different times. Katrine had asked Xenia if Helena was crazy, and Xenia told her about PINCing. Katrine laughed at the memory, and then at the thought of being on the receiving end of her first Catalain PINC. She was sure she'd earned it.

"I brought this for you," Katrine said, handing her niece a plastic bag containing clear lip gloss and mascara the same brown shade as Tara's long lashes. Katrine had picked up both from the Apothecary on her way to the bead shop. She'd also brought along a book she'd brought from Europe, a guide containing color photos of the best restaurants, museums, and nightclubs in London. She'd topped the bag off with a peach-colored silk camisole that she'd never worn but had loved too much to leave behind. "You might want to hide it. Is your mom home?"

Tara accepted the bag and peeked in, her large eyes growing wider. "Yeah!"

"She's probably busy, and I—"

Jasmine appeared at Tara's side, her eyebrows arched. For the briefest moment, Katrine thought she saw happy surprise in Jasmine's expression, but it might have been the lighting. In any case, it had been fleeting. Tara closed the bag and hid it on her opposite side, but Jasmine was too focused on her sister to notice.

"We're just sitting down to eat," Jasmine said. "Why don't you come join us?"

Katrine followed without complaint. The interior of the house was as bad as the outside. It felt empty and repetitive, like a sitcom stage set between takes—plain furniture, knick knack shelves, everything done in soft colors. The dining room was painted beige, and the table at the center lacked any decoration save for the salt and pepper shakers shaped like the front (salt) and back (pepper) of a pig.

"It's lasagna," Jasmine said.

"Great! Is Dean here?"

Did Jasmine's face stiffen? "He's on the road."

Katrine felt rather than heard the pain in her sister's voice. Was that why Jasmine was so distant, because she was having problems with her marriage? They had always kept in contact through letters and occasional phone calls, and Jasmine had never let on that there was trouble. Wait—when was the last time Katrine had called her sister?

Katrine took a seat at the dinner table across from Tara. "Did you two have a nice date night?" she asked.

"We did." Jasmine's lips were tight. "I cooked, and then we went out and saw the town orchestra play at the city park. It was fun. You enjoyed the movie?"

Katrine glanced at Tara. The girl must not have mentioned Katrine's meltdown. Her heart warmed to her niece even more. "It was fine." She held out her plate for a square of lasagna and pointed at a pile of green and blue fuzziness, about the size of a loaf of bread, at a side table. "What's that?"

"Mom and I are learning to make felt," Tara said. "Those are supposed to be slippers." She hadn't taken her eyes off of her aunt.

Katrine's lip quirked. "They look partially digested."

Tara laughed, and then swallowed the noise as she glanced nervously at her mom. Jasmine and Katrine stuttered through small talk about the weather and Katrine's new job at the *Gazette* as Katrine choked down her meal, moving bits around so it'd look like she'd eaten more than she had. It wasn't that it was bad. The gummy plainness of it, though, when compared to the majesty of the feasts Jasmine used to create, was hard to swallow.

"Dean on the road a lot?" Katrine asked.

"Six days a week," Jasmine said. "Sometimes more."

"You miss him?"

"Yes," Tara said.

Katrine nodded. She cleared her throat and directed her attention back to Jasmine, reaching out again for a connection. "I visited Ursula."

"Aren't you living there?" Jasmine asked.

"You know what I mean. She's always out in her shop, just like back in the day. Taking care of the whole town, unless they happen to live under her roof. I should be grateful. The last thing I want right now is to talk. I already feel like I'm going crazy."

Katrine was washed with a wave of dizziness. It was the speed required to navigate between the closeness she used to share with her sister and the reality of the distance between them now. It hurt.

Jasmine only shrugged.

Katrine wondered if they'd ever be on the same side of the river again. She studied her sister, worried by this new version of her, this angry, deflated shadow of her sister's previous self. How long had she been like this, and Katrine oblivious to it? Jasmine's best features were her liquid eyes, and even these looked different. Katrine had teased her growing up that they were cow eyes, they were so big. It was a lighthearted joking, though. They had been everything to each other. Ursula had been working. The aunts were around and had plenty of love to offer, but everyone was tertiary in their universe.

Katrine knew that she had a reputation as being popular in high school, but the truth was she and Jasmine had both been teased for being Catalain witches. Heather had led the worst of it, but they didn't fit in well with any group. Katrine's job at the theater had bought her a handful of friends, and her looks garnered dates and a nomination for whatever school pageant was happening, but at the end of the day, the two of them had only each other.

They'd been best friends, protectors, united. They'd promised each other they'd always be that, and Katrine had assumed that bond was unbreakable, even after she had fallen in love and gone off to college. She'd figured Jasmine would break up with her high school sweetheart and see the world, too. She hadn't. She'd stayed in suffocating Faith Falls, a town Katrine couldn't bear the thought of returning to. Katrine grew ashamed, realizing she couldn't remember the last time she'd had a meaningful conversation with her sister.

It was time to fix this. Katrine glanced at Tara. "Will you clear the table, honey?"

"Sure." Tara nodded and disappeared into the kitchen with a stack of plates covered in half-eaten lasagna.

Katrine glanced at Jasmine and Jasmine stared at the table. "What's up, Jazzy? Why are you so distant? I feel like I don't even know you. I know I've been gone for a while, but I'm back, and it was you who called me home. Let's make up for lost time."

Jasmine didn't respond. Katrine wished for river agates but lacking those, decided to coax her with a story to pull her out of the sad temper, just as she'd done when they were children. "Remember when I came down with the chicken pox in eighth grade?"

Jasmine patted her mouth with her napkin, still not making eye contact. "It was terrible."

Katrine nodded in agreement, pulling out details in the hopes of finding where the sister she remembered had gone. "I was covered in the bumps, and they were all full of pus. Then they blistered and scabbed over and itched so bad I wanted to cut off my skin. You took care of me, cooking garlic chicken soup for me, dabbing me with calamine lotion, telling me I'd be pretty again. I thought it'd last forever, but then I woke up one morning in a bed of scabs that I had sloughed like snowflakes."

Jasmine smiled, but it was a smile that hurt to look at.

Katrine felt the pain emanating from her sister, so sinister and complete that she found it difficult to breathe. She indicated the house, and the felt slippers, and the congealed pan of lasagna. She couldn't take it any longer, and put her hand over Jasmine's, their first physical contact since Katrine had left. "What's happened to you? What's happened to us?"

When their hands touched, she caught just a lick of the memory that Jasmine was trying to bury, had been trying to bury since she was ten, now with the help of those bitter smooth capsules. And that was the price Jasmine was willing to pay ten times over so she didn't have to remember the burning soup, and the snakes, and the man, and his words like knives (*Every time the snakes rise, I'll be here to take the power away from every one of you goddamned witches. You will never have a better man than me, not one of you Catalain women down the line. Not one good man*).

Katrine was falling into the horror of the memory, grabbing flesh, hoping not to sink too deeply, her stomach in her chest, when Jasmine slammed the door on her thoughts with such force that Katrine's chair almost tipped over. She had to pull her hand from her sister's to catch her balance. Her breath burned in her lungs.

"What was that?" Katrine's voice was hoarse, a razor whisper.

Jasmine appeared startled before hooding her eyes. "I don't know what you're talking about."

"That memory!" Katrine couldn't catch her breath. "What happened? And why haven't you let me see it before?" Everything that had been in Katrine's head before—Adam, flirting, Faith Falls, apologies—left to make room for the horror of the snakes, but the scrap of thought kept slipping from her vision.

Jasmine blinked rapidly. "I don't know what you're talking about."

A horrible thought, almost darker than the slip of memory she'd witnessed in her sister, entered her mind. The lasagna pushed back against her throat, a bloody, gluey, meaty mess. She gagged against it. "We used to know everything about each other, Jasmine. *Everything.* Why don't I have this memory of yours? You looked young. That means we were still living at home. *Together.*"

Tears slid down Jasmine's face, but she didn't answer. She didn't need to.

"*You took it away.*" The reality fell on Katrine like gravedigger's dirt. "You fed me something that took away my memory of someone hurting you, and then you pushed me away, halfway across the world. Away from my family. Away from *you.*" Her voice was a whisper. "How old were we?"

Jasmine shook her head, her hair falling in her face.

Katrine fought so hard for the vision that sweat broke out across her temple. Too-serious Jasmine, who'd entered the world ready to sacrifice for others, who loved her sister more than she loved herself, had been ten, Katrine eight. But then the memory wriggled loose again. "What happened?"

Jasmine wiped at her tears, her hands vibrating like hummingbird wings. Her voice sounded high and unnatural. "I don't know what you're talking about."

The blatant lie, the thought of Jasmine cooking food designed to banish her from her hometown, Jasmine's unwillingness to face the horrible memory, share it with her sister, free herself from it, all of it pushed against Katrine's throat. "Someone attacked you, didn't they? And you cooked your magic so none of us would know what had happened to you, and you..." Katrine's voice rose. "You made me eat something that drove me away, so I'd never know."

"No," Jasmine mumbled. Her face was swimming in tears so thick she appeared to be underwater. "I didn't want you to get hurt. You can't understand."

"No, I don't, Jasmine, *because you didn't tell me.*" Katrine continued, well past the point of hearing. "I missed your wedding, and my niece being born, and *my family* because of you."

Jasmine paled, her eyes suddenly so dark that she her face looked like a skull. "You could break it when you wanted to," she whispered. "You could have come back, if you wanted to see us bad enough because look. Here you are."

Something deep and elemental rumbled underfoot. It felt like the shifting of a giant, hibernating animal. Katrine ignored it, her words flying like darts. "I'm only here because you called me home. And now you're jerking me around."

All the pain Jasmine had had to face alone, all the years that Katrine had lost with her family, it was too much. She scrambled toward the bathroom, but she didn't make it. She threw up the red lasagna all over Jasmine's plain gray carpeting.

Jasmine rushed to her side, trying to hold her sister and stay apart from her all at the same time. "I'm sorry. I thought it was the best thing."

Katrine wiped her mouth. "You were wrong."

She couldn't stay in this box of a house even a moment longer. She left her sister, again, but this time without the push of Jasmine's magic. She felt more alone than she had her entire life. What meal was it that her sister had cooked for her to make her forget, all these years? It must have been quite a feast. She could almost taste the roasting caramel pork, crusty, chewy sourdough, spiced green beans, cucumber cups filled with a delicate salad of watercress and mint. The shrapnel of the reclaimed memory left ash in her mouth, and she fought to keep her remaining bile down.

Still, she thought back, desperate, trying to hang onto the slipperiness of the memory buried under all the power of Jasmine's cooking magic. It was a terrible secret Jasmine had hidden from them all, an act so horrible that Jasmine had pushed her only confidant away. Surely Jasmine had done it to protect her sister, out of habit, without even knowing what she was doing. But she should have known. She should have been brave enough to tell Katrine, and to let her stay and help.

Panic was threatening Katrine from the edges. She tried to outrun it in her car and found herself outside a familiar building, about to ask out a person she'd never thought she'd go to willingly.

The Catalain Book of Secrets:
Protection Spell

Use this spell if someone in your life is wishing you harm, trying to injure you, or introducing dark energy into your life. First, step inside a circle. You can create this circle with anything handy: towels, string, scarves, salt, etc. Once inside, envision white light surrounding you.

Next, picture the person meaning harm as being trapped inside a clear, soapy bubble. Hold this image in your head and chant the following three times:

Any bad you do will return thrice to you.
All words of hate become your own fate.
Likewise, all good you do will reflect
back true.
Any kindness you create will heal
this strait.

CHAPTER 22

Ursula

"Ursula, this is Leslie. Leslie, Ursula."

Ursula held out her hand to the latest of Xenia's lovers. Most of them hailed from the surrounding towns, as Xenia claimed that all the women in the Faith Falls' pool were too uptight. Leslie looked anything but. She was twenty-five if she was a day, with caramel-colored skin and eyes like toasted almonds.

"Pleased to meet you," Ursula said.

"And you." Leslie had a slight Mexican accent.

"We're heading to Fargo to dance," Xenia said, tossing Ursula a wink. "And we have a hotel room, so don't wait up."

"Have fun." As Ursula watched them walk out the door, she realized she didn't want to be alone tonight. She made her way to Helena's room, stopping on the other side. Her hand was poised to knock when she heard the singing. It was a light tune, happy. Helena was reaching a crescendo when the doorbell rang.

"I got it," Ursula said loud enough for Helena to hear. She made her way back down the stairs and was surprised to discover Artemis on the other side. "Hello?"

He had a handful of pink carnations. "I'm here for Helena."

Ursula bit her tongue. She stepped aside, allowing him to witness a blushing Helena sashay down the stairs.

"We'll be out late!" she said as she passed Ursula, enveloping her in a cloud of cinnamon and sugar.

And like that, Ursula was alone. She too felt the elemental shifting beginning underfoot, but to her, it arrived as memories crowding in, dark ones. But then, shot through the middle of those like a silver promise, she remembered a man, someone who had been able to hold most of the shadows at bay. She grabbed her coat and slipped into the night.

§

She watched him outside his bay window. He reclined in his easy chair, sipping a beer and paging through the newspaper. The TV flickered on his face. His wife sat stiffly on the couch, a book open on her lap. It appeared to be a Bible.

Ursula was hypnotized by the scene for several minutes. She hadn't visited the house in three decades. When she couldn't stand the waiting, she went to the front door and rang the bell.

Michael Baum, Meredith's husband, answered it. His bland face slipped into white shock. "Ursula?" He glanced over his shoulder. "Is everything all right?"

"I want you, Michael." Her voice was measured. "I want what we used to have." It had been glorious, their six months together. The sex had been good, but it was the way he'd made her feel precious that had kept her coming back.

He stepped outside the door and closed it behind him. His eyes were sad. "What we used to have?"

She kept her cool stare on him.

"Ursula, it was an affair. It's over. We can't go back."

Still, she didn't move.

"Go home," he said, as if she were a stray animal. He opened his mouth to say more, thought better of it, and retreated into the house.

She stood for a breath of heartbeats, and then returned to her car to seek out the plumber. No one answered his door, and she didn't know whether to be grateful or angry. She had nowhere to go but to her cottage, though the tightness at her throat was growing unbearable. Outside her own door, she almost stepped on a fat snake lolling in the sun. It was all she could do not to scream. They were the one creature she couldn't stomach.

She stepped gingerly around the reptile, muttering a protection spell, and entered her cottage. She was reaching for a botany book when a knock came at the door, heavy as a reaper's blade. She jumped, the accumulated tension of her day coming to a head. She collected herself, willing her heartbeat to slow. She was safe in her moss-covered workshop. Probably, it was just a client with a question. But then why did the air suddenly seem too close?

She moved toward the door.

And then she stopped, scolding herself for being so silly but unable to go any further before she heard the voice on the other side. Inhaling deeply to calm herself, she addressed the knock. "Yes?" she called through the door. A blue moon cooled the sky overheard, spilling into her cottage windows.

A pause followed. Had she imagined the knock?

"Let me in, or I'll huff, and I'll puff, and I'll blow this place down!" The voice belonged to a stranger, and the laughter that followed was uneasy.

Ursula flinched. All the day's misfires seemed to be coming down to this moment. Whoever was on the other side of the door was bringing bad with him. Her hand went to her throat, which it always did, of its own accord, when she was scared. She stepped to the entrance, her hips bumping against cluttered tables. Her movements were jerky, her reluctance to open the workshop door a living thing. But she'd never turned anyone away from her cottage and she wouldn't start tonight, not with the blue moon bearing witness.

When she finally pulled open the door, the hinges groaned, spilling the liquid yellow of the full moon over the threshold. August's musky, green smell kissed the tender skin of her neck, shivering her. A tall figure stood backlit in her doorway.

He was not big, but he had a presence. It might be that he was brutally handsome in a way that made Ursula think of sex and knives, or the cowboy hat tipped over his raven eyes, maybe even the guitar slung over his back like a promise, but no, those were distractions. It was his energy, black, angry but smiling on the surface, squirming under his smooth, tanned skin and puffing out his flesh.

Stomach in her throat, Ursula's mind raced to her daughters and her granddaughter. She hoped fervently for their safety, a ridiculous thought. All three were removed from this. Still, cold oil slid down her spine. She'd had clients come to her from all walks of life, some who made poorer choices than others. She didn't judge as she mixed the anti-anxiety tincture for the woman she knew beat her children, or question the man who came to her straight from his prison release and requested a sleeping draught that would work where all others had failed. Her job wasn't to choose or control, but rather to give what was asked of her. Something about this man, though, rattled her.

"What can I do for you?" Ursula asked. Her heartbeat was uneven, but her gaze behind rimless glasses remained cool. The force on her neck grew tight, a boa constrictor.

His lazy smile grew wider, his expression cocky, almost sensuous. He was used to getting what he wanted. "Well, you don't look like a witch at all! You look more like my mom." He laughed and held out his hand. "Name is John. I'm new to town. I have a little problem and was told you're the one to see."

She took his hand, just to be sure. When their flesh touched, his strong grip swallowed hers, the dead-cold worms of his sickness crawled up her arm. Dropping his hand, she whispered a warding spell, and the myopic, seeking grubs that had been squirming from his body to hers clenched and fell, squealing and smelling of burning hair. For a haunted moment, she thought of her father, and his curse, but she dismissed the fear and the sick pounding of her heart. The snakes had already come and gone once since his death, in 1985, and nothing had come of it. The dying man's words held no power.

Swallowing the sour spit in her mouth, she stepped to the side. Probably, the man was unaware how much evil lurked inside him. Ursula tried for pity and failed.

"Have a seat," she said. She couldn't shake the thought of Katrine and Jasmine and her precious granddaughter, Tara, as she listened to what he'd come for.

The Catalain Book of Secrets:
Acceptance Potion

Our spirits come into our bodies in full acceptance. As we grow, we forget that we are of the elements. If you are not feeling accepted, either in your own skin or by those around you, a simple acceptance potion that you drink at the new moon can reconnect you to your birthright.

Potion:

1 part geranium
1 part blue tansy
1 part neroli

Combine all three ingredients in a blue jar. Suspend it over a fire of rosewood. Drop frankincense and sandalwood into the rosewood fire, and recite the following spell three times:

I am of fire
I am of air
I am of earth
I am of water
I am whole

Let the fire burn itself out naturally.
When the blue glass is cool to the touch, apply
the potion to your wrists. You will return to
your state of self-acceptance, and subsequently
be accepted by others exactly
as you are.

Chapter 23

Katrine

Katrine parked her borrowed car outside the newspaper office, feeling like a fool. Heather Lewis was probably not even inside, and if she was, why would Katrine want to spend time with her? The woman had made it her life mission to ruin Katrine's high school career, and in her down time, had picked on Jasmine. She probably ate kittens for breakfast. Yet, who else did Katrine have to go to? Certainly not her family when her own sister was the one who'd sent her away. She barely knew Ren. The closest thing she had to a friend in this town was her tormentor.

She sighed and exited her car. *This is the beauty of having nothing to lose.*

She smiled at Stephanie, the receptionist. "Heather in?"

"Of course! Fightin' the good fight." She tipped her head toward the hallway. "Go on back."

Katrine paused just on the other side of the open doorway, took a deep breath, planted a smile on her face, and popped in.

Heather jumped, guiltily clicking something closed on her computer screen. "Katrine! Back already. How'd the interview go?"

Katrine felt sixteen years old all over again. "Fine, I guess. Hey, you want to go to the Rabbit Hole with me and catch the band? I'll buy you a drink."

A peculiar expression crossed Heather's face, somewhere between confusion and gas. "You're asking *me* to go out?"

Katrine began to turn. "Forget it. It was stupid."

"Wait!"

Katrine stopped and glanced back at Heather.

"I have a lot of work to do," Heather began.

"Like I said, it was dumb. I—"

Heather held up her hand. "I'm lying. I don't have any work to do. I was online searching for photos of John Stamos." She had the good grace to look mildly ashamed. "You remember that actor? I had the biggest crush on him. This is what my life has come to, by the way."

The unexpected honesty threw off Katrine's guard. She was dumbfounded to feel the hot salt of tears streaking her face. *My own sister sent me away, and I think she was right. I could have broken the spell and come back earlier if I'd wanted to bad enough.* The crying grew deeper.

Heather made her way around the desk, grabbing a handful of tissues.

"Hey, hey hey. No need to cry, though I have this effect on people. I'm a load of fun at parties." She paused with her hand outstretched, then put her arms around Katrine. "It must be quite a change to come back to Faith Falls after London. Probably you have reverse culture shock. As in, you left culture, and now you're stuck here."

"You ever have problems with your family?" Katrine asked, her breath hitched. She let Heather's floral perfume envelop her. "Problems so big that you don't think there's any starting over?"

"Oh, honey," Heather said, grabbing Katrine by the hand and pulling her out the door. "Let me buy *you* a drink."

§

"Gawd, he's hot." Heather took a swig off her third rum and diet cola, staring rapt at the leader singer of the 32-20 Blues Band as he belted out honey-smooth promises in his deep, husky voice. His incongruous cowboy hat only added to his sexiness. "And there's something wicked about him."

"Too wicked," Katrine said. He had been making eyes at her since they'd arrived, which had been about half an hour after Katrine and Heather had gone back to Heather's place to get cleaned up.

He was sexy, certainly, but the more she watched him, the more Katrine sensed something odd about him. It felt like he was looking through her, almost puncturing her glamour in a way no one had before. Plus, there was something about his eyes that made her shorthairs stand at attention. They were jeweled, like the eyes of a snake. Looking straight into them was unsettling.

Besides, she was having too good a time with Heather to think about men. The woman knew everyone in town and was not afraid to gossip. The only topic that was off-limits seemed to be her divorce. Katrine was playing her cards closer to her chest—Adam was the only outsider she'd ever told the truth about the Catalain magic, and she certainly wasn't going to reveal what she'd just learned about Jasmine—but Heather commiserated with Katrine's feeling disconnected from her mom and sister.

"Too wicked? Is there such a thing?" Heather held her nearly-empty drink up to the waitress, signaling for another. "You want a refill?"

Katrine glanced at her red wine, her first and only. "Sure. Why not?" She caught the waitress' eye herself, noticing a familiar face at the bar. It was an Asian woman in her 50s, and she had a bit of a blue glow around her, suggesting that she'd visited Ursula at some point. Katrine placed her as the owner of the Great Hunan, and turned her attention back to Heather, who was swaying in her seat as the band started playing a sexy, sultry song with a drum beat that thumped pleasantly in Katrine's lower stomach.

"You know my mom hates your mom."

Katrine raised an eyebrow. "The usual?"

"If you mean because my dad and your mom had an affair, then yes. Is there anyone in this town your mom *hasn't* slept with?" Heather put her hand over her mouth, but it was to cover a burp. "Sorry if that was too harsh."

"She definitely gets around. What about your mom? What's she like?"

"Imagine if Imelda Marcos, Hitler, and Tammy Faye Bakker had a threesome. Their love child would be my mother."

Katrine spit out her mouthful of wine. She couldn't help it. "She can't be that bad!"

"Worse. So maybe you should think before you whine. Someone always has it crappier than you do."

Katrine thought of Ren, and the perspective he'd given her on her heartbreak without even knowing he'd done it. "You're right. Want to dance?"

"Love to. Just don't block my sight of that hot guitar-playing wizard."

Katrine returned her glance to him and shivered. His cowboy hat was slung over his eyes, and despite her trepidations, the way he smiled at her when he caught her look made her tingle. She couldn't tell if it was because she felt appreciated or hunted, but in either case, she was beginning to fantasize about what sort of lover he'd be—rough, she bet—when the Asian woman with the blue glow was suddenly blocking her view of him. She was dancing with a woman with gorgeous dreadlocks who was also shimmering with a blue glow. Katrine was used to seeing the shadow of her mother's magic around town, but had never seen it so focused. It was almost like they were trying to come between her and the band. And then there was the glow around the singer in the cowboy hat, only it was purple, like someone had thrown a cup of blood into the blue glow her mother's magic left.

Katrine moved so she could see the singer better. There was something captivating about him, something underneath that pulsing purple glow. He was damn good-looking, with those long-lashed jewel eyes so dark they appeared black and a cocky mouth that tilted in a way sure to make his audience feel like they were in on something. She was familiar with his type, and was done with it. Still, she felt her hips grow looser and was considering dancing closer to the stage when she was jostled so hard that she spilled part of her drink. She glanced over to see the Asian woman dancing next to her.

"So sorry," the woman said.

"That's okay," Katrine responded, shaking the wine off her hand. Her eyes were immediately drawn back to the guitar player, as were nearly every other woman's in the bar. The band switched songs, and suddenly, Katrine felt herself locked into the tractor beam of his stare, his lips moving as he sang just for her, the two of them locked together in a wall of sound, bodies gyrating around them. The band transitioned from blues to something a little faster, dripping with sex, driven by a grinding, dirty guitar riff. A woman toward the front of the bar actually moaned.

"Did you hear that?" Heather asked, hands in the air and lost in laughter. "I think she just came! See what happens when you don't get out of a small town? A little blues music turns everything into an orgy."

But Katrine couldn't hear her over the spell now being woven around her ears, dancing liquid through her blood on a warm bass beat, pulsing with the sex-soaked rhythm of the drums, circling, circling with guitar, and driven home hot on the words of the guitar player. He was singing about the best woman he ever met, his eyes locked on Katrine's, and for a moment, irrationally, she wanted to be that woman. She found herself dancing toward the stage, a fish on a line, moving her hips to match the beat that was building toward climax, feeling every lick of the guitar on her flesh.

"Katrine?" Heather grabbed her wrist, her face puzzled. "Where are you going?"

Katrine pulled her wrist loose, the thick, hot music filling her ears and guiding her toward the stage. The guitar player's smile grew wider, and he tipped his hat lower over his eyes and began to grind with the beat. Another woman moaned, but he had eyes only for Katrine, hungry, glittering.

She would have made it to the stage except the Asian woman was back, this time colliding with such force that she knocked the drink fully out of Katrine's hands, spilling red wine down the front of her dress.

"Oh! I'm so clumsy!" She looked upset enough to cry. "I wreck your dress!"

The music grew quieter, dryer, now just notes and words, the spell broken.

Katrine shook her head, dazed. The woman with dreadlocks, who had been dancing nearby, rushed over to Katrine's side. "Shoot, I hate it when that happens! Wine, right? Let me help you get it off. I used to work at a dry cleaner."

She led Katrine toward the bathroom. Heather followed, dancing the whole way.

"He's all yours," Katrine said, nodding over her shoulder toward the band. Feeling back to herself, she made a vow to find out what kind of red wine they served here. It must be powerful stuff. "I'm done with trouble."

Across town, in the closed and locked old Stearns Bank, the spectacled rabbit darted out of the grandfather's clock, chiming midnight.

Underground, the massive, hibernating ball of snakes shifted uneasily.

CHAPTER 24

Tara

Tara's own muffled scream woke her. She was sitting upright when her eyes snapped open, blankets as tight as a noose around her, blood roaring in her ears, breath shallow and harsh. Blinking rapidly, she made out shapes: a chair holding her favorite childhood doll. Her dresser, found at a garage sale and redone by her mom. The window to their backyard, the one she'd swung in since she was a toddler and only just recently grown too big for.

So why the terror? She squeezed her eyes closed again, and she saw it.

Her grandma Ursula, her heart broken loose from her chest and blood on her hands.

Katrine squeezed inside a small jar. Tara's own mother holding that jar.

A black-eyed man with a guitar.

And snakes. Dear Lord, there were so many snakes.

They were speaking, a slithering, rustling sibilance, wet tongues and dry skin scraping against one another.

You will never have a better man than me, not one of you Catalain women down the line. I'll come back and take the power away from every one of you goddamned witches.

The Catalain Book of Secrets: Poison

There is a story whispered of a Catalain woman who was so frightened for her daughters' future that she poisoned her husband. This wasn't unusual in a time when women were considered property and men treated them worse than animals. It also wasn't unheard of for a woman to choose poison over divorce; the former looked like natural death whereas the latter was a moral issue.

The most common form of "home" poison is castor oil beans boiled in the same pot as brown beans, combined with a dash of oleander and mandrake root. Add salt and bacon, and the poison will be undetectable. If the poison needs to be administered in liquid form, mix a ¼ teaspoon hemlock with the same amount of honey and lavender. If it is then mixed in a bitter liquid, like coffee or beer, neither the recipient nor the law will have a reason to suspect.

Winter

CHAPTER 25

Ursula

The impending dawn was 34 degrees below zero, a temperature that either crushed your spirit or turned it to steel. A mist of water sprayed into this air would hit the ground as tinkling crystals. A local joke had it that if you whistled in weather this raw, your music would freeze on your lips and drop to the ground as note-shaped ice cubes, to pop and thaw in a chorus of sound come spring.

Ursula stepped into the morning bundled in a thick pair of mittens, and layers of fleece and down. Three minutes' exposure would kill bare flesh, turn it as black as the plague, yet it was a magical, alien, snow-globe perfect world. Hardpacked snow squeaked under her boots, the piercing sound of the earth crying out. Overhead, prismatic icicles dangled from the street lamps and refracted light in kaleidoscopic patterns of yellow and white. The air smelled bleach-clean and sparkled with charged ions.

She was just in time. The winter sun had begun to rise. It hurt to look at. Not only would extended gazing ice-burn her eyes, but also a sunrise at this temperature was such a rich orange-gold, it humbled a person. It was a whiskey-liquid ball of fiery hope, dragging with it otherworldly purples and magentas and then tangerines the higher it rose until it rested in the sky as if it had always been there. Ursula had not missed a sunrise since the day, at age twelve, that she had mixed the poison that had killed her father. She'd vowed then that nothing would ever come between her and the sun awakening.

It had been an odd summer and then fall, with Katrine coming home. Christmas would be interesting. But then, it always was when you gathered any number of Catalains under a single roof. She would finish her Christmas shopping later this week.

But first, Ursula needed to pray.

She crunched and squeaked her way to Our Lady of the Lakes Catholic Church two miles from the Queen Anne, and entered through the unadorned metal door on the side. It'd never been locked in all the years she'd been worshipping.

The interior was heavy with the scent of frankincense and the clack-thump of marble-encased air. She unwound layers of clothing as she walked to the vestibule, lighting a votive candle from the flickering wick of another one. She whispered a prayer for her mother, sisters, two daughters, and her granddaughter. None of them knew where she went in the mornings, nor would they understand why. She wasn't sure even she knew, except that she'd found herself wandering around the church the morning after she'd help murder her father, and going inside had comforted her. She'd kept up the routine, always attending in secret.

Every time, in addition to praying for her family, she prayed to erase the memory of her father's accusing death stare, to forgive herself. It never worked. She also said a mother's plea, the only request that mattered to her: *please don't make my children pay for my mistakes.*

Crossing her chest, she made her way to the front pew, dipping her knee and crossing herself again before entering. The wood was warm and worn. She pulled out the kneeling bench and leaned forward. Bowing her head, she slid a quartz rosary from her pocket. The cross hung over the back of her hand, a flaccid thing. She'd bought it at the drugstore when she'd moved back home. She massaged each bead in turn, releasing the secret smell of roses, emptying her mind as she moved from one bead to the next.

She finished her meditation and stood, feeling oddly, pleasantly empty, like she did every time. She walked the two miles home, entering her car rather than her house when she arrived home. The Toyota was parked in the garage and its core heater plugged in, but it still took some coaxing to turn over. She let it warm for ten minutes before unplugging it from the wall and backing out. The motel was 40 miles away, on the outskirts of Alexandria.

She pulled into the lot. His car was in front of room 23. She parked next to it.

The motel room door was unlocked. She stepped through it, closing her eyes and taking in his scent. She stood like that, leaning against the door, until he spoke.

"I didn't know if you'd come."

She opened her eyes, glancing toward the bed. He was stretched out on it, a book opened on his lap. His expression was both pained and hopeful. There was none of the guilty excitement she'd gotten used to in other men. She shed her layers as she walked toward him, mittens here, scarf there, parka falling to the ground like a snake's skin.

It had taken many private meetings to convince Michael Baum to meet her here today. She knew he didn't love her, and that he never would. She was aware that he did love Meredith, even if the woman wasn't reciprocating the affection. She would begin to love him again, once Ursula was done with him. Ursula would make sure of it.

Out of her winter clothes, she pulled her shirt off. The move was practical, not sensuous. She unzipped her pants and dropped them to the floor. He watched her eyes as she advanced, not even looking away when she stepped out of her panties. When she reached him, she put her hand on his zipper and opened his trousers. She reached for him confidently and leaned forward to put him in her mouth. He groaned. The noise excited her, and she took him deeper. His hips bucked.

"Ursula," he whispered. He wound his hands through her short hair, reaching for one of her full breasts. "Jesus, Ursula. I've needed you."

That was why she'd come. In the winter of her heart, it was the closest she'd ever come to being loved.

Chapter 26

Katrine

"You don't think it's too cold?"

"It's always too cold. It's Minnesota."

Katrine stood on the edge of the rink with her sister. It had taken every bit of her persuasive power to coax Jasmine to the ice. As children, they had owned one pair of skates between them, every year a new pair as their feet grew but only a single set because money was tight. They weren't deterred. They spent two or three days a week at the public rink in the Faith Falls city park. They'd finish their homework, grab the skates, and walk the mile downtown, taking turns gliding across the ice, cheering each other from the sidelines.

Katrine had been trying to get Jasmine out of the house weekly since she'd thrown up on her carpeting. The horror she'd witnessed that day in Jasmine's memory—the hot pain, vivid violet shame, the reeking snakes—haunted her. Jasmine wouldn't give up that secret, and Katrine needed her to. It was standing between them. She missed her connection with Jasmine like a limb. She yearned for the tightening of the air around them as both of them returned to the balloon of sisterhood.

It was almost with a sense of desperation that Jasmine turned her down every time, as if she were afraid of how much it'd hurt if she got too close and lost it again. Today, however, Velda had taken Tara shopping, giving Jasmine nothing to hide behind.

"I don't remember how to skate," Jasmine said for the twentieth time.

"Like riding a bike." Katrine walked to the warming house, and Jasmine had no choice but to follow. Skaters packed the pond behind the warming house. The crystalline atmosphere sparkled, turning the skating rink into a diamond mine. The slice of blades on ice carved the air. Winter laughter needled them, searching for warmth inside the folds of coats and curves of mittens. It was a glorious day.

Katrine stopped just outside the squat structure. "Hey, should we rent a single set, just like old times?"

Jasmine smiled back, and the sun rose for Katrine. In that moment, she wanted Jasmine to share her secret more than she'd ever wanted anything in her life. It was all that was standing between them. She couldn't make her, though, and suspected that Jasmine had interred it in her deepest self, that the secret had grown blood and bone around itself and to remove it would require the rending of flesh. Yet, she'd keep trying. Jasmine didn't need to carry it alone, even if she was the big sister.

"Jasmine—"

"No."

Katrine stopped, her mouth open, and then decided not to finish the thought. She entered the warming house, waited her turn, and handed the teenage boy behind the counter a $20 when they got to the front. "Two size 8s."

She waited until they were alone in the corner of the warming house to finish the question. "Just answer one thing: is this…thing, this memory…is it why you started taking the anti-depressants? And why you sent me away rather than give me a chance to help?"

Jasmine sighed. It was an echo of a sound. "That's two questions. Let's skate."

Katrine followed her onto the ice. She wouldn't give up on Jasmine, no matter how long it took to draw her out. At first she wobbled on the rink, but soon the muscle memory returned. It wasn't long before she was skating around the edges, relishing the sensation of flying on the ground, the pricks of air piercing her cheeks and reminding her she was alive, the exquisite, tender equilibrium of the skate blade. It brought to mind the fragile balance she and Jasmine had found.

She glanced guiltily at her sister skating alongside her and was surprised by the Christmas-Day smile on her sister's face. She almost cried for the beauty of it. She reached for Jasmine's mittened hand, and they skated like this, two sisters against the world, for this tenuous moment.

§

"Did you hear that Ursula is sleeping with Michael? Michael Baum?"

"Heather's dad?" Katrine asked over steaming hot chocolate.

"Yup."

"Christ." Katrine was used to rumors of her mom sleeping around and so was unsurprised as Jasmine told her that Dean had seen Michael and Ursula's cars next to each other when he'd pulled in for gas next to the Alexandria "L" Motel. Still, she was mortified. Why couldn't her mother be more discreet?

"Yup," Jasmine said. "She's one of the powerhouses in town. If she finds out they're having an affair, she's going to come after us."

"Us?" Katrine raised her eyebrows. She tried it on for size and found it fit. She was feeling like a Catalain again, bit by bit.

She took another sip of her hot chocolate, thinking of the creamy drink Jasmine used to make from cocoa powder, real vanilla syrup, crystals of white sugar, whole milk, and a dash of fresh-ground cinnamon. It had tasted like puppy love and drinking it used to make Jasmine and Katrine giggle so hard that their eyes watered. She missed Jasmine's power with an ache like heartbreak. Aunt Helena had the cooking gift with her candy, and Jasmine had had it with everything else. For the first time, Katrine sensed that for Jasmine to reclaim that power would mean reclaiming the memory of what had happened to her.

"What bothers me most about Ursula is that she doesn't have any boundaries. She'll sleep with *anyone.*"

Katrine nodded, trying to distance herself from her mother, just as she had always done. "Guess that hasn't changed. Want another spin around the rink?"

"You won't try to play crack the whip?"

Katrine made an "x" across her chest. "Cross my heart."

CHAPTER 27

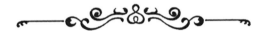

Tara

"Your mom and dad are coming to Ursula's for Christmas again this year?" Velda had taken her great-granddaughter Christmas shopping every year since the child was old enough to use a toilet. She ostensibly helped her pick out presents for the entire family, but given the number of questions she asked, Tara suspected it was more of a yearly fishing trip.

Tara's mittens rested empty on her lap, and she pretended to study a hangnail. "Yep."

"Think you all will stay around longer than usual this year?"

Tara dropped her hand and stared out her window. Because her great-grandma drove a '73 Mercury Cougar, there was enough space between the two of them to strap in a decorated Christmas tree. Today the distance felt physical as well as emotional. "I think so."

Tara wanted to tell Velda that she didn't want to jinx it. Her mom had been steadily growing happier than Tara had ever seen her, the swelling on her wound receding in the tiniest of increments.

Her dad hadn't moved back in, but he'd started taking meals with them. Everything really did seem better with Katrine around. The sky was brighter, food tasted better, laughter healed more deeply. Tara loved Katrine. She wanted *to be* Katrine. She worried that if she let anyone know how happy she'd been since her aunt came back, that it'd all be taken away from her.

"What aren't you telling me?"

Tara shrugged. She knew her grandma wouldn't let up until she gave her something. "The bricks around mom's heart don't look as red as they used to, like they're not so hot to the touch. They've been cooling a little bit every day since Katrine and mom had a fight at our house."

Velda nodded. She was aware of Tara's talent. When she'd first realized that the child could see into the center of each person's greatest pain, she'd had one request: *Don't tell me what you see inside of me.* Tara knew her great-grandma preferred to look outward rather than in, and that perspective seemed to have served her just fine.

"Maybe she's cooking up something new in there, something that doesn't require as much heat."

Tara returned to studying her fingernails.

Velda patted her back. "You know where we're going?"

"Christmas shopping."

"Yes," Velda said, covering both lanes of the road as she turned right. "To Seven Daughters. I imagine you're old enough now for one of Xenia's dresses."

Tara's eyes widened, and she tugged at her hand-me-down winter jacket. Underneath, she was wearing a too-large cowboy shirt over too-short Wrangler jeans. "Mom won't let me."

"Pfft. You let me handle Jasmine. I was thinking we should pick up a dress for her, too. Think Xenia does rush orders?"

Tara closed her eyes and saw a whole world of chartreuse, gold, and cream where before there'd only been shades of brown. "At Christmas-time?" She shook her head. "Besides, mom would never wear a Xenia dress. Too expensive."

"She wouldn't be the one buying it, would she?"

They had to circle Elm Street four times until they located two empty spots front to back, big enough for the Cougar. The air was still too cold for snow, but it was so clear Tara could see the blue when walking through it, and the downtown was bustling with merry shoppers. No store was busier than Seven Daughters, despite a slump in business last fall when those three women had stood outside the door, trying to deter customers. It had worked, but only for a while.

As they walked, people stopped in their tracks when they spotted Velda, hoping to catch her eye and exchange a word with her. Tara observed her great-grandma crank up her charm as habitually as she breathed. She would never grow used to how much each interaction cost her great-grandma, how each time Velda encountered another person, she had to make herself insignificant and tuck her spirit in a cupboard so she had room for the other person to inhabit her.

"Hello, Linda! How is your granddaughter? Wonderful! Oh yes, Seven Daughters is the best-kept secret in town. You can bet I'm proud of all my girls." She kept up a steady stream of chatter as they entered the store, which was so packed that they had to gently touch people's backs to get them to make room.

"To the kitchen," Velda called over her shoulder, grabbing Tara's hand as she threaded the crowds.

Tara loved the bustle, the steady chatter of people out shopping, the smells of mint, chocolate, and honey. She followed Velda to the kitchen in back, prepping herself to see a flurry of activity as Helena strove to keep up with her holiday orders. Still, she couldn't hold back the gasp when they entered the normally-immaculate room.

Velda also stopped in her tracks. "What in the name of Peace is going on back here?"

The kitchen where Helena crafted her candies was as packed as the store floor. Eight women and two men wore full-on aprons and chef's hats, tubes of frosting and pots of sugar sprinkles perched in their hands. Make that eight women, one man, and a teenage boy. The room smelled of fresh butter and gingerbread.

Helena separated herself from the cookie-decorating group. In her apron, she appeared as round and cheery as Betty Crocker. "Hi, Velda. And Tara!" She hurried over to hug her great-niece, gesturing behind her. "This is the second-to- last of our End Times Training classes that you helped out for way back when, only we're taking a break from the conclusion of the world to bake Christmas cookies." She shared a teasing wink with Tara.

Velda smiled toward the tall man with big ears who was speckling a pan of gingerbread stars with edible glitter. "Who's he?"

Helena glanced over her shoulder. "Ren Cunningham. He owns the watch store next door."

"Easy on the eyes, right?" Velda nudged Tara.

Tara jerked and flushed. She cut her eyes to the floor, but it was too late. Both her great-aunt and her great-grandma had caught her staring not at the tall man with the big ears but at the teenage boy. He was gangly and loose-jointed, his chin and nose dusted with flour. Tara was sure he must smell like cookies up close, and the thought made her blush an even deeper scarlet.

"Tara, do you want to meet Leo?" Helena asked. "He's our helper. He's about your age, I think."

Tara shook her head, and her golden hair fell into her eyes. She mumbled something about wanting to look at dresses and ran toward the kitchen door so fast that she upset a tray of pfeffernüsse. The clattering drew the attention of the cookie makers, and Leo glanced up, locking eyes with Tara for just a moment before the door swung closed behind her.

§

Velda took Tara for cheeseburgers and hot fudge malts at the A & W before driving her home. "You know, it smells like love is in the air," Velda said when they were within minutes of the square house.

Tara scrunched lower in her seat. She'd managed to avoid any sort of meaningful conversation with her great-grandma. She was confused by the rush of emotions she was feeling, and she wanted to be alone in her room to sort it all out. Her stuffed animals on her bed, her journal in hand, she would make sense of this. She knew she was small and bony for her age, her long flax hair straight. Her elfin ears poked out on each side. They were pointy, like her nose and chin beneath her too-big owl eyes. Yet, something about the way that boy had looked at her had made her feel liquid and beautiful.

"I sure wouldn't want to miss out," Velda continued.

Tara sat up a hair, her curiosity winning over her instincts. "Are you in love with someone?"

Velda laughed. "Not me, child. I took a vow many years ago never to fall for love again. But it is fun to *be* loved. After spending the better part of this afternoon watching you moon-pie over that boy at Seven Daughters, I have a hankering for some romance. I believe I'll stop by your grandma's for a potion before I go home."

Tara would remember the crunch of the snow under the Cougar's tires as they pulled into her driveway. It sounded like rabbits screaming. "Do you get elixirs from grandma very often?"

Velda put the car into park. "Nope. This'll be the second time."

CHAPTER 28

Ursula

When Velda marched through the cottage door, knocking snow off her boots, Ursula felt her blood run cold and then drain out of her. Velda had never before visited her in her workshop.

"It's me," Velda had said.

Ursula stood behind the table where'd she'd been distilling anise, watching flakes dust her mother's white hair, the setting sun outlining her petite shape. The air smelled like metal. Ursula and Velda had connected one day in their lives, the day they'd conspired to murder. "What do you want?"

Velda pushed past her oldest daughter. "What everyone wants when they come here."

Ursula listened to her mother's request, wondering why now of all times, promising herself she would say no, she would finally stand up to Velda, she was old enough after all and her own person, had been her own person since she'd begun raising herself back in March of 1965, but…soon enough, she felt the soothing comfort of Velda's charm wash over her, and she was unable to resist the full power of her mother even though she was cognizant of the self-hatred burning through her cells.

She shrank to twelve all over again as she stirred the wild pink rose petals, clover honey, and brandywine under her mother's watchful eyes, a little girl who wasn't and would never be good enough. Ursula concentrated the liquids, strained the clear amber liquid into a pink jar, and corked it.

"Why do you even need this?" Her voice sounded whiny to her. She knew the answer to her question: Katrine was back in town, and her magic was making people reach for more than they thought they could. "Can't you just use your regular charm?"

Velda took the jar as she licked her lips. "This is an especially tough nut to crack. I think he might actually love his wife."

Ursula swallowed, her jaw set. "If he drinks all of this and you are the next woman he sees, he'll be overcome with desire for you."

Velda nodded. "Exactly what I want." She put out her hand.

Ursula dropped the still-warm bottle into it. She did not want to know the name of the man who would be swallowing it. She consoled herself with the knowledge that at least this time, it wasn't poison, and that because it was winter, the snakes couldn't come.

When Velda left, Ursula felt wrong and ugly, so she opened the *Book of Secrets*. Despite turning to the first page, the book fell open in the middle. The borders of the paper were hand-painted with tiny lavender and pink petals threaded with finger-shaped leaves of dark emerald. The writing was elegant.

The Catalain Book of Secrets: Rue

Rue is a natural remedy for curses and negativity. Dried rue tied in a red bag and hung over your door will dispel bad luck and welcome powerful good.

Ursula said a word of thanks. Leaving the book open, she strode to her wall of apothecary's drawers and opened the third from the left, seventh from the top. She pulled out a sprig, wrapped it in a scrap of red velvet, and bound it with a golden cord. She walked to the cottage door, dragging a chair, and opened the door so she could balance the chair over the threshold. A frigid gust of blue air entered, confronted the peppery, witchy wall of heated air inside the cottage, and retreated.

Ursula spotted a woman who wasn't after a love potion navigating the snow-sentry path to her laboratory. The woman slithered as though her skin was all that held her bones together.

Ursula was still feeling out of sorts from Velda's visit. "Yes?"

The woman stopped, her eyes afraid but her jaw set. She seemed to be expecting anger or impatience. Her face was bland, as if it were missing glasses or more permanent features, and her ears stuck out like teapot handles. "Ursula Catalain?"

"Yes?" Ursula repeated. She ran her fingers through her hair, realizing that a stalk of rue had found its way behind her ear. She pulled it out.

"My husband and I are new to town. I live over in the Havership Development? I must have taken a wrong turn. I've heard about you but don't really need a spell. I was just driving and got lost, and your lights back here were the only ones on."

Ursula glanced at the Queen Anne through the front window. All the lights looked like they were off. Damned house. It had conspired with the night to send this woman to her. She was the worst kind of client, a person who needed help but wasn't willing to come out and ask for it. "I'll get you," Ursula said to the house in a tired voice.

The woman looked over her shoulder, confused but not frightened. "Who are you talking to?"

"No one. I was just making some tea. Would you like to join me?" You can only help those who ask for it, but there were tricks for hurrying them to that point.

"I really should be going," the woman said without conviction. "I was on my way to a class. It starts in twenty minutes."

Ursula didn't move a muscle.

"But I suppose, if the water is hot…"

Ursula sighed and pulled the chair out of the way so the woman could enter. She closed the door behind her. A bit of winter caught in the space between jamb and door, and there was an angry squeak. She always had hot water ready. She grabbed peppermint leaves from their drawer, then two mugs from a high shelf.

"Are you a chemist?" the woman asked, staring at the wall of bottles and the other of tiny, labeled drawers. Ursula's work table was covered with three hotplates, knives and leaves, pots of oil and alcohol, and, over all that, towered intricate glass tubing leading to beakers shimmering with liquids.

Ursula poured steaming water from a beaker into each of the glasses, not answering the question. The woman would see what she wanted to see. She handed the woman a mug. She reached for honey and squirted a dollop into her tea before offering it to the woman. "You and your husband enjoying Faith Falls?"

"Yes." She accepted the honey, glancing at Ursula. "But he wouldn't approve of me being here."

Ursula was beginning to get the picture. "Here" was not a specific place; rather it was anywhere he wasn't. "How are you?"

The question worked as a lancet, piercing the woman's protection and letting the words flow hot. "I was sick for a whole year when I was 13. I'll never get that year back. I think it would have been my favorite. They say your wedding day is the best day of your life, but I wished I had been sick for mine, sick and young with my mom to feed me soup and make sure I didn't get too lost inside myself. It's not that my husband is bad. He's loud, and angry, and cruel, but he's got this energy. He's the red in my gray. He's always been that way, grabbing life and letting it know who's boss. But he lost his job, and we had to move, and I don't know anyone, and I thought, just maybe thought, that I could do something for myself. I lied to my husband and told him I was going to check out an evening service at the Catholic church so I could get away to the class."

Ursula realized what it was about the woman's face that seemed off. It wasn't a permanent feature she was missing. Rather, there was an asymmetrical, unnatural smoothness to her, as if someone has broken every bone in her face and reset it from memory. "You want to make some red of your own?"

The woman nodded into her tea. Her hands were shaking. "Can you help me?" Her voice was a husk, a tender slip of dried paper offered to a world that had burned her.

Ursula couldn't take her eyes off the pudding of the woman's face. "Yes."

In the end, she gave the woman a placebo because she needed permission, not a spell. That's all she gave most of them: permission to use their own magic.

The Catalain Book of Secrets:
Self-love Potion

This spell is simple. Under a full moon, gather rose hips and petals from wild pink roses. Also, have on hand saffron, red wine, sage, water, and a moonstone. Put all ingredients in a pot in a 1:1 ratio over medium heat. Allow the mixture to come to a boil, stirring the entire time. As soon as rolling bubbles begin, remove the pot from the heat. Cool, then strain. Reserve the moonstone to sleep on that night. Drink the liquid. The next face you look at will reflect your true beauty back to you.

p.s. The Law of Helping Others

Only enter a house through an open door. There are always windows, or locks to be broken, but if the door isn't open, it's not time to enter. This is the same when helping others. It's only possible to provide help when it's asked for. The rest of the time, all you can give is love.

CHAPTER 29

Katrine

She was working for the newspaper and grudgingly enjoying it. She'd been out with Heather a handful of times, and felt they were building a friendship. Black-eyed John had asked her out twice, and she'd turned him down both times. There wasn't a morning she didn't think of Adam, didn't wish he'd show up and whisk her away to the life they'd once shared, but reaching out to Jasmine made that hurt less. In fact, every minute she spent in her sister's company felt like balm. Plus, the winter air held more love particles today than usual. That energy drove her to Jasmine's house as the sun was setting.

Katrine didn't bother knocking. "Hello?" She crossed into the living room, a smile on her face. It fell to the floor when Tara raced into the room, her face white.

Katrine rushed to her niece. "What is it?"

Tara pointed behind her, unable to speak. Katrine raced into the kitchen, preparing for the worst. Instead, she found Dean and Jasmine on the floor, husband on wife, locked in the most passionate of embraces, oblivious to the world. She clamped her hand over her mouth to keep from hooting and backed out of the room. She grabbed her ashen niece's hand and led her out the door.

It wasn't until they were buckled in the car that she let out her breath and started laughing so hard that her jaw hurt.

"How can you laugh?!? Did you see what they were doing? Gawd. It's like that image is burned into my eyelids."

Katrine held up her hand, fighting for breath. "I'm so sorry. That is a horrible thing to have to see your parents doing. I'd tell you about the time I walked in on Ursula, or Xenia, or even Helena, but I'm confident that wouldn't make you feel better."

"How can they still *do* that? They're so old."

Katrine let another peal of laughter escape as she backed out of the driveway. "I won't take that personally. And be glad that they still do that."

Tara looked doubtful.

"Okay, be glad that they love each other enough to do that."

Tara appeared to taste those words. Not for the first time, Katrine wished she could get inside her niece's head.

"You know," Tara began, "I don't think they've done it for a while." Her cheeks blushed violently, and she fought through the stammering. "I don't mean because it looked like they were out of practice or anything. I mean I don't think they've been close like that for a long time."

She grew quiet. "Except, I'd be okay not seeing it for a while."

Katrine couldn't help it. The giggles overtook her again.

For a dear moment, all was in balance in Faith Falls. But the snakes were on their way, just as they'd come every 25 years since time remembered.

CHAPTER 30

The Queen Anne

Xenia and Helena were busy arranging the nativity scene on the front porch. Xenia had received the charming, half-scale set in exchange for a shimmering periwinkle dress crafted by hand sewing strips of beads onto a simple jersey pattern. The customer had been staring at the dress through the window of Seven Daughters for three weeks, until Xenia came out to ask her what she needed. After much cajoling, the woman confessed that her beloved daughter was getting married, but she was a single mother who'd spent all her limited income on the wedding and had nothing left over for herself.

Xenia had been waiting for the owner of the lavender blue dress to show up since she'd sewn it three years earlier. It was a relief to get it off her hands. She would have been just as happy to give it away, but the woman insisted on some form of payment. When she revealed that she was an artist who specialized in painting wooden statues, the exchange for the nativity scene had been agreed upon. While not Christian, Xenia and Helena enjoyed a good tradition as much as the next person.

"Want to help me move this manger?" Xenia asked. "What are you doing, anyhow?"

"I was brushing the stuffed donkeys."

"You aren't supposed to brush donkeys."

Helena poohed her. "You don't know that. Have you ever owned a donkey?"

"Of course. I'm a wise woman," Xenia said, indicating the robes she'd worn for Christmas in case any carolers stopped by. She and Helena were brewing mulled cider and had insulated cups ready to distribute. "I know all there is to know about donkeys."

"Well, then you know they need to be brushed. A lot."

Meanwhile, inside, Ursula was cooking.

"You sure you don't need help with the turkey?" Katrine stood at the threshold of the kitchen, a room which smelled like roasting meats and sage, and was ten degrees warmer than the rest of the house. Garland was strung over the doorway, and the table behind her had been set for a feast. Ursula was peeking in the oven and releasing a perfume of fresh-baking bread and roasting turkey.

"I'm fine," Ursula replied. "You can relax."

Katrine was relaxing. In fact, she was happy. It didn't mean she was healed, or that she'd gotten her sister to share the memory of the event so horrible that she'd cast a spell to push Katrine away, but it did mean she was building something in Faith Falls. Not a life, exactly, but a safe resting spot. On top of slowly reconnecting with Jasmine, Katrine had grown close to her niece, taking her out for day trips to window shop, or grab lunch at Great Hunan or Mort's Diner, or sneak a makeover at the Herberger's counter that they'd scrub off before returning home. This felt like stolen time to Katrine, a way she could rescue her niece if not her sister.

Ursula had invited Jasmine to cook with her this year, as she did every year. When Jasmine turned her down, as she always did, Ursula had begun cooking the feast on her own. She didn't even allow Helena to help. She roasted a turkey stuffed with pearl onions, lemons, and sage. She baked a ham drizzled in honey and spiked with cloves, which caramelized to a sweet-salty crust as it rested on the counter.

Her corn-bread dressing was bursting with slivered sweetbreads and almonds, creamy and crunchy and comforting. The center island was lined with three different kinds of salads, cream for peas, candied yams glazed with browned butter, and six kinds of pie: pumpkin, cherry, mincemeat, apple, lemon meringue, and French silk. None of her magic aided her in cooking, but she was a mother, and she poured all the love she had for Jasmine and Katrine into this meal, hoping they would recognize it. She didn't know this, of course. She just cooked.

Velda strode through the front door without knocking, brushing back the green and silver garland that had caught on her shoulder.

"I'm here!" she called. A Santa hat perched on her head. "Merry Christmas!"

Artemis followed, pausing to tap the snow off his boots before removing her coat. The affair she'd required Ursula's love potion for had come and gone, at least for Velda, like her trysts always did. Artemis had remained a constant calm friend throughout this last one, and she'd been happy to invite him to Christmas. He hung her parka on the coat rack alongside his, balancing the bottle of champagne in his hand. It was wrapped in deep blue foil with a forest green bow.

"Get you a drink?" he asked Velda.

She nodded and made her way to the dining room, tossing an "I'm hungry" at the kitchen on her way. The table was set for ten. Velda took her position at the head of the table and awaited food and drink to arrive.

"Merry Christmas, Velda," Xenia said, pausing to push her mother's Santa hat into place. "Did you see the Nativity scene on the porch?"

"See it? I felt like I was *in* it. Did you have to put it so near the front door? People will talk, you know. They'll say the Catalains have found God."

Xenia chuckled. "I don't think we have to worry about that."

"We'll eat as soon as Jasmine and her family arrive," Ursula said, appearing through the swinging kitchen door holding a bowl of bacon vinegar spinach salad. The tangy, salty scent of it curled into the corners of the room. "They said they'd be here by seven."

"Do we have to wait?" Velda asked.

The doorbell answered her. The room tensed for a moment. Jasmine had arrived.

"Hi, Grandma!" Tara had only sporadically adopted the family tradition of referring to her relatives by their given names. "I made green bean casserole. We're staying late today!"

Jasmine's smile was tentative. Dean had his hand at the small of her back and urged her forward. He had agreed to join them for Christmas, even though he was still living in his apartment. "Thank you for inviting us," he said.

"It'll only take ten minutes to crisp the French fried onions in the oven," Tara said. She was beaming, her cheeks rosy with joy. "We even brought presents!"

Ursula heard all of this with an echo. She realized she'd have her whole family under her roof for Christmas. She'd known it, but until Jasmine had appeared, she hadn't trusted it. Her limbs felt loose like honey. She accepted the green bean casserole and turned so no one could see her naked expression. "Make yourselves comfortable," she called over her shoulder. "Dinner in ten."

Helena glided down the stairs. She took one look at the entryway and her smile grew even wider. After hugging the new arrivals, she hurried to the dining room to flip the Christmas CD. Frank Sinatra singing "O Little Town of Bethlehem" followed her into the entryway, where everyone but Dean, who had run to the car to retrieve the gifts, was standing.

"Come on, gang!" she said, her good cheer back in force. "Let's wash up and head to the table."

Katrine had wandered in. She was enthralled with the idea of being with her sister at Christmas. The thought was a kernel, budding green energy, taking root just below her stomach. It was one of many colors she'd allowed inside her since she'd returned home, and she didn't want to smother it. For some reason, she thought of the Christmas of 1976. She had received a Lifelike Baby, and Jasmine had gotten a Sears Holiday II typewriter. It was funny because Katrine had grown up to be the writer and Jasmine the mom. Katrine wondered whether it was those gifts, or their lives, that had gotten switched.

"Come and eat!" Velda hollered.

They filed from the large, garland-strung foyer into the dining room, performing an awkward shuffle until they'd all found their seats.

"Leslie will be arriving as soon as she gets off work," Xenia said. "She said to apologize in advance."

"Dean would like to say grace," Jasmine said.

Dean appeared surprised by this declaration, but he moved ahead. Tara kept one eye open so she could watch what everybody else did. Velda didn't stop scooping creamed peas over her mashed potatoes, but the rest of the guests crossed their hands and dipped their heads until Dean was done.

"Amen," he said.

"Thank you for coming," Ursula said in a shy voice at the end of the blessing, her eyes on Jasmine. "I'm glad you'll be staying late."

"It was Tara's idea," Jasmine said. "We have our own family tradition, usually."

"I'm sorry to intrude on your tradition," Ursula said.

Velda snorted. "Those words are meant to be a door, not a shield, Ursula. You can be gracious, can't you? Now pass the rolls."

Tara felt her mother sitting forward in response to the spark of tension from Velda, ready to bolt. A chunk of pinched turkey caught in her throat. Their "tradition" had been to come to Ursula's, have an uncomfortable Christmas dinner, and then return home to her mother moping as they sat around their own small tree. She'd held out hope that Jasmine would continue to heal, the bricks on her heart cooling and crumbling, just as they had since her and Katrine had fought over the lasagna. It was going that direction, but Tara was hyperaware that this all could be taken from her at any minute if her mom grew as skittish as she used to be. She tried to change the feel of the room.

"Aunt Katrine, Mom said that one Christmas you two stayed up late to see Santa Claus," Tara began, the words tumbling out in a worried heap. "She said you rigged up a Polaroid camera so in case you fell asleep, he'd trip the wire and it would snap a picture of him. Said you both fell asleep before eleven, and the next morning, the Polaroid had taken a picture, but you couldn't find the snapshot anywhere."

Both girls had fallen asleep by 10:30, sooty at the edges from crawling into the cool fireplace to set up the tripwire. If they'd been awake when the snapshot was taken, they would have witnessed a frozen moment of Ursula setting out presents and covering her girls with a handsewn quilt before retiring to bed.

"I think that was your idea," Katrine said to her sister, knowing it wasn't. She held her breath. She hadn't teased her sister in over a decade.

Jasmine tensed, then snorted. "Anything trouble was always your idea."

Katrine's relief was palpable. She moved the ball forward. "What about the time one of us wanted to sleep on the roof during a full moon?"

Jasmine's eyes grew wide, despite herself. She flashed a worried glance at Dean. "I forgot about that. Can you believe how stupid that was?"

"I don't know," Katrine said. "I thought it was pretty cool."

The frogs had roused her that summer night, singing an urgent song outside her window. She'd slipped out of bed, intending to cuddle with her sister like she did whenever she awoke out of sorts. When Jasmine couldn't be found in her bed, Katrine searched the third floor before spotting the sheet tucked into the rooftop window to hold it ajar. She'd opened the window and crawled out, seventy feet off the ground. The moon had been bright enough to read by that night, which meant it was easy to see how long a fall it'd be to the ground.

Katrine had held her breath and curled her toes onto the edges of the dormer and inched out, not daring to look down. On the other side of the sloped roof, she'd swung a leg and arm over, trusting there'd be something to grab onto. There was. She found herself on the widow's walk, Jasmine wide awake and staring at the stars, which seemed as close as her own heart. Katrine curled next to her, and they had passed the night there, not saying a word to each other.

The corners of Jasmine's mouth curled at the memory. "That was fifth grade. Remember elementary school? You were so popular. Heather still talks about it."

Katrine dropped her fork with such force that it took a chip out of her plate. She barked a laugh. "Heather hated me. And except for a couple of friends who hung around me because I could get them into the theater for free, I was as popular as crabs in elementary *and* high school."

"Really, Katrine," Jasmine said. Her voice was dismissive.

"*Really*, Jasmine." Katrine didn't know where Jasmine's anger was coming from, but she suddenly felt more than happy to match it.

"You know, I think I'll have some of that wine," Jasmine said.

This drew Dean's attention, though only for a moment. He handed his wife the bottle of merlot in front of him before digging into his mashed potatoes.

Helena clapped her hands. "I remember you both being as pretty as pictures in school. I'm sure you were both popular."

Katrine's cheeks were pulled tight. "You were the amazing one, Jasmine. You earned the good grades, kept this house running. You're the reason I had a lunch to bring to school or my hair combed before I walked out the door."

"Katrine," Xenia snapped, "that is an exaggeration."

Jasmine took a deep pull from her wine. "Is it?"

Ursula cleared her throat, and the house couldn't help but lean forward. The pressure caused a carved wooden bird to fall off a nearby shelf, and everyone at the table jumped. Would Ursula finally stand up for herself? Would she tell her daughters how after a full day working twelve and sometimes thirteen hours, seven days a week, she checked on them in bed, not missing visiting them a single night of their lives that they spent under her roof, brushing aside their hair and kissing their warm cheeks? Would she explain that she had gutted and remodeled this house to give them safe shelter to grow up in? Would she admit that she'd never had a long-term relationship, never even introduced her girls to one of her paramours, because she wanted them always confident that they were the most precious people in her world?

"Your aunts were in the house for you, and I was always nearby," Ursula said.

The houselights flickered. No. She would not stand up for herself. She would not become Velda.

"But no father was around, also because of you," Jasmine said in triumph, refilling her glass. This confrontation, starting between Jasmine and Katrine, and hopping like a nimble spark to Ursula, had been a long time brewing. The air in the room began to sing like water in a tea kettle.

Ursula blinked, and continued to eat.

"Plenty of good men around, though," Helena said, her voice strained, frantic to change the flow of conversation. "Ursula, do you remember that Connor fellow you dated back in the 70s, the one who always brought you flower seeds? I liked him. Whatever happened to him?"

Ursula was ever-so-slowly curling the tablecloth into her clenched hand, the gesture unconscious, the dishes moving toward her. She brought a morsel of ham to her mouth.

"I know!" Xenia said, glad for a change of subject. "He ended up opening a nursery in Iowa. A friend of a friend saw him when she went home to visit family."

Katrine, who'd been gearing up to jump in the ring, was startled out of the fight. "You dated, Mom? I thought you just slept around."

Dean clenched his jaw and glanced at his wife and daughter. Artemis sat straighter in his chair. The air crackled. The lights flickered again, went fully off for a second, then returned.

"Must be a power surge," Dean said, looking around. "I'll check out your fuses if it happens again.

"I'm sorry if my lifestyle bothered you," Ursula said. Her voice was a winter waterfall.

The air smelled of ozone, and then crackled, the tension released. Ursula had refused to claim the fight. Jasmine and Katrine were not yet done with it, however. They both stood, ready to say something to the entire table.

What words they would have chosen, only the house knew, for at that moment, the doorbell rang.

§

The carolers crowded on the front porch of the Queen Anne. Meredith Baum was scowling inside her winter bonnet. She didn't want to be here, but she went where God-via-her-pastor directed her to go.

"They have a nativity scene," Michelle Jakowski whispered into her mitten.

The woman with the beautiful black, gold, and copper dreadlocks and the gold-flecked tiger eyes, one staring off from the other, nodded. The metal in her hair clinked. She was also surprised by the nativity scene. She'd joined Immanuel Lutheran Church after leaving Ursula's cottage last summer, and she now read the nativity scene as a sign that it had been the right choice. Nothing else had come of that meeting, and she'd almost regretted going, if she'd been the type given to regret. As it was, she saw it as an entertaining use of half an hour and $250.

She wasn't sure what she'd been expecting. For the Catalain witch to look into a crystal ball and tell her that she must go on safari to Africa, or for Ursula to read her palm and tell her that a tall handsome stranger was to come into her life? It was foolishness that had sent her to Ursula in the first place, complaining of a life too perfect to continue.

That day, she'd accepted the tiny ruby-colored glass bottle Ursula had handed her and held it until her body had warmed it, as Ursula had instructed. Within a half hour of walking and warming, she'd found herself on the edge of downtown, across from the Immanuel Lutheran church. Her eye traveled its peak as she tipped the warm liquid into her mouth. It poured down her throat, tasting of crushed aspirin and ear wax.

A powerful coughing attack shook her, and she'd entered the church in hopes of finding water. There was a bubbler in the vestibule and a choir practicing in the interior. The music filled her so full that it spilled out her eyes in warm, laughing tears. Her parents were atheists. Her life had been full of books and love and logic, but never music that she could breathe in through her heart. She'd tossed the scarlet bottle in a plastic-lined garbage can by the pamphlet rack and joined the church on the spot.

"Somebody is taking good care of the donkeys," she replied to Michelle. "Look at how their fur glistens."

Michelle nodded and stood straighter. All the women demonstrated impeccable posture tonight, tummies in and breasts out as if their winter coats didn't desex each of them. Ren Cunningham was the cause. He had shown up for Christmas Eve caroling with his two teenage daughters and a guitar that he apparently could only play three chords on. He was the hottest prospect in town, a widower with beautiful eyes and a kind heart, and here he was, offering to spend an evening singing with women.

Meredith knocked on the front door of the Queen Anne. The carolers huddled inside a held breath: *Everyone knows Ursula is sleeping with Meredith's husband, and they're about to come face to face!*

Velda opened the massive oak door. She appeared imperious, but then her face softened. Immediately the carolers felt appreciated.

They wanted to sing their best for her. They were beautiful, and valued, and they needed to prove to Velda that they knew that.

Helena showed up next. "Carolers!" she called over her shoulder. She turned back to the church group, her excitement plain. "Let me get you all some hot cider."

She bustled into the house, leaving room for Tara to squeeze out, followed by Katrine and Jasmine. Jasmine blanched when she saw Meredith, an elder in her church, but it was too late to hide.

"Home for Christmas?" Meredith asked, her brows arched.

Jasmine nodded and stared at her hands.

Katrine noticed this. She also recognized the woman's eyes and facial structure. "You're Heather's mother?" she asked, holding out her hand. She wasn't surprised when she and Meredith's hands touched and the images came to her: brown-yellow, constipation, fear.

"What are you going to sing?" Tara asked, breathless.

Overhead, stars salted the sky, brighter even than the twinkle lights reflecting off the diamond-eye snow crystals. Ren strummed his guitar. Katrine felt her eyes drawn to him, and she grew breathless. Besides the drive back from the movie theater, he'd been on the periphery of her interactions in town: leaving a restaurant as she was entering, crossing paths in the baking supplies aisle, at the bowling alley with his daughters when she came there to interview the owner. His crooked nose and a broad smile ignited pleasant bubbles in her stomach. She couldn't hold his glance and so looked away, but she was drawn back. *Time.* That's all she could read on him. Waterfalls of moments cascading into bubbling streams of flowing, beautiful possibility. It was disconcerting.

"'Silent Night?'" Meredith asked. She didn't wait for an answer.

The carolers hit their notes with such precision, and the air was so clear and cold, it was a magnificent science to hear them. Helena stepped out with trays full of steaming mugs of cider, and Artemis brought coats, scarves, and mittens for Dean, Jasmine, Tara, and Katrine. While the carolers sang in voices so pure that it almost hurt to hear them, a soft snow began to fall one perfect flake at a time, turning the multicolored twinkle lights edging the porch into diamonds, sapphires, and emeralds.

Dean held Jasmine, who held Tara. Helena rested her head on Xenia's shoulder. Artemis smiled and sipped hot chocolate with a splash of peppermint schnapps. Katrine closed her eyes so she wouldn't feel vertigo as the music Ren made blended with the music that he was.

The house noted all of this with the deep appreciation that can only be felt under the clear, starry sky of a Christmas Eve.

CHAPTER 31

Ursula

The stress of the evening sent Ursula to her workshop. She could still hear the singing, but it seemed less invasive. The moon lit her path as she walked and reflected the falling crystals, lighting up each like a fairy lamp. She was too far in her own heart to notice.

"Mmmhmm."

The polite throat-clearing startled her, but she wouldn't show it. She tipped her head at the man standing in front of the door to her cottage. He wore a hunter's cap, which covered most of his face. It wasn't until she was standing in front of him that she observed that he wasn't a man at all, but a boy whose bones were growing faster than his skin. He stepped to the side, and she unlocked the door and flicked on the lights. She neither invited him in nor shut the door behind her.

She heard him step in and waited for him to speak as she bustled around her herbs, checking quantities in the apothecary drawers, rearranging beakers, sweeping Artemisia clippings into a pile, brushing off loose seeds that clung to the black velvet of her dress. He didn't. Several minutes passed. She was impressed with his patience. She finally turned. "Yes?"

She studied him head to toe and was caught off guard by the smile that made itself at home on her face. The teenage boy had removed his hat and held it in his hand. His coat was draped over his arm. He was wearing brown corduroys and a green sweater, and he reminded her of a plant. It wasn't just his appearance— hair curling like tender artichoke leaves over his collar, eyes blue and bright like bachelor's buttons, a strong, craggy branch of a nose, rose-colored lips—but also his presence. He was calm, and he made the air around him easier to breath.

He was a good man, or would be, if nothing got to him before he grew up.

"My name is Leo." He held out his hand. "I'm in love with your granddaughter."

CHAPTER 32

Katrine

Katrine was *seeing* Ren for the first time, the whole of him, as he strummed his guitar between his two singing daughters. The man was golden chords with sapphire eyes, the laughter of someone you love and fresh rain and a warm fire on a snowy day. She felt something tugging just below her heart, a pain so exquisite that it could only be healing.

Next to her, Tara gasped. Katrine looked toward her. The girl's eyes were as wide as wheels and glued on Katrine's chest. Katrine looked down. Could her niece see what Katrine was feeling?

A deep voice interrupted the singing. "Carolers!" It was the lead singer of the 32-20 Blues Band, a shovel over his shoulder, his breath coming in mighty plumes. Katrine felt a blend of excitement and shock at seeing him here, at the steps of her home. She hadn't seen him since that night at the Rabbit Hole with Heather, hadn't even known he lived in Faith Falls. Most of the singers broke away from the song, but Ren and his girls continued to the end of "Joy to the World" before turning their attention to him.

"Decided I'd shovel sidewalks for Christmas, but didn't know I'd get music with it."

Meredith stepped forward, her hand out. "I don't believe we've met. Meredith Baum."

"John Trempeleau, humble musician, trying to make up for some sins by doing a kindness on Christmas." He looked up at the falling snowflakes, caught one in his hand, and offered it to Meredith. "I figure that's the message this snow was sending me."

"Would you like some cider?" Helena asked from the porch.

John turned his eyes toward her, but they hooked on Katrine. A broad, perfect smile transformed his face. "I know you. You came to one of my shows. I'd never forget a face like that."

Katrine felt the tension between Ren, and Meredith, and John, and the house. Above all that, she sensed Jasmine trembling in her husband's arms. Did her sister know John? Was she simply cold? "How many sidewalks have you shoveled so far?"

Did his smile slip for a moment? "This is the first. I was going to start at the end of the block and work my way down when I heard the music. I thought there must be angels here." He winked toward the singers. Two of the women blushed. Velda, however, watched him with a rare intensity.

"Don't let me stop you," he said, dropping his shovel to the snow. "I have a lot of houses to get to tonight."

"You're a musician, you said?" Meredith was leaning toward John. "Maybe you'd like to sing a song with us before you shovel? We could use another deep voice to balance us."

"I wouldn't want to disrupt your style."

"Please," one of the female carolers said. Katrine recognized her from the Rabbit Hole the first night she'd gone there with Heather.

John pretended his shovel handle was a microphone and swiveled his hips like Elvis. Meredith jumped back, and the female carolers squealed in delight.

"A-one, a-two, a-one-two-three-four," John sang in his gravelly voice, fingers in the air counting off, head tipped forward over his shovel-microphone, hips cocked suggestively. He launched into "Santa Claus Is Back in Town," infusing it with such sexual rawness that the snow at his feet began to melt. Katrine couldn't help the tug she felt toward him. He was magnetic. She found herself wondering what he was doing later that night when the house creaked, and a load of snow slipped over the side and onto his head.

"Whoa!" He laughed and jumped back, brushing the snow off. Several of the carolers, Meredith included, jumped forward to help. He let them, smiling into the eyes of each. "Guess that's what happens when it's snowing," he said.

"We should probably get moving," Ren suggested, avoiding Katrine's eyes. "We have a lot of other houses to get to tonight."

Meredith took her hands off of John's coat and blinked. "Of course!" She clapped her mittens. "On to the next house!" The carolers followed her down the sidewalk, dazed ducklings, many of whom glanced longingly over their shoulders at John.

"I'll probably follow the music," he said to the Catalains left on the porch. "As soon as I finish your sidewalk."

§

"He had eyes for you."

"Who?" Katrine asked. She and Jasmine were sitting on the couch in front of the roaring fireplace, their legs twined together just as they had been when they were children. The table and kitchen were cleaned up. Everyone had long since gone to bed, including Dean, who had taken Tara home. Katrine had talked Jasmine into spending the night with her at the house, for old time's sake, and it felt like the greatest gift she'd ever received when Jasmine agreed.

Jasmine didn't tell her she was staying because ever since the carolers had left, the words were firing too rapidly in her head to silence them without Katrine's presence. *I will take your power when the snakes rise. Your children will pay for this, and their children.* "The shoveler. What was his name? John?"

"John Trempeleau, he said. I saw him play at the Rabbit Hole last fall."

"He made me feel funny."

Katrine laughed. "Those funny feelings are perfectly normal, honey," she said, doing her best imitation of Mrs. Diego, their nasally health and home economics teacher.

Jasmine swatted her sister's foot. "Not like that, dummy. There was something off about him. And he looked familiar, though I'm sure we've never met. It was creepy. And did you see how Velda was looking at him? Like she'd rather see him dead than happy?"

"Yeah, you're exaggerating, but I think he's trouble, too. I wouldn't touch him with a ten-foot pole. You gotta admit that he's pretty cute, though."

Jasmine raised her eyebrows. "Cute? Did you look at Ren Cunningham? *That's* cute."

Katrine sighed. "He is cute. And far too good for me. I only date losers, remember? Besides, I'm not even officially divorced yet."

"Hey, Katrine?"

"Yeah?"

"What happened?"

Katrine thought of their childhood, her weak magic, the series of troubled men she'd dated, her husband cheating on her, her attraction to both John and Ren even though she knew better, the spell Jasmine had cast to banish her before she'd forsaken her beautiful cooking magic, this house that felt like a living thing around them.

"Who the hell knows, Jazzy? At least we found our way back to each other."

The Catalain Book of Secrets: Sisters

Nothing multiplies your power like a sister.

Spring

Chapter 33

Ursula

Spring weather visited the first week in March—prematurely, for Minnesota—arriving as yellow as daffodils and lightning. The backyard of the Queen Anne was thick with gangs of robins pecking at the thawing lawn, drunk on winter-fermented berries, chattering and chirping. Teenagers who held hands and walked the streets were dusted in hormones as thick as pollen.

Yet, something was on its way, and you didn't need to be a witch to sense it. People jumped at memories. Dogs growled for no reason, and all creatures smaller than a cat disappeared, gone into hiding.

Ursula was not immune to the scratchy feeling in the air, but she always grew tender to the world as the anniversary of her father's murder neared. She buried herself in work to escape the circling memories. Today, she was nose deep in an ancient botany book the library had tracked down for her, the one she'd tried to read the night the cowboy had visited, a musty treasure with gold flaking off the edges of the page, when something outside the cottage door drew her attention.

She knew Michael was coming to visit her. They'd set the date at the end of their last one, but this was too early to be him. Would he stand her up if he came and found her busy with clients? She yanked open the cottage door. Dean stood on the other side. Impatience turned to alarm. Dean had never come to the house on his own and certainly never set foot into the cottage.

"What's wrong?"

He wore his cap low over his eyes. His hands hung at his sides almost like a child's. "Can I come in?"

Ursula stepped aside, allowing in the man and the clean scent of spring. Her relationship with her son-in-law had been superficial. That's how Jasmine wanted it, and Ursula supported every one of Jasmine's decisions, whether or not she agreed with them. She found Dean to be dull, but stable. She hoped she wouldn't discover anything else on this visit.

He glanced around the interior of the cottage, his face registering mild surprise. "This place looks smaller from the outside. And not so warm." He unzipped his parka to reveal a dress shirt underneath. Ursula didn't know whether to be charmed or worried that he'd dressed up for this visit.

"Can I make you some tea?"

He shook his head. "I came for a spell."

Ursula's throat tightened. She'd heard appeals over the years that had defied logical and morality equally—requests for leprotic poisons to drip on the genitals of exes, potions to turn enemies into bugs, a spell to make a cheater invisible. She'd thought nothing could shock her anymore. She'd been wrong.

"I can see what you're thinking," Dean said. "But everyone in town knows about the Catalain magic, even if we don't talk about it at my house. I don't know if it's true or not, but I figure the worst that can come of this is that I get your blessing."

"What spell do you want?"

He closed his eyes as if he were gathering nerve, or remembering something painful. "I want Jasmine to find the courage to be happy. I want Tara to be safe. Things have been so good since Katrine came back to town, and I want to keep them that way. Can you give me something that'll do that?"

Ursula hadn't been aware that she'd been holding her breath. "I can't stop time."

"No, I'm not asking for that." He clenched his hands, maybe in frustration. "I just want to protect them both. It's foolish, but I feel something bad coming. Almost like an itch you can't scratch, you know? But one that hurts."

Ursula's green eyes shone. She'd underestimated this man. She wouldn't make things worse by interfering. "I can't help you."

He lifted his cap and ran his hands through his hair, a frustrated gesture. "Yeah, it was stupid to come. I drive truck. I don't believe in magic." He turned so quickly that he upended a burning candle, spilling wax all over the front of his dress shirt. "Dammit!"

"Take it off," Ursula commanded. "If I get some hyssop on it right away, it won't ruin it."

He sighed, dipping his fingers into the hardening wax. "This is my best shirt. I got some on my pants, too." Reluctantly, he stripped off his parka and then top. The hot wax had left a red streak over his heart. Ursula whispered a protection spell and went about mixing the tincture needed to bleed the wax from his shirt and the front of his trousers. Then she started to scrub.

She was so intent on her task that she didn't see Michael glance in her window, witness her bent at the waist in front of a shirtless man, and leave.

CHAPTER 34

Jasmine

Jasmine was thinking how wonderful it was that she and Dean had grown closer. He hadn't moved back home yet, but they were working toward that. Nothing could stand in their way, she was she sure of it. She stopped by ValuCo to pick up toilet paper and other groceries and was trying to balance them all on one hip and open the car door with her free hand. It wasn't going well.

"Need help?"

She didn't recognize the man wearing the cowboy hat right away. She just knew he made her feel unsafe. She glanced around the parking lot, seeking for help.

He laughed and raised his hands in the air. "I'm not going to steal your toilet paper, ma'am." He squinted and leaned closer. "Hey, I saw you at that big ol' house on Christmas. When I came by and shoveled? You're Katrine's sister, aren't you?"

Jasmine nodded, the memory of him clicking into place. He appeared different wearing his Stetson. She grew ashamed that she'd judged him so quickly, or was it a different emotion she was feeling? Whatever it was, her blood was pumping fast enough to make her queasy. "Yes."

He held out his hand. She reached for it. When they touched, her panic returned, this time so thick that it blinded her. *I'll come back with the snakes and take the power away from every one of you goddamned witches. You will never have a better man than me, not one of you Catalain women down the line. Not one good man. I will be back. Your children will pay for this, and their children.*

She swayed, started to fall, but he propped her up. "Name is John." His grip remained tight. "You okay?"

She yanked her hand back, and the nausea cleared. "Fine," she said, running her hand over her face.

"That's good, because you look a little pale." He pushed his hat back to get a better look. "Probably this weather. It isn't right for it to be so warm in March, you know? Say, speaking of your sister, can I ask if she's single?"

Jasmine forced her stomach back down her throat. Her life had been so good since Katrine had returned. Why did it feel like this man was going to take that away? She was being ridiculous. It was a beautiful sunny day. She was in a public parking lot. This was not the man who had hurt her, could not be. That man would be in his 50s. "I don't want to talk about her personal life."

He laughed in a way that made her feel abashed. "I didn't mean to pry. I just wanted to ask her out, that's all. Can you blame a guy?" He looped his thumbs into his jeans and rocked on his heels. "How about this? How about you let me know if she's still working at the paper. You can do that, right? In fact, I imagine that's public information."

Jasmine didn't want to answer him. "She does."

"And what's her favorite flower? Gardenias, I bet."

"Exactly. She loves gardenias." She didn't know what had provoked her lie.

He chuckled. "See? That wasn't so bad. You sure you don't need help with your groceries?"

She managed a smile. "I'm okay. Thanks."

"All right, then. Have a good day, and don't get too warm! It's supposed to top 70 degrees today."

Jasmine watched his retreating back, suddenly very much wanting to check on Katrine and make sure she was okay. Car loaded, she made her way to the Queen Anne. The entire town seemed intent on keeping her from her destination—every car in front of her drove ten miles under the speed limit, a stray dog crossed the road, construction rerouted her five miles and across the river—but finally, she pulled in.

Dean's car was parked in the driveway. She was surprised, and then relieved. He was spending the day with Tara and so must be inside with her, which meant her whole family was here, and she could make sure they were *all* safe. She suddenly, desperately craved a protection spell. She'd never before asked Ursula for a potion, but now was the time. She raced to the back of the house, took the corner at the gate, and ran straight into Michael Baum with such force that she fell on her ass on the sidewalk.

He was so flustered that he almost didn't offer her a hand. When he did, the words spilled out of him. "I wouldn't go back there. Your mom's with a new lover. Some things never change, eh? I don't know why I thought they would."

Once Jasmine was to her feet, he took off. His car door slammed and his tires squealed, and still she stood in the sidewalk, glancing toward the front door of the cottage. Her organs felt dipped in an ice bath, and everything in her screamed to turn around and enter the Queen Anne rather than the cottage, but her feet propelled her toward the off-kilter workshop.

Each step forward pushed her through air that buzzed with warning, but she couldn't stop herself. Step. Another step. She reached for the doorknob, the hair on her neck piercing her skin like pins. She thought better of it, almost turned around, but then she found herself at the cottage window.

Dean's back was to her.

His shirt was off.

She couldn't see her mother's face, only that she was crouched forward, on her knees in front of Jasmine's husband, her hands working furiously.

She reeled back, her mouth a perfect circle of horror.

Your mom's with a new lover.

The ground rumbled underfoot.

She didn't want the memory. She'd given up her power so she'd never have to fully remember it again. She'd distanced herself from her family as much as she could in this town, she'd cast a spell to push her sister away so she wouldn't be violated as Jasmine had been, and she'd raised her own daughter without magic to protect her. She'd swallowed the anti-depressants. She'd buried the secret as deep as she could.

And then she'd let down her guard, and let Katrine back in. That had tipped the balance, and look what that had wrought. Her mother had seduced Jasmine's very own husband. The bile pushed against her throat, a hot acid that brought with it the memory that she'd worked so hard to suppress.

Tart, creamy avgolemeno is simmering on the stove. It's Xenia's favorite. She's got bread rising and will make a salad. The snakes are slithering outside on the ground, rasping like sandpaper in the too-hot spring day. She doesn't know how Katrine can be outside in that, but once she had learned Jasmine needed saffron to make her favorite flourless orange cake, there'd been no stopping her.

There is a bee, a honeybee, that tries to whisper to Jasmine when she turns to knead the bread dough. She fans it away. She is complete in the kitchen, happy, her true self in the right place at the right time.

Her soup smells so good, Velda once said, that it would raise the dead from their graves. She doesn't know about that, but she likes the scent of the chicken bubbling in the rich, velvet broth. She is kneading the bread when her neck prickles. There is someone at the door.

That was as much of the memory as Jasmine could bear. She let the hissing back into her brain, the keening sound that had started on the other side of her ornamental pig shelves when Katrine first returned to town. It was horrible, this sound, and it would kill her, but at least it drowned out the past. She turned her back on her cheating husband and drove home.

CHAPTER 35

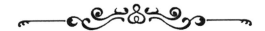

Katrine

Jasmine hadn't returned her calls for five days. It was like she had dropped off the earth. Katrine was worried. She would have known what to do with old Jasmine. New, brittle Jasmine was different. She broke easily. Katrine didn't want to risk that, and so she turned to something that had calmed her back when she was growing up.

This is why she was on her knees.

A gardening trowel, a spade, and a compost bag rested on one side of her, and Rum River ran nearby on the other. The silver water sluiced and whistled through ornate ice sculptures at its banks, reveling in the freedom of an early spring. The air smelled of thaw and hope. The ground cracked and moaned. Katrine wrote the sound off to the unusual warm-up.

"You reclaimed the whole plot, didn't you?" she asked no one in particular.

Her gloved hands pulled at the fern, clearing the overgrown spot where she'd tended her own garden as a child. Growing up, she hadn't wanted to ask Ursula for anything and certainly had no interest in letting her mom know she thought she might enjoy gardening. Rather, she'd cleared a patch by the river, where she'd had some luck growing cucumbers and watermelons. Her peas, beans, and tomatoes had never taken off.

As a child, she would bring the successful veggies to Jasmine to cook, maybe an underripe watermelon one year, a handful of scraggly cukes the next. She liked that she had to sneak to her garden, that she was the only one who knew of its existence. The secret made her feel safe.

The beautiful, early spring welcomed Katrine back to her little garden perched between the woods and the river behind the Queen Anne. It was too early for any sort of planting, but something about yanking at the weeds and creating order scratched at a deep itch. Her brain, which still sometimes cycled on thoughts of Adam, what he had done to her, what he was doing without her, began to empty, leaving a sweet, quiet rhythm in its wake. Pull horsetail. Scratch dirt. Get at the root of the crabgrass. Scratch dirt.

Thoughts of Jasmine and why she hadn't returned Katrine's calls would enter, or the question of what she was doing in Faith Falls and how long she'd stay would flit through, but the harmony of working the soil would gently shoo them away. She was encased in the comfort of practical action, her mind empty.

"Ursula would give you a patch of your garden if you told her you wanted it," she said to herself out loud, in response to a breeze riffling the dried leaves still clinging to the oaks above. She heard her voice and laughed. "Who am I kidding? Ursula would shit her pants if she knew I liked gardening. Best to not get her hopes up."

Katrine returned to her digging.

"Whatcha doin'?"

Katrine jumped. She turned to see her niece standing behind her in an oversized yellow parka. She brushed dirt off her knees and glanced behind Tara. "Are you alone?"

"Yup." Tara tugged her cap tighter on her blonde curls. Though it was warm for March, patches of half-melted snow still littered the ground like brittle glass. "Are you gardening? Ursula'd probably let you use some of hers, you know."

"How'd you find me?"

"I stopped by the house, and no one was there so I came to the river."

"Your mom with you?"

"She's sleeping."

Katrine's stomach dropped. "What? It's past noon. Is she okay?"

Tara shrugged. Her face was pinched.

"Tara?" The child's quiet made Katrine uneasy. The soil that moments before had felt warm and welcoming now sucked at her shoes, the cold seeping into her body.

Tara shook her head, opened her mouth, closed it, and then opened it again. "She went shopping five days ago. She hasn't been the same since."

"How do you mean?"

"She stays in bed all day. She says she hears hissing, like snakes. I got her aspirin and said she should go to the doctor. She made me promise not to tell dad. He doesn't live with us anymore, so it's just me and mom."

Katrine knew this, though Jasmine had never told her. She'd seen Dean and Jasmine growing closer, though, and had hoped husband and wife would be living under the same roof before the summer. "Hissing?"

"She won't shower. She won't eat the food I bring her. I don't even know if she drinks water." Tara bit her lip, looking anywhere but Katrine's face.

Katrine pulled her niece into a hug. "Let's go into the house, make some hot chocolate, and figure out what to do, okay?"

She felt Tara nod, but barely over the shaking sobs the girl finally released.

§

She'd gotten herself cleaned up and fed Tara some hot cocoa and cookies before driving her to the grocery store to pick up more food for her and her mom. There, they did more talking. From what she could gather, Jasmine and Dean had had a terrible fight, and it had knocked Jasmine for a loop, though Tara made Katrine swear she wouldn't tell anyone. It was concern for her mom that had driven her to Katrine.

When Katrine drove Tara home, her niece had insisted she not come in, had made her promise not to tell anyone else about how weird Jasmine was behaving. She said she didn't want to betray her mom. Katrine had agreed on one condition: if Jasmine wasn't up and around in 48 hours, Katrine would come in and drag her back into the world. This compromise seemed to relieve Tara, though it left Katrine unsettled.

After dropping off Tara, she'd gone into the newspaper office, where Heather had handed her her latest assignment. Covering the spring Sadie Hawkins dance at the high school wasn't the worst way to spend an evening, she figured. She was almost looking forward to it. As much as she was confused about living in Faith Falls, there was comfort here. A little bit at a time, she was finding her way back to herself, though the progress was glacial.

"Can you spare a photographer, or do you want me to snap pics, too?"

"Sorry. Kevin is covering a baseball game. It's all on you. Now, get going. The dance starts in an hour, and I want shots of the decorations before the gym fills up."

Katrine reached for the digital camera Heather offered her. She was rekindling her love of writing through the Faith Falls newspaper, of all places. She'd reconnected with her aunts and even filled in at their store a couple times. She and Ursula had a prickly relationship, but what was new there? Jasmine was in a low spot, but the two of them had grown so much closer that Katrine was confident she could help her sister through it, once she could convince Jasmine to finally unburden herself of her terrible secret. Katrine knew what it was as confidently as she knew that Jasmine had to be the one to reveal it to set herself free. And she hadn't texted Adam since her slip-up last fall, and was only thinking about him every other day rather than every day. The door was opening. Cracks of sunlight were streaming in.

On her way to the dance, tooling through the streets of Faith Falls in her new-to-her raspberry-red Honda Civic with 145,732 miles on it, she observed that the early, warm spring was acting like a tonic on the townspeople. Strangers waved at her, couples held hands. It was difficult to fight the promise of life in the air, the sun's warmth stopping to caress her cheek on its way to heat the earth, the vibrating hum of buds preparing to pop.

She found herself smiling when the townspeople's unprotected squirrel thoughts came to her, sweet morsels of *hope time to put in the garden I think I love her opportunity finally passion new business green.* She shut off the random input of other's brain meanderings, as she'd learned to do while still in grade school to keep herself from tipping into crazy, and pulled into the high school parking lot. The dance wasn't set to start for an hour, so she nabbed a parking spot close to the back entrance.

Her old high school. It was like visiting the person she used to be. Slipping through the propped-open double doors of the gym, the musky-tart smell of contact sports and industrial cleaners brought her back to the first wrestling match she'd attended. Heather had been there as well, head of the cheerleading squad. Katrine had tried to look cool, slipping out to smoke Virginia Slims that Heddy Larsen had pinched from her mom, then prancing back in lightheaded and reeking of tobacco. She'd thought life was so difficult back then. It almost made her laugh. If teenaged Katrine could see herself now, working for her worst-enemy-cum-newest-friend and scarred by battles of her own making, she'd be humbled.

The pep squad had done a passable job decorating the gym with blue and gold streamers, the school colors. The wooden bleachers had been pushed back. Folding tables lined half of the far wall, full of sweating canned soda and bottles of water, each available for $1 as a 4H fundraiser. A DJ was setting up his booth near the soda, and a janitor was stringing up a single disco ball, a glittering uvula dangling in the warm mouth of the gym.

"Are you here to dance?"

Katrine pulled herself from the musty, innocuous world of memories. She was surprised to find Ren standing next to her, and even more startled to discover she was blushing. She'd thought of him more than she'd cared to admit since he'd caroled at the Queen Anne, asking Xenia and Helena about him, hoping against hope that he'd felt the same zing as she had when their eyes met, that he would maybe track her down and ask her out. He hadn't, and she'd accepted that as her fate and even had the wisdom to be grateful. She would learn to stand on her own.

But here he was, in his tall, sturdy glory, his soft blue eyes crinkling at the edges, his hands stuffed into his jean pockets. Part of her was screaming at her to hide, to protect herself from any potential pain. Instead, she held up her camera. "I'm here as an official representative of the *Faith Falls Gazette*."

His eyes scanned the gym. Other than the janitor's pants riding a little lower than decorum dictated, the space was the picture of small town security, with hopes and dreams writ large in crepe paper and hand-penned banners decorated with sayings like

"We've Got Spirit, Yes We Do." He cocked an eyebrow. "I presume this isn't investigative reporting?"

She smiled. It was his words combined with the easiness about him. When he brushed his curly hair back from his forehead, her eyes were drawn to his fantastic long hands, the fingers strong and straight. "Pretty straightforward human interest piece, though I've heard talk about a student strike if the cafeteria doesn't stop microwaving the hamburgers. Some things never change. You didn't go to high school here, did you?"

He shook his head. The same lock of hair fell into his eyes, and he brushed it away absentmindedly. "Born and raised in Duluth. Met my late wife in college, and we moved here when I got a chance to buy the store downtown."

She felt a twinge at the mention of his wife. She did not pry. "So, what brings you to the dance?"

He pointed at the nametag on his chest. "Chaperone. Both my daughters are attending, and I want to make sure they stay a ruler's width from any boys. Don't tell 'em I said that."

She drew an "X" across her chest with her pointer finger. "I wouldn't dare."

A woman on the other side of the gym waved at Ren. Katrine recognized her as Mrs. Tappe, the same English teacher who'd been here in Katrine's tenure.

"Oops. Guess I better get to work."

Katrine watched him amble away, her heart hammering in her chest.

Bright, chattering teenagers began filing in. The lights were dimmed and the disco ball lit, and pop songs as empty and smooth as soap bubbles filled the gym. Katrine snapped occasional photos and got blurbs from teenagers, but her eyes were drawn to Ren. She didn't want a relationship. She had to figure some stuff out for herself, by herself. But she felt better knowing he was in the world.

She was asking a young woman with pretty brown eyes about her college plans in the fall when her shoulder was tapped. She turned to see Ren holding out a hand.

"May I have this dance?"

A mercifully slow song was playing. Most of the teen boys had gravitated to one side of the gym, the girls to the other, leaving the long-term couples in the middle, swaying and clinging.

She felt flustered. He recognized it. "This is purely a fact-finding mission," he said, holding up his hands. He nodded over his shoulder. "See the girl dancing with the boy in the blue t-shirt? That's my oldest daughter."

"Hold my camera and notebook?" she asked the girl she'd been interviewing.

Katrine found herself whisked onto the dance floor. A wave of anxiety washed over her. She didn't want to be in his arms. Would he feel what had been done to her? Would she sense darkness in him? But the fear passed. He held her, but not so close that their bodies touched, a firm hand on the small of her back, the other clasping her right hand. He led, but gently.

For the first time in her life, Katrine imagined what it'd be like to feel safe with a man. The idea laughed with joy, and the song skipped, replaced by an upbeat Michael Jackson tune from her youth.

She began to walk off the floor but was surprised when Ren didn't follow her. She turned to see him still dancing, in a way. Everything sort of came loose on him. His body vibrated with the music, full of silliness and innocence, his hands in the air, and Katrine saw him without her eyes. Strength radiated from him.

She returned to dance by his side, feeling some of the rebelliousness she had honed in this school two decades earlier but somehow lost the last few years. She was aware of teenagers rolling their eyes and of both of Ren's daughters looking mortified, and even of Heather's mother staring imperiously at them from the line of chaperones, but the attention made the moment sweeter.

His eyes closed, he rotated his upper body, his hips gyrating and his thumbs up, swaying and smiling.

It was the most honest thing she'd ever witnessed. She felt herself begin to fall, and for once, she didn't fight it. She let herself believe that finally, maybe, it was just possible that she would get a happy ending.

Chapter 36

Jasmine

The hissing sibilance that she'd first heard on the other side of her basement wall after her sister came back to Faith Falls had returned with a vengeance when she witnessed Dean inside her mother's cottage. The sound had scratched itself into every cell in her body, a tiny distant tune that could not be escaped no matter where she went or what she thought.

Its pitch was somewhere between a baby's cry and the squeak crunch of the yarns of a cheap wet sweater rubbing against one another. She couldn't sleep for it, could barely eat. It was pushing her to the brink of insanity, a place where her mind vibrated so fast it was as if it stood still.

She had been drinking steadily since she'd witnessed Dean at the cottage, doubling her dose of antidepressants, staying in bed, but even in those rare snatches where her body quit from exhaustion, she still dreamed of the snake song on the other side of the brick wall.

Dean had left on a long haul after she'd confronted him about Ursula. He'd denied he was having an affair with her mother, but what else could he say? Tara was worried for her, she recognized that. She walked on the edges of the room, scared to speak to Jasmine for fear she'd jump down her throat.

This morning, Jasmine had caught a glimpse of herself in a hallway mirror and jumped. Her eyes were sunken, her lips a tight gash across the lower half of her face. She'd thrown the mirror away. But it wasn't enough. The hissing continued, an itch that couldn't be scratched, a dream destroyed, a lover killed.

On an unnaturally warm March day, the intensity of it finally drove her to act. "Tara, we're going to Ursula's."

Tara twitched. But she followed her mom.

Jasmine didn't have a plan, just a sense that Ursula was to blame for everything bad that had ever happened to her. She felt jittery, and she didn't know if it was the last of the green and white pills she'd swallowed that were doing it to her. It was time, though, time for her to do something drastic to leave both the memory and the hissing behind.

The ground rumbled as she walked, and so she ran to the car, Tara hustling to keep up. Jasmine didn't speak the entire ride. Jasmine, the woman who had protected her daughter from every harm, sewed her clothes, cooked her meals, tucked her in at night, home-schooled her so the world couldn't damage her beautiful spirit as it had clipped her own wings, could not hold a single thought for the hissing in her head. The noise faded the farther from the Sam Street tunnels that she drove, but it never disappeared.

She believed if she could put a name to it, like the lyrics of a distant song, she might be free, but just when she thought she recognized a string of notes or a clear word, the hideous sound would switch tenor. In her lowest moments, it was enough to make her consider slicing off her ears and if that didn't work, sticking the sharp silver point of the blade in the remaining cavity and scouring until only black and silence existed.

Tara's presence kept her from this drastic act. She didn't want her daughter to find her in that state. But her tenuous grasp to even her daughter was fading, and she knew there was one person who might be able help her.

And it was the last person she wanted to ask.

They drove to the Queen Anne, the nasty, shrill sibilance beating at Jasmine's bruised brain. A heavy rain had begun. The air smelled like crushed worms.

When they arrived, she ordered Tara to wait in the car. She slammed her door and ran up the porch. Whipping open the heavy oak door, she continued to the kitchen, where she discovered Velda, Helena, Xenia, Katrine, and Ursula gathered around the breakfast nook table in some sort of uneasy silence.

She looked around the table at their shocked faces. Helena and Xenia had jumped to their feet, but they seemed unsure of whether to approach her. The secret burned against her throat. If she didn't release it now, she would explode into a million quivering pieces. "I was raped when I was ten. I think he was one of your *clients*, Ursula. Not one of you bothered to notice I was different afterward. You didn't even *know*."

At these words, a brick fell out of the structure guarding her heart. A cooling air rushed in, but it didn't stand a chance against the blazing fire of Jasmine's pain. "I wanted to protect Katrine, and save all of you from feeling like you had failed me, but I guess…" Her voice broke. When she spoke again, the words quivered. "I thought you would know. I thought if you loved me enough, you would figure out my secret." Her voice cracked.

She pulled her heavy, sharp eyes to Ursula. "And I know you seduced Dean in your workshop." She swayed where she was standing. She thought she had fight in her, but it was only desperation. "Please don't take my husband from me."

"Oh baby," Helena said, rising, her arms out. Xenia and Katrine followed right behind her. Ursula, an expression of pure horror on her face, stayed put. Velda stood next to her.

There was a scratching at the entrance to the kitchen. Jasmine glanced behind her, embraced by her sister and aunts. The hissing in her head hadn't stopped. If anything, it had grown louder, each sibilant beat accompanying her slow swivel until she was looking into the terrified eyes of her daughter. "Tara!"

The girl's face was an exclamation point of shock.

"How long have you been standing there?" Jasmine asked. There was no need. It was written on Tara's face. She had heard everything. She turned and ran, leaving melting, boot-tread-shaped puddles of water.

"Tara!" Jasmine ran after her, her aunts, mother, and grandmother close behind. But they were too slow. Tara had disappeared.

CHAPTER 37

Ursula

She felt Xenia watching her. "I'm fine."

Xenia shined her flashlight on Ursula's face. "You look pale."

It was after 8:00, dark, the air smelling murky, like thaw and fish. They were walking the slippery banks of the Rum River, hollering Tara's name. Artemis and Helena were on the far side, and Ursula and Xenia searched the side closest to the house. Velda and Katrine were driving up and down side streets, and Jasmine was at the house, phoning any person Tara might have run to. The ground had grown so noisy that Ursula wondered if these were earthquakes. But of course she knew they weren't. She knew the snakes were on their way.

"It's the reflection of the moon," Ursula said.

"It's more than that," Xenia said. "You look nervous, like a conservative in a think tank."

Her attempt at humor didn't go unrewarded. A small smile tipped at Ursula's lips. "Worried, more like it. How far could that girl have gone?"

"How far would you run if you recognized that your mother was losing her mind, and heard that she'd been molested as a child, and realized there was nothing you could do to save her? Oh, and by the way, you thought your grandma was screwing your dad?"

Ursula sighed. "So far that I don't know if I'd ever come back."

"Do you think she knew what we were talking about before she and Jasmine came? Her eyes sure looked like it."

Ursula shuddered. They all sensed that Jasmine had gone over an edge, but didn't know what had driven her. Ursula had deduced that Jasmine had become afraid of herself. Power unclaimed turns on its owner. Jasmine had not used her magic for over a decade, and it was making her crazy. When Ursula had consulted the *Book of Secrets*, it had opened to this page:

The Catalain Book of Secrets:
Revoking Power:

Every person enters the world with a gift at exactly the strength they need it, though some families can pass on extra magic like they pass on eye color or allergies. Some are born knowing their gift, others need to discover it or grow into it. Not infrequently, a gift can be used for destruction, or left feral and turn against its owner. In these cases, it may be necessary to revoke the person's power.

This dangerous operation is irreversible. It should only be done when no other option remains.

To strip a person of their gift requires all the living female relatives to be present in a single room along with the person whose power will be expunged. The female relatives need to cross four of their fingers and two of their toes and mutter a single word in unison, three times: sever.

It is done.

And so, Ursula had called a meeting of the Catalain women to talk about Jasmine. They'd been horrified, and then despondent. Having your power stripped was a horrible fate, but Ursula didn't see any other route if she was to save Jasmine from herself. Ursula was crushed to find out it was even more than that, that her daughter had been molested and thought that her own mother would steal her husband. It was too much to comprehend at the moment, with Tara missing.

"Tara has a gift, probably more than one," Ursula told Xenia as they walked the bank, bathing the cold, sloping earth with their flashlights. It wasn't unheard of for a Catalain to be blessed with multiple powers. Jasmine had made them promise not to speak to Tara about it, but one needn't be a witch to recognize the girl was gifted. "I hope those skills protect her tonight."

And to herself: *so many damned secrets in this family. So many. They rip us apart.*

CHAPTER 38

Tara

Tara had been planning to run away ever since she'd talked to Katrine about her mom. In fact, she'd hidden a packed bag in the trunk of her mom's car under the emergency kit: $22 she'd saved from odd jobs she'd done for her grandma over the months, an empty blue glass jar, a change of clothes including a silk jacket Katrine had given her that was too beautiful to wear, and her diary. She knew she would need to escape, she just didn't know when.

The shift in her mom's sickness had initiated her planning. Jasmine never told her daughter what was devilling her, but Tara saw it rise up when Katrine returned, ease slightly, and then multiply inside her mother since the fight between her and her dad. Her mother was flinging herself against her pain, fighting with all her strength and losing like an insect against a flytrap. What Jasmine didn't recognize, what would have killed her if she had known, was that her daughter was so bound to her that she lived this battle as if it were her own. Tara realized that if she didn't run far enough away, she'd be sucked in along with her mom and be lost forever.

She hadn't known that her mom had been molested, but she'd observed the resulting trauma from the inside while she was incubating in the warm red of Jasmine's womb. Jasmine's particular trauma was an absence where there should have been something, like a face without a nose, but what had been stolen from her was more essential, at her core. When Jasmine started taking medication, the absence just grew lonelier and larger, until last week when it became a pulsing vacuum that occupied more space inside Jasmine than her own spirit did.

Tara was terrified by this, and by the many ways her world was crashing around her. She knew about her mom's pain just as she knew that Ursula had a hand in helping Velda kill Tara's great-grandfather. Tara couldn't ever remember not knowing that because unlike most people, Ursula didn't hide her sickness. It was there, in plain sight, shaped like what it was: the potion that killed her own father. She lived inside the blue bottle at her center, separated from all the joy she could possess.

Tara noticed tonight that the bottle had an impressive crack in it, but it was too soon to tell if it was a breaking or a healing. Katrine had stopped tugging at the fishhook through her heart—with the exception of Christmas Eve when she'd pulled the correct end while looking at Ren sing—but she hadn't yet realized she could remove it all together. Even the earth was beginning to rumble like an animal with a belly ache. It was all wrong. Everything good around Tara was slipping away.

And then, the man with the cowboy hat had shown up. He'd come caroling at Christmas, and she had recognized her great-grandfather curled inside of him like a filthy baby. She'd wanted to say something, to Katrine, to her mom, to anyone, but she'd been born and raised on the understanding that you hold secrets close, and you certainly do not reveal the confidences of your family.

But since, the man with the cowboy hat had started following her, showing up in the corner of her vision. She understood he was coming for her. That knowledge left her mouth dry.

It was her friend Brittany, her mom's friend Michelle's daughter, who'd shown Tara the secret entrance to Tivadar Samaras' underground tunnels connecting the houses, including her own. The entrance on the edge of town once had a whole house resting on top of it, but then the owners had moved, and the market had been slow, and it became cheaper to raze the house than fix it up. Someone bought the lot and never rebuilt, and the forest began to reclaim its own.

Brittany had heard from a friend who heard it from a friend that you could still access the tunnels from the door in the weedy, mucky basement at the center of the lot, and Tara had discovered it was true while searching before she'd gone to see Katrine.

Always a planner, in addition to stocking her backpack, she'd stored cans of ravioli and bottles of water down there along with an old purple sleeping bag her mom thought she'd thrown out. Now, flashlight in hand, she dropped into Samaras' subterranean world, prepared to stay until the world returned to normal.

CHAPTER 39

Ursula

Tara'd been missing for over forty-eight hours when the boy who'd claimed to love her granddaughter showed up at her front door.

"Hi. I work at Seven Daughters?"

Ursula was quiet.

"It's closed, and I'm wondering what's up. Are Helena or Xenia here?"

"They're out looking for Tara."

He clenched his fists. "She's gone?"

Ursula regarded him with glittering eyes. "Ran away."

"I'm a friend of hers now."

Ursula could see he was lying, knew he hadn't taken the love potion she'd made for him. It didn't take magic to intuit either. First, the boy was a terrible liar, all twitches and pinballing eye contact. Second, if he'd taken the potion, he would have known Tara had run away because the two of them would be joined at the hip. Ursula found herself liking the boy even more. Still, a lie could not be tolerated. She watched him until he couldn't hold it in any longer.

It didn't take him long to break. His words rushed out. "That's not true. We're not friends. I haven't even talked to her yet. But I'd like to help. When'd she run away?"

Ursula felt a smile tug at her corners. A good man, at least a young one, is as predictable as a puppy. "Two nights ago."

"Did you call the police?"

Ursula sighed, any temporary lightness erased. "Yes. There's not much they can do that we haven't."

"Leo!" Xenia slipped past her sister. "What are you doing here?"

"I went to work. It's closed."

"Of course. It was closed yesterday, too, but you didn't work so you wouldn't have known that. We have much more important concerns now. We need to find Tara."

"I want to help."

Xenia stepped aside to guide him through a massive foyer to the massive kitchen. Copper-bottom pans hung from a rack in the center of the giant room, perched over an island scattered with sandwich fixings: a mustard pot, tomatoes, ham and cheese. Glass-front cupboards lined three of the walls. Spices, dishware, and exotic cooking tools peeked out at him. The gigantic cook stove had the curving porcelain look of an antique, but he saw the modern gas line leading to it. The smell of the space shifted depending where a person stood—blueberry muffins here, roast pork there. A breakfast nook curved into the far wall.

The rest of the family had been eating a quick meal standing around the island before they left to search again. Ursula could see he felt comforted by their strength until his glance landed on Jasmine. She was cradled in Dean's arms, and she was bony, crazed-looking, an eyeless creature unearthed. The sight of her condition stopped Ursula's heart every time she saw it.

He glanced over at Katrine and she stared back. Ursula was impressed to see him stand tall despite quavering in his fingers. Katrine's full stare could strip a man to his core.

"Where have you all looked?" he asked.

Helena heard his voice and glanced up. "Leo!" She rushed over to put her arms around him. "We've looked everywhere. Along the river. At all her friends'. Up and down every street. The library, Target, the bus station. We've looked everywhere."

"Everywhere an adult would," Leo said, out the door before Helena's words had cooled.

Chapter 40

Katrine

She'd been searching for Tara for two days, resting in fits and cuts. Jasmine was slipping away. Katrine could feel it, had known before Ursula explained the plan to revoke Jasmine's gift.

Tara must have known what was going to happen to her mom, too. Katrine recognized her niece's power of observation. She was certain Tara had run to save Jasmine, and something that felt like steel girded Katrine's heart. Her niece had courage, but in the end, Katrine knew Ursula was right. If Jasmine was going crazy because she refused to use her magic, drastic means were required to save her.

She found herself wishing Ren was by her side. It was such an unexpected thought, but so natural. He was someone she could trust. Someone she could lean on. The awareness gave her strength and was dominating her brain when her cellphone rang.

She listened to Meredith, Heather Lewis' mother, gibber in an excited rush. Tara had been spotted! Katrine's heart soared. When Meredith's call came, she'd been driving up and down the streets of the haunted Avignon neighborhood searching for her beloved niece. She was so tired that her eyelids were quivering, but the good news gave her a burst of energy.

Car screeching, she carved an illegal U-turn and raced the three miles to Immanuel Lutheran. The evening was unseasonably warm, nearly 60 degrees. Her car bumped a little as she drove, as if she were hitting tiny potholes.

It wasn't until she screeched into a parking spot in front of the church that she saw she'd been driving over tiny snakes. *What the hell?* But she didn't have time. Her feet barely touched the ground as she flew up the church's steps, and she didn't register Heather's car out front. It was not until she was inside the hushed apse that she realized that Meredith had never meant for her to find Tara. She'd sent her to get her heart broken.

And there they were, in the middle of the aisle.

Heather, in the comforting arms of Ren.

She couldn't have known that Meredith had orchestrated this scene by telling Ren and Heather the same lie she'd told Katrine to bring her to the church, an ugly little plan designed to hurt a Catalain as much as Ursula had hurt her. She couldn't have known that after unexpectedly finding one another in the church, Ren and Heather had offered each other the comfort of neighbors searching for a lost child and nothing more, that after the embrace, they would both go their separate ways in search of Tara. Katrine only saw what was in front of her eyes and so backed out silently, her stomach a brick of charcoal.

She stumbled down the stone steps. The air was charged and scented with moldering leaves and splinters of bright green. The snakes were running thick, slithering and tripping her. Twice she almost fell before she made it to her car.

Once inside, she locked the door, her chest filled with hardening cement, her blood slugging through her veins. The crescent moon shone on her like a Cheshire grin, and underneath that wicked light, reptiles flowed, hissing, rubbing leather against each other, squirming, making her see what she didn't want to see. In that moment, the weight of her family struggles and the loss of her silly schoolgirl hope that Ren would sweep her off her feet crushed her. She put her head in hands.

A knock at her driver's side window startled her.

She glanced up.

John stood there, his black eyes glowing like answers, a guitar strapped over his back. She fell into his wicked smile.

The Catalain Book of Secrets:
Ending a Curse

A curse can be borne, reversed, or removed. To bear it, do nothing, but know that the power of a curse lies in how much of your life it takes, even when it doesn't have to. Think of the woman cursed with the nose of a pig who rejected her suitor, certain that he was making fun of her by professing his love. What is worse—the curse, or what we let it do to us?

Beware if you choose to reverse a curse. Sending it back to its owner keeps the energy between the two of you, like a child's game of catch. If reversal seems the best path, it's a simple process:

1. Fashion a poppet out of white cotton. Stuff it with flax seeds and angelica root.

2. Carve your name in a purple candle. Anoint the candle with uncrossing oil.

3. Light the candle. While it burns, sprinkle the poppet with garlic powder and say this three times: curse, your parent calls you home.

4. Meditate until the candle has burnt itself out. See the curse returning to its creator, and see the effect the curse has on his or her life. Also, see your life free of the curse, and feel the accompanying joy.

Once the candle has burnt itself out, the curse will be off of you and on the person who placed it. Prepare to sleep with one eye open, because a living curse is a fickle nomad, and it's got your scent.

If you can, it is always better to remove the curse entirely. However, this is an arduous, dangerous undertaking. Be sure to have three times as much gathered power as the power of the curse, remembering that a curse gathers strength over time. If the power of the curse exceeds the power of those gathered to remove it, the curse will transfer to all present. Follow these instructions to destroy a curse:

1. Create a circle with salt.

2. Gather all the power you can. Douse them with oil of agrimony. Have them form a ring around the circle of salt.

3. Draw the curser into the salt circle. She or he does not have to be conscious. If she or he has died, you can put an item dear to them in the salt circle instead, though this method is not guaranteed.

4. Once the curser or their representative item is in the salt circle, have the power hold hands around and chant the following:

With the power of my blood,
   And the strength of my verse.
   I reclaim my own path,
   And I destroy your curse.
   Air.
   Earth.

Water.

Fire.

As these words are spoken,

This curse is forever broken.

Curse removal is a gruesome process when it works, as the curse must unstitch itself from the flesh of the person who made it as well as the one who has borne it. They don't always survive.

CHAPTER 41

Katrine

He told her he'd been out walking when the snakes started bubbling up from the ground. He asked for a ride home. She drove him back to his apartment, veering to miss the bump and pop of reptiles under her wheels before realizing such a thing was impossible. She shouldn't be with him. He was dangerous. Still, when he asked her to come up for a drink, she said yes.

Outside his apartment, she exited through her driver's side window and balanced on her hood, trying to get inside without wading through them. He tossed her over his shoulder and carried her up the exterior staircase to his second-floor apartment.

He set her down outside the door and unlocked it, stepping aside to let her in first. She stepped over the threshold. He closed the door behind her. A plug-in room freshener emanated the cloying smell of funeral gardenias. She would never be able to smell that flower again without feeling sick.

He took off his hat. She thought he looked vulnerable without it, but so painfully handsome that she thought he could read her mind when she looked at him. "They come every twenty-five years, but I'll never get used to them."

"Hunh?" He set his guitar on the couch.

"The snakes." She felt like she was hyperventilating. She wasn't supposed to be here.

He went to a window and pushed back a curtain. "They can't stay forever." His chuckle was low, almost a growl. "I've heard of frogs falling from the sky, and blackbirds raining down, but I've never heard of so many snakes coming out at once." He turned, his black eyes piercing her. "Have you?"

She shook her head. "No, only here. I think it has something to do with the warm weather. They'll probably disappear as quickly as they came. You're not from here originally?"

The question seemed to amuse him, but he didn't answer it. Instead he stepped away from the window. She felt like she was falling, and put out her hand to steady herself. "Am I bothering you, being here?" she asked. It was a reflexive question.

"No. Can I get you that drink?" He glanced at her sideways.

"Sure."

She removed her coat and sat on the leather couch, putting her head between her knees to restore her balance. The apartment walls were close and bare, probably the same harsh white that the landlord had painted them between tenants.

John ambled into the kitchen, flicking on his stereo as he passed it. She heard the hiss of two beers opening. She folded and then refolded her white linen coat. A hunting magazine lay open and face up on the table in front of her. He'd been reading. Bruce Springsteen was singing about small towns. She accepted the cool brown bottle when he handed it to her.

"Thanks." She swallowed half of it. Outside, the wind of history and fear rose up, whipping against the windows of the apartment, enlisting branches to get Katrine's attention, blowing children's toys from the yard into the street in the hopes of waking her up. The snakes grew sibilant. She chose not to listen.

John watched her, his black eyes hooded. "I've got more beer if you need it."

For the first time since she'd met him, she focused her attention on him fully and held it, scanning him from top to bottom. He was vibrating with a sexual energy too strong to read anything underneath it, a hot thick thing that reached right back out to her. She accepted it. She wanted to feel good. Her mind wouldn't, but her body could. And they were safe up here, away from the snakes.

She stood and strode to the bedroom, her breath sharp and scented with beer. He didn't let her reach the bed. He was behind her, his corded arm wrapped around her waist. He shoved her hair away and kissed her neck. She moved into it, turning until his hot mouth was on hers.

He helped her to the floor. His weight on her was good. It made her feel like someone else was in charge. She bucked her hips, and he moaned in the back of his throat, a growl more than a word. He unbuttoned her shirt, yanked it off, and pulled her bra down to her waist. She'd have an abrasion circling her ribcage from the force of it, but for now, she welcomed the pain, just as she welcomed his mouth on her breasts, his bites, his hand thrusting into her jeans.

He pulled his hand out to undo the snap on her pants. His breath was ragged.

She hadn't had sex with anyone since Adam. Adam, who had followed her their entire relationship with an eraser, forgetting everything she had done for him. It made it so easy for him to move on. She wanted so badly to feel some other man's mark on her. It would push Adam farther away. It would have to. It would heave every thought away so she could just *be*. She shoved John's hands away and wiggled out of her jeans. She tried to stand, wearing only underwear and her bra around her waist, intending to step to the bed. He yanked her back down.

"We're going to do it here."

He used enough force to throw her off balance, and she landed next to him on the carpet. She grazed her elbow on the edge of a table. "Stop it," she said. She'd meant his roughness, but her words inflamed something in him. She saw it flare up for a moment, in his eyes. They were shark-black, and something crawled in them like beetles in a hole.

He recovered himself, but it was too late. She'd seen it.

She pictured Ren and his honest strength, and she felt sick that she was in John's apartment. So what if Ren and Heather were dating? Good for them. It didn't mean she needed to be here. She inhaled soul deep. It was the sound of a death row pardon.

"I have to go." She pulled her bra up, adjusting it before sliding the straps over her shoulders.

"What?" He sat on his haunches, his voice incredulous. His erection pushed against his pants like a ridiculous spear. Outside, the wind picked up, screaming its warning. *Listen. Please listen.*

But she didn't need to. She was strong. This was her body. She was going to take it outside now. "You heard me."

"Hold on." He started to reach for her shoulder, noted her expression, and instead held up both hands. "We were just having fun."

She reached for her shirt, not arguing. Her body felt light because she had realized something: she could comfort herself. She didn't need to be here, or anyplace like here, ever again.

"I can make you feel good."

She felt his eyes on her blue silk panties, still wet from the earlier passion. "I don't want to—"

"We'll just have fun," he promised. He put a hand on her ankle. The heat was incredible. He snaked it up her calf. "This is just about making you feel good. I don't need anything out of it, baby."

She didn't stop his hand, or his mouth as it moved over hers, kissing her, softly reigniting the passion. *Maybe. Just for a minute.* He moved his warm mouth down, to her stomach. His kisses were light, his tongue stirring electricity. She didn't stop him as his kisses moved lower, or as he maneuvered himself between her legs. His fingers hooked the sides of her panties. He sat up to pull them along the length of her legs, returning to kiss a soft circle around her belly button. His mouth moved lower, licking her, his hand stroking her inner thigh.

She tried to keep still, but it was hard. His mouth was so close. The anticipation danced along her nerves like heat lightning. She closed her eyes, her mouth curving in a soft smile. She would let him go down on her. Her body would find relief, and it might just clear her head. What would that cost her?

But then her eyes opened. She didn't know what it was—the tenor of the snake song outside the window? The insistent scraping of the branches against the building finally getting to her?—but she was no longer blind. She witnessed his pulsating evil clearly. All the heat in her belly disappeared, replaced by slicing fear.

She twisted her hips to get him off.

It was too late.

In the moment that followed, she felt the backdraft that precedes horror.

It pushed against her throat, but she couldn't pull away fast enough. He was on top of her, thrusting into her, one hand splayed next to her head, pulling at her hair, the other pushing at her shoulder. It took him thirty seconds, and he was ejaculating inside of her. He whispered ugly words, ridiculous words, as he came: *I will take your power when the snakes rise. Your children will pay for this, and their children. I will return to make you pay. Not one of you can stop me.*

And then he was spent. He fell, his weight pinning her, the spasms wracking his body. He lay there until they passed, then pushed himself onto his back.

"It's times like this I wished I still smoked," he said, his voice husky.

Her brain couldn't piece it together, couldn't understand what had just happened. It was her substantial, tenacious heart that commanded her. *Pull on your underwear, then your pants, then your shirt, girl. Get out of here. Don't let him take anything more from you.*

"You leaving so quick?" he asked. "Like I said, I've got more beer."

She couldn't look at him. If she had, she would have seen a layer of innocence slathered on so thick that he believed it himself. Dressed, coat yanked on, she stumbled out of his apartment. She felt dirty and small. The hope that she'd been nurturing the past three months fled like a hunted thing.

Once outside, she ran until her breath was raw, slipping and sliding over the reptiles, sometimes falling to join them, always getting back up and running some more. On the other end of town, police sirens rang out, but no one was out in the Avignon neighborhood, or on any other street she ran through. The snakes were keeping them inside. When her breath cut at her, she walked, numb, until the tears came.

She hadn't protected her sister from being molested, hadn't even known about it, had left town as soon as she'd graduated, and had blundered from one disastrous relationship to another since then. Jasmine masking her power with anti-depressants was no worse than Katrine misusing hers. In fact, it was a step up. At least

Jasmine wasn't pretending. And now, Katrine's arrogance had cost her something she could never get back: her own body, and the right to decide what was done to it.

Her heart tugged at her like a supplicant as she walked. The pungent scent of the reptiles girded her ankles. She ignored both. She deserved everything that had ever happened to her. She had the power to see, and she'd closed her eyes at every opportunity. The tears intensified, and she felt herself drawn to Rum River just around the bend, water calling water. Her female relatives should wrest her minor power away rather than Jasmine's. Any hard-won peace that she'd felt since returning to Faith Falls dissolved in the acid bath of her thoughts.

She wondered what Adam was doing at that moment. Sitting in front of a fire with a glass of wine, Lucy wrapped in his arms as Heather had been in Ren's? She was happy for the latter pair. Ren was far better off with Heather than he ever would be with her. What about Tara? Was she safe? Tears rose at the thought. She'd spent enough time with Tara. She should have sensed her fear. She'd failed everyone.

The tang of the spring-thawed river caught her nose. She was back in her neighborhood, the twenty blocks between here and Avignon traveled in a blur. She chose not to walk within view of the Queen Anne (*don't look at me, I'm ugly*), instead treading through a neighbor's yard, the snakes thinning the nearer to the water she drew. The sly shard of moon shone on the rushing water of the Rum River. It was spring-high, frothy, sharp. Katrine didn't slow.

She waded straight in.

The biting temperature of the water stole her breath, and then the force of it stripped her balance. Her body scraped along the bottom of the river, fierce whirlpools whipping her head around and shoving her back into the calmer edges, only to yank her back toward the raging center. It was icy black. The water penetrated her nose and mouth and pushed into her lungs. She had no urge to fight it. Her heart kept her down like an anchor, a red muscle cast in lead. She was soul-tired, wearier than she imagined a person could be, and nothing felt more natural than following the flow.

What has John stolen from me?

She kept her eyes closed and thought of life's extremes. Fire to water, with nothing she could call her own to stand on, not for any length of time. She extended her arms and legs. A rock chewed her right ankle. Blood spilled from the gash and churned into the current, diluting from salty red to formless pink to racing silver, becoming clear river water diving through waving weeds and fish gills.

She felt a tug, a pull to follow her blood. She opened her eyes to the confusing murkiness and took a deep breath of river. The water burned like fire in her lungs. It felt good against the breathtaking cold.

When she had taunted Jasmine as a girl, telling her sister she was a liverless chicken-licker for not joining her in the chicken drop, she'd been terrified herself. She'd wanted Jasmine next to her. Even though Katrine would jump in again and again, her fear never lessened. She was always sure the next time would be the time the falls would win, and she'd be sucked over like that bag of puppies. But she kept jumping in. *Why?* The question trailed out with her blood as her head scraped against a rock and the cold forced her deeper into herself. It felt so good to stop fighting.

I'm doing the chicken drop, Jasmine, and I'm not chicken this time.

CHAPTER 42

Tara

Sleeping in a protected cove of the dank tunnel had not been difficult the first night. She had her sleeping bag and the heat of risk to keep her sheltered. The tunnels were quiet except for the sound of water dripping and the occasional skitter of rodent feet. When her dreams came, they resembled the roots of trees. The following day was spent reading and crying. The second night was much harder than the first, laced with nightmares and groaning sounds. She decided to spend the next day exploring, using a roll of string she'd brought to lead her back to her nesting spot.

The tunnel floors were musty, hard-packed dirt, their walls cold, crumbling red brick that shed copper-colored dust when she trailed her fingers along them. The smell of damp and earth was strong. Old wiring lay exposed in the walls and the ceiling, empty light sockets staring down like eyes. Someone had spray-painted "sex, hugs, and rock and roll" on a wall and traced a white heart around it. Her flashlight caught all of this in epileptic bursts but mostly, it lit the area exactly four feet in front of her in a yellow circle that she followed until she found herself in front of the door that led to her house.

The doors at each tunnel terminus had numbers above them fashioned of nickel-sized pieces of blue and white tile. Her house number was 2227. All but the tail of the third "two" was intact. She reached out to the mildewed wooden door made of once-powerful oak grown spongy with time and moisture. On the other side was more wood, fresher, nailed there by her father on her mother's command, and on the other side of that, brick laid on brick and cemented in place to keep out all the dark.

Tara put her ear to the wet wood. It felt cold and tingled, like a snake's kiss. Up close, the rotting wood smelled like the deep of a fall forest. Could she hear crying? Laughter? But that was a trick. The three layers of protection over the tunnel entrance were too thick to let any noise through.

Loneliness held her, a smothering embrace that made her sleepy. Was it nighttime? She'd spent the whole day navigating the tunnels. She should rest. She was winding her string back up when she heard the scrape of a door opening, followed by the heavy breathing of a man.

She thought immediately of the demon in the cowboy hat, coming for her, coming for every last one of the Catalain women. He was at his most powerful tonight, and he was done waiting.

CHAPTER 43

Ursula

Ursula sat up in bed, the scream echoing in her flesh. It took her several beats to realize the shriek was hers. Once she became oriented, she reacted without hesitation, not even slowing to grab her glasses. She shot from her first-floor bedroom where she had gone to steal an hour of sleep before resuming the search for Tara and charged out of the house and down to the river in her frayed pajamas, her hair flying around her like bats. She was sobbing, yelling as she ran, screaming Katrine's name.

The night air smelled like freshly-dug dirt. The crescent moon leered.

Ursula stumbled to the edge of the river, icy mud squishing between her toes, and didn't stop until she caught sight of the white jacket. She dove in, stroking powerfully, gliding between rocks, and catching her daughter just before the falls, twenty descending feet of rocks and pools. Using the branches of a fallen tree that had spanned the river since she was a girl, she pulled them both to shore.

The mud made a sucking squish under her knees when she knelt down at Katrine's side, both of them shivering with exertion and cold. She pushed the stringy hair out of her daughter's face and slapped her between the shoulders as hard as she could, fear and confusion powering the blow. She didn't stop when Katrine started gasping, either, not right away.

The coughs erupted into big wet burps chased by buckets of silvery vomit. The moonglow caught the tepid, chrome streaks as they fled down the mud bank to their source. Katrine heaved on her side, her back arching with every tremor. The painful spasms continued until Katrine fell onto her face, too tired to hold her eyes open. "Leave me here."

Ursula's hair was plastered to her cheeks. Her breath puffed out in cumulus clouds. "What the hell were you doing in the river?"

Katrine pulled herself up to a sitting position. It felt like trying to balance a bowling ball on noodles. It hurt to talk. "I had a right to make up my mind about him, but he didn't tell me the truth."

"Adam?"

"Sure. Let's start with him." Katrine tried to chuckle, but it morphed into a juicy retching.

"You couldn't have known." Ursula spoke firmly, but she was shivering.

Katrine was still. The house snapped as if it was moving closer to hear her response. Even the river was listening. She sighed, and when she spoke, it was with the gravitas of old wisdom. "I could have. I can see the truth of people. That's my gift."

Ursula started coughing. It began as a wheeze but grew until her whole body was vibrating with it. Her mother was laughing. "Is that what you thought your gift was, all these years?" Ursula asked. "To see the truth in people?" She laughed even more, the sound hoarse but full.

Katrine appeared deeply offended. "I should think I'd know my own power."

"Then you have a lot to learn." Ursula shook her head and rubbed Katrine's cold arm. "Besides, being unfaithful wasn't the truth of him. That's why you didn't see it. Things like that are a part of a person, a part that they work hard to hide, but it isn't all of them. Not by a long shot."

Ursula had to tread carefully. Her laughter had started with surprise, but she'd held onto it to nurture the one thing that could save Katrine: anger. She knew that if a person stared too long at the dark strands that made up a moment, they were lost. It's what was killing Jasmine, and she'd be damned if she'd let it devour either of her girls.

Katrine hugged her knees. "I make terrible choices with men. I want a new story."

"You can't have the trees without the worms." Ursula studied her beautiful child, all headstrong will and careening intuition. She stroked her shivering head. "Let's go inside."

"I'm damaged," Katrine said. She hiccupped. "I let John..." She switched tacks, a yelp of hysterical laughter startling out of her mouth. "Forget John. You know what's even worse? Adam is a selfish monster, but I miss him. I miss him most in the places I least expect it, like the grocery store when I see his favorite food and realize I have no one to cook for."

Ursula held her daughter for the first time in years. "You're going to be okay."

"I let him bleed me."

Ursula took her daughter by the chin and turned her head so they were nose to nose. "They can hurt you, but they can't break you. Ever. You're stronger than you know."

Katrine sighed, and it sounded like a ship being retrieved from the bottom of the ocean. "Hey, if I ever consider another relationship again, I'm going to take him to a psychologist to get him checked out the way you take a used car you're considering buying to a mechanic."

Ursula smiled in the dark because in that moment she knew Katrine was going to be okay. She would help her sad and weary daughter into the house, where she would bathe her and rub balm on her wounds and brew a potion to heal her heart.

"And mom?"

Ursula helped her to her feet. "Yes?"

"What the hell is the deal with the snakes? They're all over Faith Falls. Thousands of them. Millions maybe."

Ursula twitched, the memories connecting. *Snakes.* "They called you home, baby. When the snakes come, it's time to face facts and clean house. That means something different for each of us, but I'm guessing you're doing it right now."

Katrine nodded, whispering the words John had breathed into her ear. *I will take your power when the snakes rise. Your children will pay for this, and their children. I will return to make you pay. Not one of you can stop me.*

"What?" Ursula asked, her heart locking. She was falling deep into the earth, a great whooshing in her ears, her eyes flooding with water and then dirt, ever deeper, into the grave she'd dug herself using secrets as the shovel. "What did you just say?"

Katrine shook her head. "The man who…took something from me tonight. That's what he said to me. You know what it means?"

Ursula sank even lower. Velda had made her promise never to tell that they'd murdered her father, but it was Ursula who'd let her shame seal that promise. That secret had festered like a poison, gathering her, and then Katrine into its green bubble. But what of Jasmine? She tried to push back against the dirt. She had to fight. "He's going to get Jasmine next. He said he'd come for my children when the snakes rose."

Katrine shook her head. "This guy doesn't even know her, except for when he stopped by last Christmas. With the carolers. You were in the shop."

Ursula couldn't stop falling. "It's not the man," she said. "It's the spirit inside of him."

Katrine's cheeks hollowed, great crystal tears carving her cheeks. Her face was a mask of horror and realization, a sun rising over a crime scene. "Then he already got her, mom. When she came into the kitchen and said she was raped as a girl? That happened last time the snakes were here. I saw them, in the little bit of the memory she allowed out."

The words doubled Ursula over. How had she not realized this already? The secret she'd kept all these years was a tumor pushing against her brain stem, blinding her. The horror was too thick to swallow.

She'd let this happen.

She'd kept the secret that allowed this to continue down the line.

She could only mouth the word: *Tara.*

CHAPTER 44

Tara

Every nerve in her body quivered, screaming at her to run, hide, protect herself, but she was trapped in the tunnels. Her terror grew shoots and then cords that wrapped around her ankles and moored her to the earth as sure as cement. She waited, trembling, for the man in the cowboy hat to come into view, strip her, hurt her, separate her from herself. Her hand went to the hem of her shirt, kneading at it.

If you can move your hands, you can move your feet. Run!

But her body wouldn't listen. And so she stood, shivering in her own fear, cold to her marrow, awaiting the executioner's blade.

Which is why, when the boy appeared, a dim flashlight wobbling in his hand, she couldn't make sense of it at first.

"Tara?"

She'd been panting. She tried to draw a breath but couldn't get her lungs around it.

He moved to step forward, turning the circle of light on her face, and stopped himself. "Are you okay?"

The air wouldn't move past her mouth. She grew lightheaded.

He almost moved forward again, concern painted on his face, but stopped himself a second time. "I will leave if you don't want me here. I'll go right now."

"No." The word released the iron cage on her chest. She drew air all the way to her belly, sucking desperately at it, grabbing for another before she was through with the first. She hoped he understood that she meant for him to stay.

"My name is Leo. I work for your great-aunts. At Seven Daughters?"

She'd recognized him as the boy she'd seen last Christmas. He'd visited many of her dreams. Seeing him, she could smell the pfeffernüsse and feel the magic of Christmas morning. She still couldn't find her tongue.

"Is someone else down here with you?"

The gentleness in his voice allowed her to breathe even more deeply. "No." She thought of the dark-eyed man in the cowboy hat, couldn't stop thinking of him. "At least, I don't think so."

He nodded, shifting his stance.

"What are you doing here?" she asked.

His smile was sheepish. "I came looking for you. I stopped by your house when I saw the store was closed, and they told me you'd run away."

She tensed, waiting for him to ask her why. Or to tell her to go home. Instead, he glanced around, flashing the walls with his feeble light.

"Looks like I remembered."

"You've been here before?" she asked.

"Once." He ran his hands through his hair and glanced down at his feet. "It was a party. I drank peach schnapps. I can still taste it anytime I'm sick." He smiled ruefully. "I don't think I'm much of a drinker. Anyways, if I am, I'd prefer to do it aboveground in the future."

A warmth melted out from her chest. She was glad she wasn't alone down here, even happier that he was the one with her. "I have a hiding spot near the entrance. Want to see it?"

"I think I passed it coming in." He paused. "It didn't look very safe. You've slept there the last two nights?"

She nodded, rolling up the ball of string to lead her back to her hidey hole. They didn't talk. When they reached her spot, she stopped in her tracks, seeing her hiding spot through his eyes. Her penlight caught a glimpse of purple—her sleeping bag. Her backpack was right behind it. She'd been foolish to think she was protected down here. Her cheeks burned. She felt very young. She didn't want to look at him.

"Wait here," he said. "I'll be back in an hour."

§

When he returned, he had wood, nails, a hammer, and two dark blankets. He explained that he wasn't as good at carpentry as his father, but he'd picked up enough. He began constructing a wall around the alcove within the cave. The recess was only knee-high. If someone was looking for it, they'd see it, but he said it was his hope that the blankets would camouflage the nook and give her a more secure hiding spot.

He was working fast, and sweat began to drip down his spine. She watched him warily, but found herself moving closer. The next time he went for a nail, she handed it to him, the smile blooming on her face.

He glanced at her as he took the nail from her hand, and his mouth dropped. Her smile was so bright that they no longer needed the flashlight.

"You're PINCing me," she said. "With wood and nails. I didn't know boys could PINC, too."

He leaned forward, drawn into her smile, and she knew he wanted to kiss her, that he'd have given up a million dollars in that moment to do it. She leaned forward, too. He'd never kissed a girl, she could tell, but she'd never kissed a boy, so they were even.

Just before their lips touched, he pulled back. "I'm sorry."

She knew what he meant. This wasn't the place or the time. She liked him even more for not kissing her, despite her disappointment. The thought made her giggle. Her laugh tickled his funny bone, and he started to laugh, too. She reached her hand out to feel his laughter in the air. It popped like soap bubbles.

"Are you hungry?" she asked, suddenly shy.

"No." His stomach growled.

She giggled again, a calliope sound, and then wiped her smile away. "Your belly sounds like the walls down here. They've been grumbling since I came. Anyhow, I have crackers. And raisins." She leaned over and rifled through her backpack before handing him a little yellow box.

He seemed reluctant to take her food, but equally uncomfortable turning down her offer. "Thanks," he finally said. He opened the top and popped a raisin in his mouth. "What's it like sleeping here?"

Words worked around her mouth like marbles until one spilled out. "Scary."

He nodded, chewing thoughtfully on his raisin. She found herself wanting to hear what he said next, wanting to hear every word that came out of his mouth from now until the end of time. She leaned forward, reaching out to him. She wanted to brush her hands against his skin, to feel it next to hers, just for an instant.

A scraping sound stopped her. It was the entrance lurching open. The sound chilled her blood.

It was the cowboy. She knew it without seeing him, the same way she knew the sun would rise tomorrow and that water always flows downhill. He'd already gotten Katrine, and now he'd sniffed Tara out like a mongoose, trapped her underground, was going to chew on her flesh.

"Run!" she screamed.

CHAPTER 45

Jasmine

The devil was at her daughter's door. Jasmine knew this. All her years devoted to protecting Tara, keeping her close, and on the night when it mattered most, Jasmine could do nothing. Her daughter was gone. The terror set her outside herself, lending her a grotesque calm.

"What happened to you two?" Her question lacked any emotion. She'd employed the words because she tripped over a memory of them being an appropriate response to bruised and bedraggled people showing up at her door.

Did Katrine, already looking like she'd fallen out of a moving car, grow even paler when she laid eyes on Jasmine? Did a dripping Ursula put her hand to her mouth in horror? It didn't matter what they saw when they looked at her. Jasmine had the knives sharpened. She'd deal with the hissing as soon as they located Tara.

"I'm not leaving you behind this time." Katrine pushed past her. "Where's Dean?"

"Driving around. Looking." The sibilant sounds were so loud that she wondered if Katrine could hear her words over them. *Sshhh, strum strum sshhh, swee, sshhh.* Was the hissing really music? Bluegrass? It almost sounded like...no, the thought slipped away again, leaving a maddening buzzing that she could not turn off. Her daughter was gone. He'd found her. Just like he'd found Jasmine, twenty-five years earlier. He was going to clip her daughter's glorious wings. She could not help her baby.

"Jasmine, look at me. Ursula never seduced Dean, and she never would. You saw her cleaning wax off of him. He was in her cottage to get a potion to keep you all together. I'm so sorry you were molested, and that I wasn't there to stop it, and that I wasn't strong enough to fight the spell that sent me away. Please let me in? We can deal with this together."

Jasmine cocked her head. She didn't understand the words. And why were snakes coming in through the door?

"You have to face it, though. Face it head on and claim your gift, or it'll kill you. You have to face yourself, Jasmine!"

Katrine cupped her hands over Jasmine's ears. They stared into each other's eyes. Jasmine got lost in Katrine's for a moment. She'd felt the absence of her sister's gaze acutely when Katrine had first left Faith Falls. Katrine's glance was a blessing. She'd been born with the ability to evolve any person in her focus. Her attention didn't just make people *feel* smarter, funnier, or kinder, as Velda's did. Katrine raised them up a level by locating and amplifying their best self. Katrine was the sun to each person's divine seeds.

She'd worked this powerful magic on Jasmine growing up. Jasmine's amazing food tasted twice as delicious and healed those who ate it in half the time when Katrine helped her cook. She'd also unknowingly applied her magic on her friends in high school, who were more popular and scored better on tests when Katrine was in the room.

Jasmine even knew via letters that Katrine had worked her talent on Adam, nurturing him from an angry, underemployed graphic artist to owner of a successful gallery who also discovered that he had a flair for cooking and didn't mind public speaking. She opened up his world for him. That he resented her power was the ultimate irony. And of course, there were people who even at their best were not worth scraping off your boot, in Velda's words. Why boots? Was the incessant hissing a marching song? Had it been military music all this time? Jasmine caught the tail end of the tune and then it slipped away. She couldn't wait to slip away.

"What?" Jasmine yelled. They were still standing in her entryway. The air had gone scratchy. Ursula's lips were moving. What was she saying? Was that more knocking at the door? Knocking, knocking, knocking, always the knocking of the bass drum, a backbeat to the rhythm guitar that took the trumpet and bleated fear and buried her alive. Knocking, knocking, knocking on the garage door, she ran away from Katrine and Ursula to grab Dean's sledgehammer.

She was going to make her own noise. She couldn't take it anymore. She was going to knock back, and then she was going to shove a knife in her ears and puncture that mighty itch. She charged down the basement stairs, sledgehammer in hand, the air around her electric with dancing, taunting hyper-hissing and the iron smell of wet metal.

She swung the hammer at the brick wall that hid the hissing creatures that had driven her mad, that were bedeviling her from behind the brick wall. The knick knack shelves were easy to destroy. They clattered to the ground, a pile of useless pig-pink pieces landing on top of wood. She swung harder, and for a moment, she matched the beat on the other side of the wall. The synchronicity was the closest thing to silence she'd felt in a week. She almost wept. Fleeing back to the garage, she gathered more hammers and a crowbar, tools clattering around her, and hurried back to the basement.

Katrine and Ursula watched her from the bottom of the stairs, open-mouthed.

Jasmine returned to the basement wall, going at it with the strength of a mother, pounding, scraping, prying, pounding, scraping, prying, every rare few minutes finding a harmony. She didn't notice Katrine had taken up the sledgehammer and Ursula a pick and both were swinging at the wall, too. Swing, pound, pry, pound, swing, pound, pry, pound.

And then, an opening in the brick. It was no larger than a plum pit, a lucky crowbar strike on soft brick. Wood appeared on the other side. The wood was the first layer that Dean had constructed when they'd bought the house, and behind that was the original tunnel door. Jasmine scrabbled to make it wider, clawing, her fingers bleeding. Katrine pushed her aside and stuck the end of the crowbar into it. With a pop, she released a whole brick.

Jasmine's eyes widened. One brick gone, and the hissing had quieted one measure rather than grown louder, and the horror of Tara alone with the monster had receded a hair.

Yanking the crowbar from her sister's hands, she worked with a ferocious intensity. Katrine lent her strength and together, they widened the hole.

They were surrounded by dust and mess, shards of cement, and with every brick smashed, the hissing grew fainter. When Katrine returned with Dean's chainsaw, Jasmine laughed and clapped. Together, they held it against the exposed wood, and they let the saw scream, slicing through the wood wall that Dean had built. Sawdust filled the air along with the scent of moldy earth. The original tunnel door on the other side of the fresh wood was so mildewed that Jasmine could push through it with her hand. The earth exhaled a breath of underground air into the basement.

She jerked her hand back and shoved her eye against the hole like an animal trapped under river ice. It was bottomless black on the other side, the ultimate screen against which to play the hissing movie that had consumed her mind. She'd been burying it for two decades plus, rarely letting down her guard, only allowing bits of it to escape, dulling these visions with medication. She couldn't keep it down any longer, and so the movie played, her eye serving as the projector displaying the image into the deep:

Ten-year-old Jasmine, flushed and pretty, leans over a simmering pot of avgolemono soup. Her dark hair is pulled back into a pony tail, her focus complete. A honeybee buzzes lazily into her line of sight. She waves it away, but it is drawn back to her sweet breath. Smiling, she lowers the burner under the soup and turns to usher the bumblebee out through the open window.

The rich, enticing smell of her soup—tender morsels of chicken bubbling in the rich, bright broth—wafts outside, but the bee stays. Jasmine doesn't mind. She is in the perfect spot at the ideal time, doing what she loves. She begins kneading bread dough, the floured ball giving way under her palms like warm flesh. She presses rhythmically, pouring her love into the dough. It's Katrine's favorite, and her face will light up when she smells it baking. Jasmine smiles at the thought, and at the image of Katrine coming back proudly holding her cucumbers, but then her neck prickles. She turns.

He is standing just inside the door, his face grim. At first she thinks he is a ghost, so dark is his form, but then he darts forward, slapping one rough hand over her mouth and sliding the other around her waist. She struggles, and her leg kicks the pot of soup to the floor. It clatters loudly. She twists, but he's too strong. He drags her into the pantry. He tightens his grip on her mouth, pinning her against the wall so he can unzip his trousers and yank down her underpants. He enters her forcefully, grunting in her ear, telling her how good she feels. The pain burns through her, splits her in two. It also makes her still. The bee has followed them. It buzzes, buzzes softly in her ear, begging her to come and play.

The man releases her. She slides to the floor. He zips his pants He laughs as he speaks the words that have introduced her nightmares for the past 25 years: I will take your power when the snakes rise. Your children will pay for this, and their children. I will return to make you pay. Not one of you can stop me.

He disappears. She lies there for minutes before straightening her panties and then her dress, pushing herself to a standing position, and limping back to the kitchen. She cleans up the soup on the ground and then she begins cooking in earnest. It keeps the horror at bay. Katrine must never know. Nobody must ever know. Because in her heart she understands it is her cooking that drew him to her. And so she will use her magic only two more times, first to hide her shame from her family and second to push her loving, curious sister away as soon as she's old enough to leave so that the man can't find her and do this to her, and then she will never use it again.

And so she cooks the feast of a lifetime, puddings and pies and meats and salads, stirring feverishly, desperately, until she has enough food to bewitch her mom, and her aunts, and most of all, her sister. Jasmine is cleaned up when they enter the kitchen, and they are enchanted by the smells of her magical food, and they walk past her, and they eat, and they turn blind to what has happened to beloved Jasmine. Her later spell, the one she casts when Katrine is 18, is so strong that it begins to push her sister away even before she finishes eating it, and before Jasmine knows it, Katrine, the only friend she's ever had, is gone from her life, living halfway across the world.

She has never known what the man's words meant, but she has lived her life around them, first sending her sister away so that she could not be hurt, and then keeping her daughter close. She'd kept the secret and the shame of it even closer, and because of that, her daughter was out in the world, in danger, as the snakes returned. It was Jasmine's fault that the man had come for Tara.

"Help me. Please," Jasmine rasped, her eye wide against the cold wood of the tunnel door. Her breath sliced her throat. The movie was playing on an endless loop. She was weeping but too numb to feel it.

Katrine gasped. She dropped her tools, pushed Jasmine aside, and began to yank barehanded at the rotting wood with a crazed intensity. Ursula joined her, the two of them working until they had cleared a hole to the tunnels large enough for Jasmine to crawl through. Katrine hoisted her up. Jasmine went feet first and dropped to the ground on the other side into the deep, into the dark recollection of it.

She was finally, completely, in the memory.

She was no longer hiding from any of it, no more clutching her guilt and shame. The secret was writhing in the confession.

Whatever it was going to do to her, it must do now. She heard Katrine crawl through the hole and felt her presence behind her. Her mother came next and held her. She wasn't going to have to face this alone. It might kill her, eradicate the last bit of *Jasmine* that was left, but she wasn't going to run anymore.

"Did you see it?" Her voice is a husk.

"I saw it," Katrine replied. "I saw the whole movie play."

"I did too, baby," Ursula said.

"I'm not going to hide it from you anymore. Not from anyone. I'm sorry."

Katrine and Ursula held her, all three of them shaking. It took Jasmine's eyes a minute to adjust.

When they did, she saw her daughter and a boy standing there, out of breath as if they'd been running. They both appeared scared, and hopeful. Cords of snakes slithered around their feet, kissing the air with their tongues. The boy held a dim flashlight pointed at the ground. Snakes began to melt away, disappearing into the walls like water down an opened drain.

"Tara." Jasmine heard herself say through a thundering quiet.

The hissing was gone.

Jasmine fell to her knees and wept, her mother, daughter, and sister holding her. The three of them were still clinging to each other when Xenia and Helena arrived moments later. Dean, when he discovered them all on a heap on the other side of his basement wall, clung to his wife and child like a saved man.

The man in the cowboy hat faded into the shadows.

The snakes would be here for 24 more hours. He was patient.

CHAPTER 46

Ursula

Around steaming cups of tea in the Queen Anne kitchen, Ursula told them everything. After all these years, it turned out it wasn't much of a story at all. It came into the world with the force of a burp:

Henry had beaten Velda, and she'd borne it, would have kept bearing it, if he hadn't set his sights on Ursula. Because he wasn't a man you left, Velda had Ursula mix the hemlock. Henry Tanager had died gruesomely, setting the curse that had cost Jasmine and Katrine their belief in their power.

Ursula should have guessed that her sisters wouldn't be surprised by the story. Xenia and Helena had simply always known and never questioned, just as they had never questioned the color of their hair or their height. Katrine and Jasmine believed the story, took the news grimly, but it was harder to convince them that the same savage spirit that had inhabited Ursula's father controlled the two men who'd come after them. Ursula knew this could happen, that evil could sleep but never died. Before she'd been forced to, though, she'd been unwilling to consider that by murdering her father, she'd released rather than destroyed whatever corrupt spark had been driving him.

"But he's not done with us," Katrine said, when Ursula was done talking. She glanced at Tara, who appeared to be in shock but otherwise not worse for the wear. She had confessed to the fact that the cowboy had found them in the tunnels, had almost had Tara in his grasp before Jasmine broke through the wall. "Right? He'll just keep coming back."

Ursula repeated the curse that had been tattooed on her heart. "I will take your power when the snakes rise. Your children will pay for this, and their children. I will return to make you pay."

Jasmine and Katrine joined in at the same time. "Not one of you can stop me." They wore identical expressions of despair.

The words had the opposite effect on Tara. "Not one of us. All of us!"

Ursula didn't understand at first. It was Leo who made it clear. "All of the Catalain women together. If everything you said is true, you have to join together to stop him."

Dawning shone across the women's faces, starting with Ursula and ending with Katrine, who had a gleam of hope to her. Even Dean nodded.

"I'll only do this if we promise no more secrets between us," Jasmine said, grabbing her daughter's hand.

Ursula sighed from the depths of her soul. "I have something to show you."

The Catalain Book of Secrets:
Scrying

The commonly-held principles of magic
are that it requires effort, it must harm
no one, it must not be performed for
selfish reasons, and it's a divine art.
Lesser known is the fact that magic and love
derive from the same element. This knowledge is
essential to the art of scrying.

Gather a tablespoon of mugwort or wormwood.
Crumble it between your palms until it is a fine
powder. Next, pour it into a square glass pan.
The mind must be free from distraction in all acts
of divination, and so release any thoughts except
for loving ones.

Rest the tip of your pointer figure into
the glass pan. With your eyes closed and
your body holding visions of love, allow
the finger to move at will. If you wish to
ask a specific question, hold it firmly

in thought, never releasing the sensation of love. Allow your finger to move until it stops.

Open your eyes. The message you seek will be inscribed in the herb powder.

CHAPTER 47

Ursula

"It just opens to a page like that?" Katrine asked. She'd tried opening the book to a different page several times, but it kept returning to the scrying spell.

Ursula nodded, placing her hand over the book. It fell open to the curse page. She leaned forward, her chest tightening. She didn't know if it was excitement or fear. "Read this."

Xenia and Helena crowded behind Katrine, Tara, Dean, Leo, and Jasmine behind Ursula. Together, they read the spell, their lips moving as they moved from one word to another. It was Xenia who broke the silence that followed, speaking matter-of-factly. "We need to call Velda."

Ursula's organs shrank. On some level, she'd known this stand-off with her mother was coming. She'd hoped it would not be tonight. She forced herself to stand tall. "We don't need her."

Tara pointed at the curse-breaking spell, her fingers dancing over the intricately-inked instructions. "We need all of us, and then some, if we can get them. It says so right here. We need three times as much power as the curse itself to undo it, and that curse has been around for a while."

Katrine nodded. "She's right, mom. We need Velda here."

Ursula shook her head, her lips drawn with a thin, colorless line. This was her cottage, her safe place, but she still couldn't find her voice. This evening, she'd broken her promise to Velda, shared the secret she swore to keep to her grave. It had been necessary. She should have dragged that demon into the sun many years earlier. That didn't mean she wanted to face Velda, though, and the disappointment that would be in her eyes, that certain feeling like the setting of a sun as Velda closed off her love forever.

Xenia grabbed one of her hands, Helena the other. They understood, as much as a person could, but they didn't know. They'd always had each other and so a steady diet of love. They hadn't been starved for it.

"Mom." Jasmine and Katrine spoke as one. "We need to get Velda."

Still, she hesitated.

"Grandma," Tara said, "he's coming for me."

Ursula crumbled. "Call her." She reached for a courage potion. It was time to stand up to her mother, once and for all.

§

"What do you mean Henry is back?" Velda was scowling, her hair in disarray, her face free of make-up. She'd been sleeping deeply when Xenia pulled her out of bed and drove her to the Queen Anne. She'd found her family, including her granddaughter's husband, crowded around the *Book of Secrets* in the garden cottage.

Ursula caught Velda up to speed, outwardly confident but trembling like jelly inside. She would do this for her daughters and for Tara, even though it was opening a wound she'd thought had healed over decades before.

Velda's expression did not shift as she listened, and Ursula wondered if the woman had ever loved anything but herself. The thought was freeing. "And he will keep coming back," she finished, "unless we deal with him tonight, before the snakes disappear."

"What kind of potion did you mix for him back in '65? A halfway one?" Her words were dipped in accusation. "I thought it was clear that I wanted him dead. Forever."

The blue bottles lining the wall of the cottage began to quiver, their molecules dancing. A faint burning smell emanated from the apothecary drawers, the odor of a forest fire right before the spark hits the pine needles. Dean and Leo glanced around, alarm written on their faces.

"She was twelve years old," Katrine said, her voice level. She ignored the vibrating bottles to focus on her grandmother. "You shouldn't have asked her to do that."

The glass jar housing Ursula's heart grew a hairline crack. She'd never had anyone stand up for her before.

Jasmine brushed Tara's hair back. "She was only a child, Velda. Not even Tara's age."

The crack grew, meeting the newest hairline crack, the two of them joining to connect with the other crack that had started when Katrine had returned from her banishment. Ursula began to smell scents she hadn't encountered since she was twelve: strawberries, lemon drops, mint. Her children were standing on her side, against her mother. They were breaking her free of the bottle of poison she'd lived in for the past five decades.

Helena and Xenia still held Ursula's hands, which were now glowing blue.

"That was wrong, Velda," Xenia said.

Helena finished her thought. "No one should ask their child to do something like that."

The glass around Ursula's heart was now shivering like the bottles on the wall, a thousand tiny cracks shooting like fevered lightning, singing through the glass.

"You should tell her you're sorry," Tara added.

A bundle of sage spontaneously burst into flame, singing and tossing orange sparks. Dean doused it with water. Velda watched it all, still scowling.

"We're wasting time," she finally said, ignoring Ursula's tender pain. "How do we kill him once and for all?"

The glass around Ursula's heart held, but barely. The *Book of Secrets* sighed. It was a sad, papery sound.

CHAPTER 48

Tara

Her mom was nearly catatonic, but they all agreed it was the only way. Tara would have to lure John to the Queen Anne. Dean and Leo would shadow her as she walked past his apartment. She was to holler up to his window (*under no circumstances do you go inside*, Katrine kept repeating, her face drawn) and convince him to come outdoors. Once he was by her side, she was to feign interest in his music, asking him if he'd come back to the Queen Anne to teach her to play the guitar. She was to tell him her whole family was away for the weekend.

"How can that work?" Katrine asked. Tara could see her aunt didn't want her near the apartment.

"It'll work," Tara said. When she'd first laid eyes on John caroling, she'd recognized him for what he was: empty, a puppet that would go where led. A black spirit was holding the strings, and that spirit wanted Tara, could only get her while the snakes still ran. He'd been forced to melt into the shadows when Ursula, Katrine, and Jasmine burst through the wall into the tunnel, but that had only flamed his hunger for the girls' flesh. Of course he'd follow her back to the Queen Anne.

Still, she couldn't stop her teeth from chattering as she waded through the snakes under the sliver of spring moon, humming to keep from thinking about what she was stepping on and thereby losing her marbles. The smell was bad, the whole world reeking so powerfully of urine and glands that it was as if Faith Falls had been sealed in a jar with the snakes. Despite the unusual heat of the spring night, she was cold to her bones.

The closer she drew to the Avignon neighborhood, the tighter her chest grew and the more her stomach flipped. The streets were deserted except for her and the snakes. She caught sight of Leo once, and it calmed her, but only until she stood outside John's window.

"Hey," she yelled, or at least meant to. But it came out as a squeak, unintelligible, a noise so tender it was swallowed by the snakesong. It didn't matter. She wouldn't have had to say anything at all. The spirit pushing John had sensed her coming.

"Hey yourself," he said, so close that he made her jump, her heart thudding.

She turned. He was leaning against a streetlamp, his cowboy hat casting a shadow, snakes making a wide berth around him. She couldn't suppress the shudder. She recognized that the skin suit he wore was handsome, but all she could see were the burning eyes inside of him, the red raw demon that craved her.

She recoiled and almost stumbled, but she didn't let herself fall. If she had, Dean and Leo would have been by her side, and this would all be over. She'd have to wait another 25 years or even more, looking over her shoulder the entire time because while the curse dictated he could only take their power while the snakes ran, he could walk the earth whenever he chose. She read all of this in the black spirit, and more, so much more that she had to clench her jaw to keep from throwing up. He was old, this demon, older than her grandfather. Ursula and Velda had done the right thing by trying to kill it fifty years earlier. But Tara didn't care about its story. She wanted the curse broken and the demon gone forever.

"My family is away," she said. She didn't need any of the rest of the story. She could read that as well. He was trembling with anticipation, his lips wet. She turned and threaded her way through the snakes. He took her hand, and it was hot and dry, far hotter than human body heat. She allowed the contact, even though his grip dove under her flesh and took hold of the glow around her heart, making it difficult to breathe.

She walked faster.

He tried to pull her into the bushes once. "Not here," she said, her heart fluttering in his grip. "Someone could see us." He was milking her innocence with his hot fist, and she would never get that back. She was all right with that. She was fourteen. She was going to shed that soon anyhow. She just didn't want him to take her power.

When the Queen Anne finally came into view, the snakes that had been avoiding John moved aside for Tara, allowing quick passage to the house. He hesitated on the steps, the puppetmaster inside of him dropping a thread, allowing the fear of the man to leak through. "You sure no one's home?"

Tara nodded and skipped up the stairs ahead of him, onto the wide, wraparound porch. The second their hands were no longer touching, her heart bloomed, careening off her ribcage. "Come on."

He was still on the bottom stair. She licked her lips, like she'd seen the lead in a romantic comedy do. When that didn't lure him onto the steps, she tossed her hair over her shoulder. This clumsy seduction turned her stomach, but it got him moving. She opened the door and danced ahead, just out of his reach. She had to get him into the kitchen. She didn't know what would happen once they got there. That part of the plan had been up to the other women.

CHAPTER 49

The Queen Anne

People began to appear on the porch of the Queen Anne, their expressions a muddy mix of confusion and determination. There was the Asian woman who owned the Great Hunan and Merry with her pudding face and the woman with the great gorgeous dreadlocks and Heather Lewis and two dozen other townspeople, all of whom shunned her during the day but had visited her cottage at night.

They each glowed the same cerulean shade. The magic they had borrowed from Ursula was calling them back to the Queen Anne. Ursula, surprised to her core at the workings of magic, decided it was time to finally accept help from others. She gave them instructions before hiding them all in the pantry or kitchen nook or dining room.

The wooden island stood in the center of the kitchen, a single bottle of beer resting on it next to a hot apple pie that Jasmine had worked furiously to bake, using muscles and thoughts she hadn't called on in two decades. The smell was heavenly, caramelized sweet apples bubbling in a delicate golden-brown crust, dusted with cinnamon.

Two chairs were open next to the island, and the whole set-up was ringed with salt. When the kitchen door swung open and Tara strode in, her eyes wild, Ursula whispered a prayer for her beautiful granddaughter and melted into the shadows, behind the basement door. She witnessed the exchange through the crack.

"You want something to drink?" Tara asked. Her voice quavered. She walked over to the moonlit island, not stopping at the light switch. Ursula hoped her granddaughter would recognize that she needed to get John to eat the pie.

"That beer looks pretty good," John said.

Ursula was surprised to recognize him, even in the dim lighting. Of course he was the cowboy who had visited her earlier, brutally handsome, but now that she could see his true red essence, she didn't know how she'd missed it the first time they'd met. He didn't look a thing like her father, Henry, but it was *him*, as plain as the toes on her feet. She began to knead at the hem of her dress, reaching for braids she hadn't worn in half a century.

"Oh, yeah!" Tara said, as if she'd just noticed the brown bottle on the island. She reached for it and held it out to him, the glass slick in her hand. "I'm sure it'd be fine for you to drink it. And eat some pie, too."

John moved so quickly that he was a blur. In less than a second, he went from just inside the kitchen door to being fully inside the room and standing beside Tara inside the salt circle. He fisted her hair with one hand and forced the bottle of beer to her lips with his other. Ursula barely contained the gasp.

"Would it be fine for *you* to drink it?" John rasped, tipping the bottle so the beer ran down Tara's face.

Tara gagged, but bless her, she wrested the bottle from his hand as if it was nothing and took a deep swallow. "Sure," she said, covering her cough with the back of her hand. "You don't need to be weird about it."

John seemed surprised, then suspicious. He glanced around the room, his eyes lingering on the crack in the basement door through which Ursula was peering. She knew he couldn't see her, but his glance in her direction stripped her bare. She was glad she was the only one who was witnessing Tara with this beast. Jasmine would not have been able to stomach it. She said a courage prayer for all of the people perching in her house, waiting for the signal.

"Aren't you going to drink some?" Tara held the bottle out to John, who still held her hair. The grip looked painful.

He took a swig, still staring angrily at the corners of the shadowy room. Ursula watched. He could have drunk every last drop. There wasn't poison in there. That hadn't worked before and wouldn't work now. She did have another plan, though, and this was the time to enact it. She reached for the basement doorknob, her heartbeat crashing in her ears. She had one chance.

"You've looked better," Velda said, her voice coming from across the kitchen.

Ursula paused, stomach in her throat, her hand on the door she was about to step through. She had been explicit. Everyone was to stay hidden unless Ursula called for them. The fewer people involved, the fewer people hurt. Velda had ignored the instructions. She would ruin everything with her selfishness, her need to face her husband. Ursula stood paralyzed, unsure how to pull this back if such a thing were possible, her pulse telling her that it wasn't possible, it was all over. She went back to watching through the crack.

John turned to the voice at the main kitchen door, a lazy, sexy smile breaking across his face. "Why, Velda. You do recognize me. I didn't think you did. You didn't say anything at Christmas when I came to shovel." He strolled out a light southern accent that hadn't been there moments before, a little bit of Mississippi honey. The cadence chilled Ursula. She recognized it as her father's.

Velda stepped further into the room and flicked on the light. She was wearing the same blue dress she'd had on ten minutes earlier, her hair in the same disheveled white curls, her peach lipstick hastily applied, but she blazed with the glorious beauty of her full power. It was like staring into the sun. Ursula leaned forward, nose to the crack, choosing to sear her eyes rather than look away.

John's jaw dropped. "I forgot how you could look, baby."

A secret smile curled at Velda's mouth. She moved forward, seventy-nine, stunning. "Did you forget anything else I can do for you?"

Tara stepped away from John, her own jaw slack. She had witnessed her great-grandma work her magic before and thought she'd seen the full extent of it. Not even close.

Velda glittered and preened, taking Tara's place in the salt circle and leaning so close to John that she could touch his shirt. He ran his free hand lovingly up her neck, cupping her chin, leaning in for a kiss. Ursula held her breath. Velda's eyes were half-closed.

"Henry," she whispered. "I've missed you."

His face was an inch away from hers before his intent came clear. He squeezed her at the throat, swiveling to shove her face into the table, taking up the beer bottle like a mace. The knife she'd been concealing in the folds of her dress clattered to the floor.

It happened so quickly that there wasn't even time to gasp. John hovered over Velda, his hand in the air, his voice sharp. "No, but you musta forgot that your goddamned magic doesn't work on me, witch." He smiled.

Ursula's body responded before her mind did. She found herself shooting out of the basement foyer, jumping forward and clinging to his back, scrabbling for the beer bottle, scratching at his eyes. He pushed Velda away, out of the circle, as easily as a sack of potatoes, to deal with Ursula. With her still on his back, he knelt down to grab Velda's knife. He yanked Ursula off his back and pushed her in front of him, crushing her in his arms. He held the glistening blade to her neck.

Tara screamed.

The kitchen suddenly filled, Xenia, Helena, Katrine, and Jasmine at the front, townspeople rushing in from every side, crowding the kitchen, terror in their eyes.

John spoke to all of them at once. "Stop. Or I slit her throat."

He said it loud, and it was a fact rather than a command. He dropped into the chair, perching Ursula on his lap like a ventriloquist's dummy, the knife drawing a lick of blood from the cream flesh of her throat. He used his free hand to take a pull from the beer bottle, his lazy smile growing broader.

"How many people do you have here, and just for little 'ol me? It looks like at least thirty. I didn't even know you knew that many people. Oh well. I do like an audience." He nodded toward Velda, who was wheezing, unable to catch her breath since he'd tossed her aside. Katrine was at her side. "That's one thing we always had in common, Velda."

"You won't do anything to her," Katrine said, trembling. "Not with all of these witnesses."

John threw his head back and laughed the hollow sound that sent ice into Ursula's blood. "I think I'll be heading out after today, anyhow, since the snakes are going. Not much fun for me without them around, though I've enjoyed hunting you this past year. After me and the snakes go, you can do what you like with this bluesman's body." He dug the knife deeper into Ursula's throat. She would not let the tears fall. She would not let her daughters see she was scared.

Helena and Xenia held each other. The townspeople shuffled uneasily. Jasmine stepped forward, grabbed Tara's hand, and pulled her daughter to her, away from the salt circle. Dean held them both. The standoff lingered in the air, thicker than oxygen, not quite solid, tasting of blood.

"This isn't what I thought I'd be getting today," John said, taking another pull from the beer. "You were a good ride, for sure." He nodded at Katrine. Her face burned.

"Your sister, too, from what I recall." Jasmine's face turned the same color as Katrine's.

"But I was hoping for a little younger meat." He tossed a look at Tara, throwing his head back and laughing at her horrified expression, never letting up on the knife at Ursula's throat.

"But you can't always get what you want." He kissed Ursula's hair. "And so, I'll have to settle for paying you back that favor from 50 years ago, eh, Ursula? But since it'll be a while before I return, I wouldn't mind a taste of that apple pie."

The room held its collective breath.

"It smells sweet enough to wake the dead." He dug his fingers in, holding a fistful of dessert, the soft apples oozing through his fingers, bleeding their sugar onto their table. "Still warm. You shouldn't have."

No one blinked. Their heartbeats suspended. This was the only chance. That had been explained clearly to the townspeople as they appeared on the porch of the Queen Anne, surprised to find themselves there, all of them notified of the Catalain need through their connection to Ursula. She'd seen it happen before, past clients showing up unannounced at holidays, appearing both shocked to find themselves knocking on the Queen Anne's front door and hopeful they'd be let in. She didn't know they'd also come to help her. She was humbled. She was also terrified that her plan wouldn't work.

John had the dripping pie flesh to his lips before he paused, pushing it to Ursula's mouth, chuckling warmly. "I'd slap my knee if I had a free hand. Fool me once, right? Dear daughter, if you don't mind, would you take a bite of this for me? Wanna make sure it isn't poisoned."

The room released its breath, mouths drawn in horror. This was not how it was supposed to happen. Yet, there was nothing they could do.

Ursula opened her mouth, and John shoved the pie in.

She chewed.

She swallowed.

A tear fell down the cheek of more than one of the people watching powerlessly.

John glanced around the room and snorted. "You all should see yourselves! You look like you're at a surprise funeral." He jiggled his knee to move Ursula. "No worries! She's still alive. As such, I believe I will enjoy myself some pie."

He nodded in satisfaction and popped an oozing corner of dessert into his mouth. The cinnamon sugar drooled down the side of his face. He closed his eyes in ecstasy. "I don't believe I've ever tasted anything quite so delicious. It's like heaven and sex, still warm."

He reached for another scoop. People blinked noisily. Jasmine cocked her head, watching with the detachment of a scientist. They had gotten him to eat the pie.

John was just beginning to chew on his second mouthful when his eyes bulged.

He jumped to his feet, pushing Ursula to the floor. Katrine reached for her and pulled her away from John, who was now scratching at his own throat, his mouth opening and closing like a landed fish. He spit the masticated pie on the floor and choked out the words. "Poison! How?"

Jasmine shook her head, her smile a grim soldier. "Not poison. Not even a potion. It's a pie I baked, just plain apple pie."

John's eyes grew tighter, his skin shading blue.

"With one tweak to the recipe," Jasmine continued. "Whoever eats the pie has their greatest wish turned against themselves."

John may have been trying to make sense of her words. He may just have been busy fighting for his life. In either case, he appeared frightfully confused.

Jasmine explained. "You wished for Ursula to be poisoned eating it. You ate the pie, and so now you will be poisoned." She shrugged as if she'd just told him he'd taken his B vitamins for the day.

John began laughing maniacally in between bursts of painful hacking. "Damn straight you witches are a lot of work. Just when I think I have it figured it out. But I'll just come back. You know I'll be back. Not one of you can stop me."

"That's where I come in," Velda said, struggling to her feet and stepping forward.

"And me." Katrine stood, pulling her mom with her.

Dean stepped forward. "And me."

Jasmine beamed at him, not letting go of his hand or Tara's. "And me."

"Me too," Heather Lewis said, moving to stand beside Katrine.

And so on, until everyone in the room had spoken, merging hands to form a circle around John. While he writhed on the floor, they chanted the curse-breaking spell. Ursula led the words, and everyone but John repeated them.

With the power of my blood,
And the strength of my verse.

Each syllable hit him like a kick, doubling him over, bubbling his flesh. He writhed in agony. The Catalain women felt the pain, too, but they held each other, passing the burning between their hands, bearing as much as they could so no one had to bear it alone.

I reclaim my own path,
And I destroy your curse.

He screamed, his face contorting and melting so he was no longer recognizably human. The air reeked of sulphur. Snakes began to flow in through the cracks, but they did not come to his aid, had never helped him. The snakes didn't take sides.

Air.
Earth.

John spasmed with such force that he broke a bone through his skin, lifted off the ground and hovered inches from the earth for several seconds, and then dropped, completely motionless. A hazy silhouette hovered above his flesh, a suggestion of a memory, the handsome, angry face of Henry. He reached toward Velda, his expression sad.

"Velda," he whispered. "Help. I love you so much."

She spit at the image. The silhouette laughed and roared up like a flame, then was sucked back into John's body. He started writhing anew.

Water.
Fire.

Green liquid leaked out of his eyes and nose, and he vomited violently. The churning green bile burned and sizzled on the floor. Still, everyone chanted, though many of the townspeople were as green as the vitriol leaving John. Only two lines remained.

As these words are spoken,
This curse is forever broken.

John's body exploded, a wet rain of oil and filth that turned to gas before it hit anything solid. Henry's molasses laugh echoed, quickly replaced by a scream. Katrine wiped her eyes. Ursula stared forward. Jasmine appeared to be in shock, as were most people in the room.

Time stopped, packing each person inside the shell of their minds.

Then, with a roar, a reformed John was dropped from the ceiling, naked as the day he was born. He landed in the middle of the salt circle, whole, unscarred, shivering and crying.

It was done. The curse was broken. Henry would not be back.

The weight of this knowledge quilted the air. Time began moving. People looked at each other, their glances confused, hopeful.

Juni, owner of Faith Falls' most popular beauty parlor, stepped forward. She'd come to Ursula two weeks earlier for a weight loss potion and was still uncertain what had called her here tonight. "I've always wanted to own a bakery but I bought a hair salon instead because fat people aren't supposed to like food." Before she was even done speaking, she clapped both hands over her mouth, horrified, unsure why she'd revealed such a personal, random thing.

But it wasn't her. When the curse broke, so did the secrets inside of every person the room, secrets that had kept them small their whole lives. The woman who wanted to swim the English Channel but had visited Ursula last January because she was afraid of water spoke next. She was still surprised that she'd turned off on Hazel and walked into this house when she'd intended to visit the all-night grocery store instead. "I don't feel like love songs are written for me anymore."

The woman with the dreadlocks was so shocked she couldn't blink her wild tiger eyes. "I've *never* felt like that."

"I'm afraid to sing!" Diane was embarrassed to discover that she'd pushed herself to the front of the gathering, almost stepping on the salt circle, and that her voice was too loud.

The air smelled like firecrackers. The floor started to rumble. Heather, who'd been taught from a young age that it was her duty to keep secrets, felt the effluvium roll out of her, a gas of words that she had no chance of stopping with her lips. "I love my mom, but I don't like her. I think I'm turning into her. First, I acted mean because I was scared, but it became a habit. I judge everyone, but no one as harshly as I judge myself." She raised a hair's breadth off the ground but felt more stable than she had her entire life.

John twitched on the ground as the secrets continued to drop like frogs from the mouths of those gathered.

"I was raped," Jasmine said, pointing at John. When she had discovered her daughter on the other side of that wall, in the grace of the silence that followed, she'd realized that Tara wanted magic in her life even more than Jasmine wanted it out of hers. Jasmine would make sure her daughter learned it on her terms, but she would no longer be a barrier. And she would no longer be the keeper of rotten secrets.

"I was ten. My family would have helped me, but I was too ashamed. I used my magic to cook a meal that would make them blind to my pain, and that would send my sister away, and then I never used my magic again."

Heads snapped toward her. The air crackled. They all bore witness to her pain. Tara slipped her warm hand into her mother's. Jasmine felt the shame pulse through her, not nearly as strong as the first time she'd confessed and nowhere near as strong as the day it'd happened, but still there, gliding up, and out, but sticking, expanding, crowding her throat. Just when she thought she would choke on the girth of it, she felt another warm grip slide into her other hand. It was Katrine's. Grateful tears coursed down Jasmine's face. They tasted like sage.

"I let John have sex with me when I didn't want him to," Katrine said. She was still holding her sister's hand. "I was too ashamed to ask him to stop. Also, my husband cheated on me and I convinced myself that I didn't know about it, but really, I'd known from the beginning that he wasn't the man for me. Oh, and my sister recently informed me that I was wrong about my gift." She squeezed Jasmine's hand. "I'm not a spotty mind reader, like I've thought my whole life, or at least that's not all I am. I'm also an empath who makes people better at whatever they want to be better at."

People nodded, lost in their own birthing secrets.

"I had my daughter mix a potion that I used to murder my husband," Velda said, drawing all attention to her with a snap. She hadn't meant to confess. Ursula orchestrating this curse breaking had released her of that burden. She'd been so goddamned pleased that her daughter had shown some spine that it had cut the guilt out of her like a surgeon's blade, as quick and painless as such an operation could. "I'm sorry, Ursula."

Ursula considered her mother. "Sorry you killed him?"

Velda shook her head. "I'm sorry I brought you into it. It's my greatest regret. But sorry I killed your father? Not for a second.

He was an absolute bastard. I miss him, though, every day of my life." She stepped into the circle and prodded John with her toe. He moaned pitifully. "Or, at least I used to. Also, I know what you think of me, Ursula mostly, but Helena and Xenia, too."

Her eyes landed on each of her daughters, a sad smile on her face. "You think I'm vain, and useless. Now stop it," she said, putting her hand out toward Helena, who was beginning to step forward. "You don't need to comfort me. I know it's true. Why do you think I fell in love with your father? He saw right through my flattery and manipulation.

And I tell you what, I've never regretted killing him, not for a second, because I needed to survive. So you can say that I'm selfish, on that you're right. But you can't say that I don't love my girls, because I do, loved them so much that I killed the one man with enough power to see the real me."

The constriction fell away from Ursula's throat and the glass jar encasing her heart shattered into a glorious blue rain. She gasped as she took her first clean breath in forty-two years. It was guilt, not the curse of her father or the promise to her mother, that had kept her silent all these years.

The air was simmering. When Xenia spoke, a burner on the stove flashed into life, sending glowing orange sparks to her feet. She stomped them out without glancing down. "I'm afraid Helena will die before me."

The warm tears burbling up in Helena's eyes doubled, and she grabbed her sister's hand. "I'm afraid of that, too. Who will take care of you?"

"My power lets me read your loose thoughts and see the pain in each of you," Tara said, smiling shyly at Leo. She paused before continuing. "It lets me see what you all look like naked, too."

A few legs were discreetly crossed. Jasmine's cheeks burned bright red. It was Katrine who caught the lightness in her niece.

She started laughing. This was the vision she'd had when she'd shook Ren's hand at the bead store, secrets shaped like frogs raining down from the sky, each one of them a vivid emerald green, women laughing as the frogs turned into butterflies just before they hit the ground, and air so clean that it smelled like water. The secrets were free, and they were as beautiful and weird as the people who'd held them.

"Just kidding," Tara said. "About the naked part."

"I-steal-nylons-from-Walgreens," Diane said, the syllables spilling out of her mouth so fast they exited as a single word. "I can't stop, and I don't know why I do it. I don't even like to wear pantyhose. They make my vagina look like it's holding up a bank."

A bark of laughter erupted from the south side of the kitchen, but when asked later, no one knew who had lit the spark. The cleansing, cool jetstream air grew wider. They weren't alone in their shame or secrets, never had been. Soon, the room was awash in belly laughs and helpless cackles, doubled-over, bunched-up, tear-filled laughing fits that colored the room dashing bits of blue and gold and tossed the oblivious, roaring men and women—a fraction of whom'd had a chance to share their secrets—off the ground as if they were popcorn, then held them in the air for as long as they laughed. From the outside, the house glowed like a firefly, and as far away as Battle Lake, people forgot why they were fighting or remembered why they'd fallen in love. When Jasmine floated into her mom, she had one question for her, something that was deviling her despite the laughter she could not contain.

"Mom," Jasmine asked as they hovered above the kitchen island. "John wished for you to be poisoned when he ate the pie. What was your greatest wish while eating it?"

Ursula was smiling so wide that her jaw hurt. She was slowly turning upside down, her dress falling into her face. She held it around her knees. "I wished for you all to forgive me. Because of your pie, it meant I got to forgive myself."

Jasmine giggled like she used to when she was a child. Ursula matched it, their girl finding its way back to both of them. The laugh grew and held everyone in the state of Minnesota.

Artemis, who had been the first to arrive after Velda, loved the mood at the heart of the storm in the Catalain kitchen and he would forever carry it in his heart, but he saw there was still work to be done. While the people in the kitchen bubbled and giggled near the ceiling, bouncing off each other like gentle balls and laughing even harder, he led John out to his car, then drove him to his place. You don't beat up a naked man, was his reasoning. Even so, John was a man who needed to be beaten up.

And so, once he had a confused but healthy, clothed John on his feet, he engaged him in an old-fashioned fistfight. John didn't know what he was fighting for, couldn't remember anything that had happened in the past year in fact, but he'd lured enough teenage girls and married women backstage after concerts to assume he had this coming. Still, he fought back. Too bad for him Artemis was the 1948 Otter Tail County bantam weight champion and hadn't forgotten what he knew back then. He beat all the fight right out of John.

While John was on the ground, flirting with consciousness, Artemis leaned over to whisper something into the vast ketchup of his brain. No one will ever know what he said, but the fact is that John gave up music that very night and took up telemarketing three states over, forever honing his communication skills.

Summer

CHAPTER 50

Katrine

In April, a drought had been declared in all of Otter Tail County, including Faith Falls. May blew in on the back of a hot, dust-bearing wind, and they'd yet to see rain. People had to blink to see where they were going, and the soil turned bone dry. Fires were forbidden. Moods were tight. The generosity that had accompanied the unusual spring warmth was replaced with a peevishness, as if people could hear the screech of parched electrons rubbing up against one another.

"Watch where you're going!" snapped Michael Baum, his fist in the air before he saw it was Bradley Willmar who had bumped into him on the corner of Lake and Elm streets. In other parts of town, the fights were impossible to stop. The grit in their eyes combined with the unrelenting nature of the wind drove the townspeople to the edge, and then past.

Heather was the only one who seemed unaffected by the wind's nagging bite, though she sometimes worried it would blow her away. She'd confided in Katrine that she felt new purpose in the six weeks since they'd broken the curse. Speaking her greatest fear had declawed the lion that was her mother and released her to create a life of her own choosing. She didn't know what that would look like yet, just that she could *do it*.

Katrine waited at a corner booth of the Great Hunan, feeling better than she had in years, and a little nervous. She didn't know what was causing the tumbling in her stomach. She saw Heather at least three days a week, and they'd gone out a number of times since last fall. They'd grown warmer over the months, culminating in Heather's spontaneous confession in the Queen Anne kitchen.

Katrine had begun to wonder if maybe Heather felt just like she did inside: inadequate, never quite belonging. She'd felt a growing kinship with the woman, one that she'd let wither when she'd spotted Ren and Heather's embrace inside Immanuel Lutheran. But now, unburdened of secrets, she wanted to build this friendship, to confess that she'd harbored a crush on Ren but that she'd come to realize her friendship with Heather was more important to her.

"Sorry I'm late." Heather slid into the naugahyde booth. Her red hair was a flawless helmet, her make-up thick enough to remove with a smack to the back of her head. "Are you getting the buffet?"

Katrine had believed, before she'd learned of her true power, that her gift had never been as useful as her sister's or Ursula's, or even Xenia or Helena's. It was unreliable, for one, as her reads often got muddied by her preconceptions. In fact, she was better at reading someone she didn't know at all than a person she was close to, and even then, their thoughts came to her sporadically. For another, if her gift revealed what she didn't want to discover, she was liable to override it, and nothing retaliates like a gift that's been ignored. Thanks to Jasmine's revelation about her true power, she'd been seeing who the person *could* be, not who they were.

Despite all this, she could still lift random thoughts from a person, and since the Equinox, that magic had become more reliable. Plus, Heather was easy to read. She was as nervous as Katrine, her extra make-up a shield. She was also lonesome, tired of raising two kids by herself, and hungry since five days ago she'd begun a low-carb diet that included skipping breakfast.

"Why are you looking at me like that?" Heather asked. "Having another Kat Attack?"

Katrine had forgotten the nickname they'd given her back in high school when she was reading people. Adam had told her she looked like she was power daydreaming, except that her pupils dilated. He was the only one outside her family that she'd ever told about her gift. "Nice."

"I'm sorry." Heather's cheeks flushed. "I shouldn't have said that."

Katrine shrugged. "It was high school. Jasmine and I were a little odd. I get it. And now that you've been to the Queen Anne, you know why."

"Thank you for letting me stay," Heather said. "It changed my life. I've never felt so light."

Diane stopped by the table. All three women smiled at one another, but they did not speak of the curse breaking. Nobody who'd been there ever would, outside of the circle of attendees. "Buffet?" she asked.

"Just tea for me," Katrine said. "And seaweed salad. Do you have that?"

Diane shook her head. "No seaweed salad. That Japanese. You want the buffet?"

Katrine grinned. "The buffet will be fine."

"Me too," Heather said. "With a diet cola."

Katrine and Heather didn't talk as they stacked their plates. Heather piled meat on hers, though almost all of it was breaded and fried. Katrine didn't comment. Back at the table, they both reached for the soy sauce at the same time.

"Can I ask?" Heather began. "Have you seen John—"

"No."

Heather raised her eyebrows and cut into her breaded chicken. "I want to kill him, you know? I get why you went back to his place with him. He's cute, and he's not from around here. Not originally, anyway. Plus, who doesn't like the wounded bad boy? We all think we can fix him, and then maybe he'll return the favor. Never works that way, though. At least, it didn't with my ex."

"He wasn't a good guy?" It was an invitation rather than a question.

Heather seemed to consider withholding the story, then she waggled her empty left hand ring finger and popped a chicken chunk into her mouth. "We've been divorced for a year now. He told me we grew apart. What the hell does that mean, anyhow? We were raising the girls, going bowling with the same friends, sleeping in the same bed. So what does that mean, growing apart?" She stabbed another mound of chicken and didn't bother cutting it.

"Probably means he's an asshole, and you're better off without him."

Heather stopped with the chicken almost inside her open mouth. Her eyebrows narrowed. "How long does it take to heal from heartbreak? Are you over Adam yet?"   Katrine thought of her and Adam sitting on opposite ends of the couch, their legs twined together as they swapped the crossword, drank café au laits, and planned their day. She remembered how he'd come up behind her and hold her while she cooked, nuzzling her neck and laughing when she'd swat at him with a spatula. She thought of how their bodies fit together like puzzle pieces, and how in the middle of the night he'd roll over and pull her into the warmth of him without fully waking up. Then she remembered how he had lied to her when she asked him why he was spending so many nights at work, or the time she'd gotten into a fender bender and he'd been too busy to drive her home from the hospital, or how he'd pick a fight every week and slam out of the flat when he didn't get his way. "Most days."

"Was he an asshole?"

"Something like that," Katrine said.

Heather covered Katrine's hand with hers. "We're going to land okay. I know it. I believe—oh!"

Katrine turned to face the front of the restaurant, where Heather was staring. There stood Ren with his daughters. He was tall, self-possessed, his smile easy. Katrine felt her heart skip its track for a moment, but she shut down that emotion before it went any higher or lower. She was going to respect Heather's relationship.

"Ren Cunningham," Heather whispered. "He is such a doll. And don't stare now because he's coming over."

Katrine shot Heather a confused look, but she didn't have time to ask her question because there was Ren, exuding strength and stability and smelling of fresh-washed sheets hung in the sun to dry.

"Hello ladies." His smile reached up to his eyes, which were locked on Katrine. "Heather, of course you know Joanie and Patty. Katrine, these are my daughters. I never got a chance to introduce you at Christmas or Sadie Hawkins."

Both girls smiled. One was shorter and round, presumably taking after her mom, and the other had Ren's lanky build. "Nice to meet you," they said in unison.

Katrine smiled back, trying not to focus on Ren. He had so much presence that it confused her. "Pleased to meet you both, too."

Heather cleared her throat. "Ren, you know that Katrine is the best reporter the paper's ever had. I was thinking she should write up a story on your store." She winked at Katrine with all the subtlety of a hand grenade.

Katrine's mouth swung open. She realized Heather was nudging her toward Ren. Had they broken up?

"That would be wonderful," Ren said. His deep voice traveled straight into Katrine's heart. "If that's okay with you."

"Sure," Katrine said, pulling her attention back to the present moment. "Should be fun. When works best for you?"

"We'll be in the store all day tomorrow," Joanie said shyly.

Diane appeared with two large carry-out bags. "Your food, Mr. Ren."

"Thank you. I…" He turned toward Katrine. Whatever he was going to say seemed to desert him. "It was nice to see you."

Their eyes met, and it was all laid out for her to see: his magnificent heart, his passion, his talent, his intelligence, his stability, his honesty. It was too much. She was sure it wasn't for her. She looked away, catching a parting glance of him with his arms around each of his daughters, laughing at something one of them had just said.

Heather leaned over the table and smacked her. "I pass you the ball, and you take a crap on it? What was that all about? He likes you!"

"But *you're* dating him!" Katrine said. "I saw you. At Immanuel. The day we found Tara."

An array of conflicting thoughts scurried across Heather's face—confusion, disbelief, humor—until one landed with a thud: resigned anger. "Let me guess. Meredith told you to go to the church that day?"

Katrine nodded.

"Ren and I aren't dating. Never have, as much as I wouldn't mind waking up next to him. Meredith set that up to make you *think* we were together. That's how she works. Don't you see how Ren looks at you? He's got it bad."

Katrine felt one emotion: joy.

And because she felt it so strongly, everyone in the restaurant felt it, such was her gift. It lifted them higher, encouraged them to call long lost loves, or reach across the table and hug the person they were with, to put down the fried meat and reach for steamed vegetables.

The rush of happiness was so powerful that it inspired Diane to stride to her car, retrieve her karaoke machine, and slam it dead center on the one free table in the entire restaurant, a double top. Customers looked up, startled by the sound. The cord just reached the outlet.

"I sing!" she declared. She didn't need to search for the song. She'd chosen it years ago. She selected the ninth track on the disk, tapping her feet to the infectious beat. Everyone in the restaurant stared at her, and she stared right back, even though her heart was beating so loud she could no longer hear.

When it was time to spout the lyrics, she nailed it.

"At first, I was afraid, I was petrified…"

CHAPTER 51

Katrine

Heather smiled at Katrine across the desk as she delivered her latest assignment. "It isn't *New York Times*-worthy, but it's a big deal in Faith Falls," she said, a chuckle in her voice.

Katrine and Heather had continued to grow close since Katrine had found out that Ren and her editor were not dating. That didn't mean Katrine was dating him either—she'd been focused on healing family wounds and growing a happiness that could never be stolen from her—but it did mean it was a possibility. Her interview with him had gone well, and she'd taken his girls and Tara to Fargo shopping on two different occasions.

She'd also contacted worried friends back in London, started taking walks at night with her mom, and gone to Jasmine's house for meals where she found, to her boundless joy, that Jasmine was cooking *real* food again. To Jasmine's surprise, Dean even preferred it to the canned stuff. Katrine'd also brought Tara along on some of her interviews. The girl had a real knack for journalism, and her enthusiasm was reminding Katrine what had drawn her to writing in the first place: stories and connections.

"Let me guess—Bradley Willmar has secured funding to outfit all the otter statues with bronze skirts?"

Heather's eyes twinkled.

"What is it?" Katrine asked, sitting up straighter.

Heather sat back, feigning concern. "I don't know. It might be too big for you. I don't want to blow your mind."

"Stop teasing!"

"Don't say I didn't warn you," Heather said, pretending to stare at her fingernails before leaning forward in excitement. "Aw shoot, here it is, and tell me if it sounds stupid. What do you think about writing a history of Faith Falls? The good, the bad, and the ugly. We'll serialize it in the paper, running a chapter each week. When you're done, you'll have enough to take to a publisher, if you want."

"The history of Faith Falls?" Katrine turned the idea over in her mind.

"It's dumb, right? It'd be the history of our families, ultimately. A portrait of small town America. Well, our version of it, anyhow. I'd particularly like to find out what happened to your great-great-grandparents, Eva and Ennis. My mom still talks about them, you know? But no one knows their story, where they came from, where they went, why. You could be the one to research it and tell it."

The more Katrine handled the idea, the more she liked it. No, the more she *loved* it. Thoughts floated around her like dandelion fluff as she considered all the directions she could take this, all the stories she could tell. "It's *fantastic*, Heather. Really. Thank you."

"Thank me when you're done. I think this is going to be more work than either of us imagines. As far as I can tell, Eva and Ennis left town without a trace."

They beamed at each other across the desk for a full minute, two ex-beauty queens tumbled around by life, the pressure leaving them both stronger and more beautiful than they'd been in their youth.

"You know what?" Katrine asked.

"What?"

"I'm glad we're friends."

Heather winked. "I bet you are. I'm pretty cool, you know."

Katrine left, chuckling. She was already outlining the first installment on the history of Faith Falls. She would research James A. Faith. She was on her way to Seven Daughters to share the exciting news with her aunts when a hot gust of wind sprayed her face with grit. She covered her eyes, trying to wipe away the stinging dirt, and felt along the storefronts with her free hand until she came to a doorknob. She pulled it open.

Her ears were filled with the muffled clicking of time.

"Katrine?"

She recognized the deep voice, even though she could not yet see. "Ren?" She panicked for a moment, blind and alone with him, and she reached out mentally from habit. He was there, concerned, steadfast. She stopped rubbing at her face and stood straight, hands at her sides, eyes closed. She trusted the moment, and him. The grit began to melt away, and she saw him inside her head. He hadn't changed. He was beautiful.

"Some dirt blew in my eyes," she said. "I didn't know where I was going."

"Wait a minute," he said.

She heard receding footsteps, a drawer sliding open, water running. In a moment, he was next to her.

"I have a warm washrag," he said, placing it in her hand.

She patted at her face with the rag, blinking a few times before opening her eyes. She'd been in his store once before, for the interview. It was one large room, timepieces in every size and shape arrayed on the floor and the walls: grandfather clocks, wall clocks, a Betty Boop lamp clock, watches, all of them clicking in perfect harmony. The overall impression was of security and order.

"Thanks," she said, handing him back the washrag. "I can see again."

"I'd like to take you out on a date sometime."

Her breath stopped for a moment. She looked at him standing close, his blue eyes wide, his expression hopeful. His words curved in the air like a heart. She traced her fingers through them. They felt like warm honey. "Why today?" she asked.

"What?"

"Why are you asking me out today?"

He shrugged. "It's the first time you've come to me on your own."

She smiled a secret smile. Faith Falls had nudged her into the watch store. She examined the situation and realized this was where she wanted to be. The wind-blown grit had done her a favor, and it occurred to her that writing the town's history was going to be even more interesting than she could have imagined. She nodded at Ren.

"That's a yes?"

"Yes," she said.

Later that night, she drove home with a silly smile on her face. She'd catch the expression, scold herself, grimace, but the smile would pop up again. She couldn't help it. Hope hadn't deserted her.

Her bliss was such that she never checked her phone, even though it glowed in her purse as she pulled into the driveway of the Queen Anne.

I'm flying to Minnesota, the message said. *I need to see you. Love, A.*

CHAPTER 52

Ursula

The person stood outside the door for so long that Ursula almost—almost—yanked it open. The warm, dry weather had gotten under her skin, coating her lips with a thin sheen of dust and forcing her to water the earth every day to keep her plants green.

Finally, the knock landed. Ursula refused to answer.

The caller didn't wait, instead turning the knob. Ursula's chest tightened when she saw it was her oldest daughter. How had she not recognized Jasmine's energy?

"Hi," Jasmine said.

The dry air heightened Ursula's sense of smell, and she noticed the absence of the sick-sweet odor of pharmaceuticals. In fact, Jasmine smelled like fresh basil.

"Hello," Ursula said. She braced herself. A barrier between her and Jasmine had been broken when they'd worked together to protect Tara, but there was still years of habit to fight against. Jasmine and her family were spending more time at the Queen Anne, but Jasmine still held Ursula at a distance. She suspected

Jasmine was here to release more of her anger. She settled in to absorb it and so was caught off guard by the question.

"Who's my father?"

Ursula unclenched in surprise. "Your father?"

"Yes. Do Katrine and I have the same father?"

"I don't know. Probably not." Ursula recognized the distaste on her daughter's face. She'd seen it before. She'd also witnessed the resignation.

"How many men have you slept with?"

Ursula held out her hands, palms up. It didn't matter how many men. She'd always kept her lovers separate from her daughters' lives, and that's all that she owed them. Knowing whose sperm had come into play would change nothing, for better or ill.

"Was my husband one of them?"

"Never."

Jasmine nodded, running her hands through her hair. "I forgive you."

"For what?" The words sounded defensive. Ursula hadn't intended that.

"For everything." With her fingers, Jasmine made the sign of a scissors cutting in front of her heart. "I release the bad. And I'm sorry for any pain I've caused you. We're starting fresh."

Cords stood out in Ursula's neck. She hadn't realized how heavy that load had been. She felt untethered without it, watching it float to the ceiling and then escaping through the cracks in a sinuous white puff.

"I need a spell," Jasmine continued, her expression defiant. The wind picked up and propelled needles of grit at the workshop's siding with such force that they fell to the earth as microscopic diamonds glittering in the white heat of the sun. "For me. I want to mute my power. I'm not ready for all of it back, and I might never be. It makes me think of…that day."

Ursula sighed and pushed her glasses up her nose. She wanted to reach out and stroke her brave daughter's cheek. She wanted to pull her into an embrace woven with lavender and almond oil and tangerine blossoms. She wanted to take away every hurt that had ever been done and repaint her daughter's flesh with the sweet peach of innocence.

"All right," she said. She turned and began to brew the potion.

"And mom—"

Ursula's breath hitched at the word. Her eyes grew hot.

"I'm thinking of growing vegetables again, but my yard is too small. Can I use a patch of yours? Katrine probably wants one, too."

CHAPTER 53

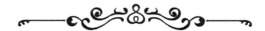

Katrine

Adam's text angered her when she discovered it, but elation quickly replaced the first emotion, then came confusion followed by more anger. Their divorce was not yet finalized because of a paperwork mix-up. She'd been waiting to scratch final signatures on it and send it to her attorney in London but had gotten too busy. At least that's what she'd told herself.

A follow-up text from Adam confirmed that he would be arriving in Minneapolis later that day and hopping a local flight to Alexandria Municipal Airport, 40 miles from Faith Falls. Katrine didn't know how to respond, so she didn't. She hadn't even been certain that she'd meet him when his plane was due in Alexandria, not until she found herself behind the wheel, navigating the back dirt roads with corners so sharp a lesser person would have signaled. Katrine had learned to drive on these roads.

The spring air was so hot that she was more liquid than solid. Gravel dust clung to the road like the molt of a snake. She passed fields full of bright green, irrigated corn and abandoned farmhouses left to the moth and rust.

Adam is coming for me.

The thought was tinged with pride and pain so sharp that it pierced her right behind her eyes. Had Adam broken up with Lucy? He must have. He must have realized that he'd made a mistake, and now he was coming for Katrine to rebuild their marriage. She hadn't told anyone where she was going or who she was meeting. Would she be bringing Adam back to Faith Falls to meet her family?

She recalled Ren dancing with her at the Sadie Hawkins event, of how relaxed and natural she felt with him, how he treated her with tenderness and respect, of the warm green light that always seemed to surround him. Tonight was supposed to be their first date. It was funny like poison ivy that Adam had reached out to her now, when she had found a good man. Adam was a known, though, familiar to her.

The car left the gravel roads and lit onto the tar, which shimmered like a mirage in the heat. The windows were rolled down, and the wind blew Katrine's loose chestnut hair around her shoulders. She was wearing a simple cotton sundress and cowboy boots, no make-up. She didn't know why she hadn't applied the usual mascara and lipstick. Maybe she didn't want to seem desperate. But she was, wasn't she? Her husband had cheated on her, and now he was coming back for her.

She pounded the steering wheel. Why was she going to meet him? Because she had to, that's why. She wanted to see his face, to hear that his infidelity hadn't been her fault. There were so many good times, and that counted for something. It had to.

In the distance, a small plane began to descend toward the local airport. Katrine didn't know if Adam was on it. She drove the last few miles and pulled into the parking lot. The airport was modest, designed for hobby pilots, with two runways and a main office, no security. She stayed in her car until the plane landed and began coasting down the runway toward the office and parking lot. The shimmer of the sun's blaze looked like it was cooking the tiny aircraft. The plane came to a stop 500 yards from the parking lot.

Its propellers slowed.

Its door opened.

A man stepped out.

It wasn't Adam. She checked herself for disappointment and found none. She was too busy holding her breath. The first passenger turned, talking to someone in the cabin, and then a second person stepped out.

This time, it was Adam.

He was here, in Minnesota. Standing across the tarmac, suitcase in hand. His shoulders were strong, his smile tentative, she could see that even from a distance. Her heart tensed. She stepped out of the car. She walked toward him. He strode toward her. She had dreamed of this moment a thousand times since returning to Faith Falls last August.

His steps were easy, confident. The closer he walked, the more she could see of him. He was wearing the soft blue button-down shirt she'd bought him for his last birthday and the sun glinted off a watch, maybe the silver Tag Heuer she'd given him on their third anniversary. The hands that held the suitcase were the same ones that had held her while he listened to her secrets and made love to her. He was smiling, his light brown, wide-set eyes fixed on her.

"Katrine."

She stopped and put out her hands, palms facing him. Two yards of space lay between them. He started to step closer, but it was as if an invisible wall had appeared in front of him. His brow furrowed. He looked confused.

"I missed you, baby," he said in his charming accent. "It's over with me and Lucy. I realized you are the woman for me, and so I ended it with her. I never should have let it happen in the first place. I was an idiot. An absolute idiot. Please forgive me. I love you."

He was sincere. She smiled. The smile turned into laughter because she knew he was *sincere*. He wanted her back in his life. She'd given him security, love, respect, admiration, money. She'd handed over everything she had, and then she scrabbled for more to give to him, and when he had it all in a pile, he'd spit on it.

She couldn't control her bubbling laughter, and it rose into the air and took flight on happy wings. She finally saw Adam exactly as he was: intelligent, selfish, handsome, unfaithful, funny, immature, and cruel. It was all there. What's better, she recognized who *she* was.

She turned and never looked back.

§

Katrine didn't reveal to Ren how she'd spent her morning. That story would unfold as their connection grew, or it wouldn't. For now, it was enough to be with him in the sultry night, the breeze lifting her hair and kissing her behind the ears.

"You know that fireflies act as a metronome, right?"

She smiled. That had happened a lot this evening, first at the Memorial Day parade as they caught the bubblegum and taffy that were tossed from the passing floats, then at dinner, then during the street dance, which they'd left to enjoy a quiet walk along Rum River, on the edges of Faith Falls City Park. The river was low due to the drought, but it was happy to see both of them.

"Hmmm," she said. The sound felt drowsy and content. Ren's strong, soft hand was holding hers.

"If by chance, a few males flash in unison, others will see it and adjust their own flashes. Soon, the entire firefly chorus is putting on a synchronized light show with no clear leader. See that?"

A copse of oak trees sheltered the edge of the park. Three tiny lights blinked at the base of the largest. Two responded. Soon, as if heeding Ren's instructions, they began to blink like a thousand twinkle lights to music only they could hear. The grass underfoot crunched like straw, and the air was so dry that she worried the insect's symphony would spark a fire.

"It's lovely," she said. She realized he was staring at her. She turned, and in his eyes she saw all of her beauty reflected back to her and magnified. He brushed his hand against her cheek. She closed her eyes. The heat of him was palpable even in the thick air.

Before she could stop it, the confession spilled out. It wasn't about her magic, or even her divorce. It was about John Trempeleau, the man who had taken the right of her body from her.

Ren stiffened as her words poured out. Before she was done speaking, he took her, and held her close. His heart beat under her cheek. When she stopped talking, when every bit of shame was laying in front of her, he spoke softly into her hair.

"You get to heal, Katrine. You get that. We all do. What you lost? It'll come back to you, stronger than you ever thought it could. Trust me, and let the people who love you carry you until you can believe it for yourself."

She tipped her face up to him, because she did trust him, had from the moment she'd first bumped into him outside of Seven Daughters, and because it felt right to take this first step with him. He leaned in, but before his lips touched hers, a warm tear of rain moistened her cheek.

Startled, she opened her eyes. "Rain!" It had been six weeks since a drop of moisture had fallen.

He glanced up, chuckling. The evening was dark, but in the yellow circles of the city park lights, tiny drops fell to earth, raising miniature dust storms. The sparse drops began to thicken, and then it started to pour. Ren grabbed her hand and began to lead her toward the picnic shelter. Laughing, she grabbed his hand, and they ran through the warm rain, splashing in puddles and smelling the richness of thirsty earth.

They ran until they reached the Queen Anne, and then they snuck in through the back door, exactly as Katrine used to do when she was sneaking home past curfew. It wasn't necessary—Ursula, Xenia, Helena, Velda, and Artemis were at the movies, and they had the house to themselves—but it was fun.

She stopped just outside her bedroom door, Ren holding her, both of them dripping on the hardwood floor. He pushed her back, pulled her close to him and kissed her passionately. His mouth traced a hot arc to her ear, and he whispered something. She said, "Hmm," and the words curved up like a smile.

She led him into her room and sat him on her bed, undressing in front of him. Her wet dress fell to the ground like a seal skin. She was down to her bra and panties when panic overtook her. It lasted only a moment, a petrifying eternal second where she wanted to leave her own body. He reached out to her, but she shook her head. He was so bright, so calm, so open. She could do this. She stripped, standing in front of him fully unclothed, at first defiant and then, finally, letting her defenses down, truly naked.

He came to her and pressed his body into hers. She could feel his hardness and was suddenly starving for him. She yanked open his shirt, ripped his zipper, pushed him into the bed. He met her desperation with warm, steady kisses, stopped her, and made her look him in the eye.

"Do you want this?" he asked. She could see the throbbing of the vein in his neck and forehead. His passion was as powerful as hers.

She nodded. "Yes. More than anything I've ever wanted before."

His entire body shivered. He pulled off his shirt, exposing broad, strong shoulders and arms, a chest covered in soft hair, and a heart that beat just for her. He leaned back over her, covering her body in kisses that brought her to the edge of absolute pleasure, then pulling away just before she climaxed, returning to kiss her mouth and whisper in her ear all the ways that he loved her.

The fruit, when it was finally ripe, was delicious, decadent, full of sweet juices and life. For the first time in her life, Katrine was safe. Her heart hummed with a sweetness like the moment just before tears, stretched out forever. She felt the promise of a baby boy moving deep inside of her, unsure how long she had been aware of it.

The sensation made her happy.

Everything would be all right.

She was home.

"i carry your heart with me"
by ee cummings

...here is the deepest secret nobody knows
(here is the root of the root and the bud of the bud
and the sky of the sky of a tree called life;which grows
higher than soul can hope or mind can hide)
and this is the wonder that's keeping the stars apart

i carry your heart(i carry it in my heart)

*Author's Note

The Catalain Book of Secrets was inspired by genetics professor
Bryan Sykes' nonfiction book, *The Seven Daughters of Eve*. In his
fascinating account, Sykes describes how, through mitochondrial
DNA, everyone of European descent can trace their common
ancestry to seven primeval clan mothers, whom he calls the seven
daughters of Eve. He bestows on them whimsical names: Velda,
Ursula, Xenia, Helena, Katrine, Jasmine, and Tara. His thesis is
that we are all connected, and he uses science to prove it. I use
fiction.

ACKNOWLEDGMENTS

I began writing this book in 2002, shortly after my husband died. It was a painful time, but I found comfort in the words and the possibility of magic. Being the mother of two small (at that time) children, life soon took over. I put away sixty or so pages that I'd written, and I didn't rediscover them until ten years later, when I was cleaning out my computer files. Falling right back in love with the words and the magic, I cozied up to my computer to type out the rest of the story. That was 2012, and I'd already published eight novels. Writing this one was different, though. Rather than directing the plot as I typed, I found myself listening for stories and weaving them together. The result was unlike anything I'd written before.

The novel has taken many evolutions since then, including three rounds of professional editing. It was ultimately turned down by traditional publishers, but I couldn't let it stay only on my computer. I felt like there was a message in the world of the Catalains, and wasn't meant just for me. And so, at the urging of Matthew Clemens and with the support of many wonderful people, I decided to create a Kickstarter campaign to self-publish. The campaign was successful beyond my wildest dreams. Here are my supporters. These people are the reason you're holding this book right now:

Stacy Reller (my first donor! because of her generosity, she forever gets to run the bead store in Faith Falls), Aimee Hix (she promised donors cookies, one of her many superpowers), Chuck Zito, Beth Ann Chiles, Sharon Fiffer, Kathleen Taylor, Suzanne Jackowski, Lisa Wilcox, Julie Hyzy, Michael Kelberer, Robin Templeton, Dina Willner, Sarah Cotter Hogroian, Dean Heitke, Shelley Manannah, Kristin Sprows, Matthew Clemens (you'll notice he's mentioned three times on this page; that is not a mistake), Becky Ernst, Tiffany Korver, Annie Alzheimer, Melissa Lee Lindsey, Melissa Jensen, LynneK, Tony Van Den Einde (thank you, honey!), Dina Stout, Diane and Ray Lourey, Connie Crose Erickson, Jenny Langford, Christine Hollermann, Kellie Tatge, Erin Mitchell, Laura-Kate Rurka, Mollu, John West, Linda Braun Kingston, Trudi Detert, Heather Koshiol, Anne Wortham, Cheryl Graves, Chantelle Aimée Osman, Linda Joffe Hull, Shannon Baker, Clare O'Donohue, Dru Ann Love, Donna Hennen, Vikki Pfeilsticker, Catriona McPherson, Sharon Short, Steve Avery, Heather Severson Tanez, Vicky Kapitzke, August McLaughlin, Keith Raffel, Shelly Gage, Sherry Roberts, Steve Whipple, Dana Cameron, Ellie Searl, Jim Thomsen, John Shaw, Susanna Calkins, Dave Wielenberg, Stanley Trollip, Michael Guillebeau, Kim Moran, Jill Svea Wargin, Barbara Moore, Laura Rae Hulka, Jamie Gaither, Vicki Stiefl, Adam Beau McFarlane, Cindy Pederson, Lynda Hilburn, Angela Trulson, Mark Basel, Jama Kehoe Bigger, Lois Reibach, Tamzin Bukowski, Edith Maxwell, Laura Weatherly, Heather Wetzel, Jessie Chandler, Joseph Roper, Lou Berney, Connie Van Den Einde Weaver, Stacy Allen, Michelle and Ryan Hennen, Jim Pohl, Peggy Brause, Alan Orloff, Bo Thunboe, Ellery Adams, Ava Nielsen, Linda Maher, Susan Schlicht, Julie Stuard Lundblad, Dorothy Nelson, Amy Glaser, Tamara Weets, Karen McBrady, Eric Hix, Dana Fredsti and David Fitzgerald, Harry Weseloh,

Loni Crowell, Jessica Spurling, Barbara Ross, Matthew Sherley, David Lyndale, Glenn Harris, Janet Cearley, Andrea Edwards, Cindy Ronken, Ann Marie Gross, Sandy Morse, Ellie Kolodzieski, Tracey Watson, Gretchen Beetner, Ben LeRoy, Corinne H. Smith, Michelle Denise Marotzke, James Ziskin, Rebecca Lane Beittel, Ann Wawrukiewicz, Sherryl O'Neill, Andrea Schraufnagel, Greg Davidson, Gina Hennen, Erika and Olivia (The Girls Next Door), Gail R. Fisher, Terri Thayer, Jessica Ruhl, Jeffrey Pearson, Mary Peterson, Richard Butler, Sheyna Galyan, Jodi Erickson-Trosdahl, Jane Burton, Hank Phillippi Ryan, Stephen Buehler, Kat Tromp, Mariella Krause, Andrea Ball Ross, Michelle Bahr, Liz Mugavero, Dawn Shawley, Sabrina Ogden, Kristen Shomion, Michael Allan Mallory, Mara Volker Trygstad, Denise VanBriggle, Karen Fraunfelder Cantwell, Bill Weinberger, Judith Griffin, Ronnette Trulson, Susan Krueger, Jan Kurtz, Jenny Kales, Maggie Caldwell, Erica Ruth Neubauer, and Theresa Rispoli.

Thank you.

Also, much thanks to Jill Marsal, who fought valiantly for this book to find a traditional publisher, and who guided me through many revisions. The same is true of my mother, Diane. Connie (Van Den Einde) Weaver, Linda Joffe Hull, Matthew Clemens, Barbara Moore, Brad Kramer, Jessica Morrell, and Shannon Baker, thank you for your feedback on this book. Tony Van Den Einde, Terri Bischoff, Christine Hollermann, Dana Fredsti, and Cindy Pederson, thank god your support for me is contagious. It's gotten me through many a low spot when this writing dream seemed ridiculous.

Great thanks also to the strong women in my life—Bernie, Diane, Donna, Suzanna, Jen, Gina, Andrea, Michelle, Amanda, Esmae, and Zoë—who taught me about kitchen magic, the power of a good red wine, and the healing spells of laughter. More importantly, thank you all for teaching me about my roots and for providing the best family a person could hope for. No less is my thanks for the good men in my life—Xander and Tony especially, but it turns out there's lots of you, like Rex, Jim, Stacy, Matthew, and Reed—who have made me feel safe and heard.

May you find the comfort, hope, entertainment, and healing in this story that I did.

There's magic enough for all of us.

The Catalain Book of Secrets series is Jessica Lourey's first venture into magical realism, a genre she's loved since she was a teenager. She's best known for her critically-acclaimed Murder-by-Month mysteries, which have earned multiple starred reviews from *Library Journal* and *Booklist,* the latter writing, "It's not easy to make people laugh while they're on the edge of their seats, but Lourey pulls it off...[A] very clever series." Jessica is a tenured professor of creative writing and sociology at a Minnesota college. When not teaching, reading, traveling, writing, or raising her two wonderful kids, you can find her dreaming of her next story. If you enjoyed *The Catalain Book of Secrets,* please check out *Seven Daughters: A Catalain Book of Secrets* novella. You can find out more about Jessica and her books at www.jessicalourey.com.

DISCUSSION QUESTIONS

1. Throughout this book, you enter the minds of four of the Catalain women: Ursula, Jasmine, Katrine, and Tara. Which character did you most identify with, and why? Was it distracting to you to move from one head to another, or did it give the story necessary depth? Would you have liked to hear the perspective of any other characters? If so, which ones and why?

2. Identify and discuss some of the reasons the inhabitants of Faith Falls might be uncomfortable with the Catalains throughout their history there.

3. Velda created a family culture in which everyone kept secrets. What do you think motivated her?

4. In what ways did Katrine and Ursula have a typical mother-daughter relationship? If there were exceptional aspects of the relationship, to what do you attribute these?

5. Why didn't Ursula confront her mother and tell her sisters or daughters that she had helped to murder her father much earlier? Could she have prevented what happened to Jasmine by doing so?

6. Discuss Jasmine's role, if any, in what happened to Katrine the night the snakes rose. Would it have ended any differently if

she had confessed what had happened to her when she was younger? Does it matter if it would have? In other words, is it ever your duty to share secrets before you're ready?

7. What do the snakes in the book symbolize to you?

8. Why did Tara run away?

9. Artemis, Leo, and Ren are all good men trying to get into the Catalain women's lives. Do you believe it is Henry Tanager's curse that initially keeps the men from getting close to the Catalains, or is it something else?

10. Who do you think wrote/is writing *The Catalain Book of Secrets* in which Ursula finds her spells?

11. Do you believe in everyday magic, like the power to make people feel something when they eat food you've cooked, or the ability to sense when someone is dangerous, or the gift of sewing clothes that hang beautifully on any body?

12. Is there ever a good reason for family members to keep secrets from one another? If so, what would the circumstances be?

13. At the end of the story, whose baby do you believe Katrine pregnant with, and what's the significance of this?

14. Would you want to read a prequel to this novel, one in which we learn the story of Eva and Ennis Catalain? Why or why not?

CPSIA information can be obtained at www.ICGtesting.com
Printed in the USA
BVOW05*0252041214

377488BV00002B/2/P